COMPLETE SHORT STORIES

Teresita Blanco

KDP

Cover design by: Art Painter
Library of Congress Control Number: 2018675309
Printed in the United States of America

CONTENTS

COMPLETE SHORT STORIES BY TERESITA BLANCO

Introduction

This is a collection of short stories based on my nightmares and dreams. I decided to compile all the stories into a complete collection. Dreams are a source of inspiration for most of my writing. It is rare for me to remember my dreams.

It is even rarer for those dreams to make sense. During the few times that my dreams have something that resembles a plot, I rework it into a short story.

Dreams with meat in their bones get turned into novels. This shows the importance of sleeping. A lot of writers have the bad habit of not sleeping. While you dream, the brain in the background is doing all the work for you.

Then when you wake up, you have everything you need to write a good story. Without more preambles, I present to you my Complete Short Stories Collection.

This book recently got a second edition. It has 10 new Short stories added to the end of the book. I hope you find them amusing.

THE BALLAD
OF EXADA

A girl is lost in the Grand Canyon. She is small and frail looking. Her white dress lies torn around the legs. She keeps walking and walking, but to no avail. She could not find her parents. As the sun began to fall, the Girl begins to lose hope. The Girl sank to the ground. The red earth stained the folding of her white dress. Tears slowly fell from her pale blue eyes. A faint wind rose and it swayed her long, curly brown hair. She felt something odd and scaly by her hand. A strange, ugly black lizard was by her. It gazed at her with its strange black eyes. His black scales shone bloodshot reddish, beneath the burning sunset. The girl stopped her crying and looked at the lizard. "Can you help me find my nana?" asked the girl.

The lizard stuck his tongue as a response. The girl said in a reptilian voice, "Yes missy, I know this place like the black of my claw." After "saying" this the lizard departed. He climbed over a nearby rock. He looked back at the girl and motioned with his head. For the whole night, the girl trailed behind the lizard. She was so tired of walking, yet the lizard urged her on. Around twilight, the girl collapsed. She was too tired, and a bit thirsty. She could not walk anymore. The lizard saw this. It quickly crawled back to the place the girl had collapse. It got over her neck and it nestled under her hair. A few minutes later, the police found the girl. Since the lizard was hiding beneath her long hair. It was easily overlooked.

The family of the girl was quickly contacted. By the time her nana arrived, the girl was already awake. Seeing the adults, the girl took the lizard from her neck and hid it in the breast pocket of her white dress. Sometime passed, by then, her family was aware of the girl's unbecoming, new pet. That Exada was such a disgusting looking pet. More than trice, her nana tried to offer the girl a new pet. One day, she brought a puppy. The girl quickly rejected it, because it frightened Exada. The cat lasted three days. However, the girl got jealous of the kitten. Exada liked to talk to the kitten more, than the girl. She made Exada choose between herself and the cat. Naturally, the girl won over Exada. In the end, only a little canary and a goldfish fish stayed. Yet, they did nothing to get the girl to lose interest in Exada.

Eventually, the nana and the butler had a brilliant idea. They figured that the girl needed some human friends. Keeping this in mind, they casually introduced Mimmy. Mimmy was the well-bred daughter of Nana. Due to her station, she had her Mimmy going to a regular school. She told the girl's father of Exada. He casually dismissed the issue. He told Nana to do what she thought was necessary. He did not mind paying for a playmate for his "Darling". As for Exada, he said that kids should be allowed their own eccentricities. As long as Exada did not interfere with her lectures, the girl was allowed to have him.

Following their plans, Mimmy started her lectures with the girl. Mimmy's mother began dressing her in fine silk. She introduced Mimmy not as her daughter, but as the girl's cousin. Nana had instructed her daughter to play the part of the good friend. This advanced home school education promised to open the doors for Mimmy. Thus, Mimmy was groomed into the perfect friend.

The girl got along well with Mimmy. She played with her dollies and her tea set with Mimmy often. One day, the girl got enough courage to introduce Exada to Mimmy. She sat Mimmy down in her chair that went with her tea play set. Amused, Mimmy kept her smirks to herself. "I want you to meet a special friend", said the girl.

"Oh! A special friend" , Mimmy sort of figured that she was going to meet the girl's imaginary friend. She was not prepared to meet Exada.

"Hello, Mimmy, it is a pleasure to meet you acquaintance" , said Exada. He reared his black head outside the window of the girl's dollhouse. Mimmy had always wondered why they never played with the doll house. Now she knew… that house belonged to Exada. Opening the front door, Exada waltzed outside the dollhouse. The girl got a mini table and chair outside the house. She got for him a plate, with a few bugs she had the groundskeeper catch for Exada's meals. Quickly, Exada "sat" in the chair. The warm summer light fell on the lizard. Coolly, Exada enjoyed its comfort. With his body all warmed up, he proceeded, "I have been told you are the Missy's cousin."

"And your point being…", responded Mimmy smirking. The girl brought a chair and sat close to Exada.

"That swine of a woman thinks me a fool. But I am onto you!" said Exada accusingly," You wish to get rid of me like all the others. However, she will not part from me! I saved her life. You cannot put a price on a child's life!"

"Cousin, it's not funny! I love you! I would never do anything to hurt you or your pest!" said Mimmy rising, but she checked her temper. Truly, she wanted to crush that lizard and give that snob a piece of her mind. However, keeping her mother's rebukes in minds she said, " Oh! You wound me so cousin and I love you ever so much."

"I will forget the fact you called me a pest…" said Exada offended. He went back indoors and refused to come out. In tears, the girl said , "I knew you would not understand". Grabbing Mimmy by the arm she said, "Get out! Get out!"

Some days passed and Nana noticed the change among the girls. Mimmy told her mother of her encounter with Exada. Annoyed, Nana tried that very night to get rid of the lizard. However, she could not find Exada inside the dollhouse. She did not suspect that Exada slept in the breast pocket of the girl. Since the campaign against Exada began, the girl took care to hide Exada in her person whenever she slept. Eventually, Nana thought her own reaction was pretty childish. She resigned herself to the un-welcome guest. After all, this Exada had bought a future for her daughter. Keeping this in mind, she told Mimmy to make peace with Exada.

A few years passed, uneventfully. Exada had become part of the family. Nana was still freaked out by the lizard. The Father had grown to like Exada. He enjoyed talking with him about the family's business. His advices time and time again had proved most fruitful. To him, Exada was the son he had always wanted. Exada had a sound business mind and an eye for money. By now, the entire household revolved around the lizard.

"How long do you think lizards live?" asked the driver.

"Who knows…" says Nana.

"Not long I wager…"responded the driver coolly.

Both were observing the girl taking Exada to the garden. She placed the black lizard, of the blue belly by the fence. He glanced at the girl with his black eyes. She smiled at him, and she imagined he smiled back at her. The girl then went back inside and got her books. She began to do her homework, outside, in the garden. Exada coolly watched her do her work. The lovebirds sung their melodies. The sky shone bright blue, under the burning summer sun.

"Ah! Exada… I love you! You're my best friend!" says the girl looking up from her homework.

"You honor me, missy!" responded Exada.

"Do you remember the first time we met?" asked the girl.

"Yes, it was in that cold barren desert. The red earth and the sky, seemed to fade into one. Both crimson, both a prison…" said Exada glancing at the blue sky.

"Do you miss your home Exada?" asked the girl.

"My home is with you Missy."

"You always know what to say to make me feel better, Exada" responded the girl.

The next day the Girl was riding inside the limo with Exada. As usual, the girl had Exada at the edge of the closed window. He was watching the scenery pass by. The road was rather bumpy. The girl worried that Exada might fall off the edge of the window. When she went to pick him up and put it in her dress, the window suddenly opened. A strong gust of wind swept Exada out of the car.

"Stop the Car!" said the Girl.

"Sorry missy, I cannot stop the car on the freeway!"

Ignoring him, the girl opened the door. The driver saw the girl's intentions. He quickly obeyed her. Running franticly, to the edge of the road, the girl discovered what was left of Exada. He was badly wounded. He had lost his tail and one of his legs. His left eye was crying blood.

"Both you and I knew that this peace was not going to last forever" said Exada.

"I don't want you to die!" said the girl.

"My time was growing near" responded Exada limping toward the sobbing Girl. "Do you remember Goldilocks?"

"Yes..."

"One day you found him upside down. The next day he was back to normal" the girl held the wounded Exada in her arms, "It seems the monkeys wanted to spare you the sight of a timely dead. The fools... despite their old age, they refuse to give death its due. They would rather you think that I was lost forever, then for you to watch me die. Alas, their childish efforts were for naught."

By now the driver had gotten out of the car. "I am sorry missy...I was just following orders."

Exada did not die right away. He agonized for four weeks before dying of his wounds. The Father even got a vet to try to save the lizard. However, his efforts were for naught. After Exada died, the girl released her canary. She gave her goldfish to Mimmy. She never had any new pets, after Exada.

In no time, the girl grew into a beautiful young lady. She never spoke about Exada, since his death. From time to time, the lady would stand by the window. With her forehead pressed against the glass. There she would sigh her youth away. One day the family returned to the Grand Canyon. By then all but the lady, had forgotten about Exada. That day the lady sported a white dress. One similar to the one she wore the day she met Exada.

Like that other time, the Lady wandered away from her family. Only this time, they never found her. Since the father had no other children, he had Mimmy replace his daughter. From time to time, whenever the sunset sky glowed red, Mimmy thinks of the Lady and her Exada. Never again will she look at the same way the pets of poor, lonely children.

MISSION JUPITER

The wizard was in an alien world. The ground looked rocky and shiny. Almost like ice. The temperature was mild. Not too cold, not too warm. There was no wind at all. Heck, there was never any wind. The air was always static. It was as if that world never rotated. The sky had a greenish, blackish phosphorescent look about it. It shimmered a lot, as if there were stars in the sky. From time to time, you saw burst of aurora borealis. The sky broke the monotony of the ground. Unlike me, the Wizard was not impressed by the sky. He was too used to the same sight. Day in and Day out, the sky looked the same. The inhabitants of his world never perceived the days passing. They were only aware of the passage of time because of their ancestors who had lived in a world like planet Earth. They carried with them the chronology of their old world.

A long time ago, their race had crash landed on Jupiter. They had originally intended to land on Earth. However, their ship broke along the way. In those days, Jupiter was just a giant ball of ice. It had barely any atmosphere. With no vegetation, heat, or air; their race was doomed to die in that barren planet. Luckily, these aliens had a great mastery of magic. Using their powers, their ancestors generated a stable atmosphere. To prevent invasions, they gave this atmosphere different layers. In essence, they created the first Auria. The only way to penetrate their planetary auria world was to enter via magic. Science could never create a machine strong enough to penetrate those layers of gas, acid and hydrogen metal. Due to this large mass, in no time Jupiter drew onto itself many nearby planets. Its gravity also destroyed a world, which became our asteroid belt.

As time passed, these aliens evolved in a way that mimicked their new environment. When this took place, we may never know. The alien's timeline is based on a faraway world, of a faraway universe. It bore no semblance to the time scale of planet Earth. Thus, day, years, hours, differed quite a bit.

After hearing this long exposition, the Wizard made his way to the human mission in Jupiter. Pointing toward it he added, "This is the reason why NASA gave up on space travel. They are ashamed to admit that they "discovered" alien life not via science, but by magic. It is a tough pill to swallow for any men devoted to science. As a matter of fact, it was my father who made first contact, in response to their silly little alien message."

By now, the Wizard was at the entrance of the Human colony. From the outside, it looked like a serious high tech bio dome. It had a lot of spikes and antennas. From time to time, the auroras would be absorbed by those rods. Once again, a product of science was being powered by magic (in this case Ether). On the bottom, there were hallways that led to an open clearing. Inside, the fake sky was deep blue, with "clouds" coming and going. "My kind prefers the earthly sky. They are tired of the surreal monotony of our world. Never changing, always static". To makes this colony more appealing to the aliens studied, the bio dome simulated earthly weather, from rain to snow. That day the dome was simulating warm summer weather.

Inside the dome, the place had an auditorium like feel. There were different floors, each, rising up a step higher. All the apartments of the aliens faced the center, B1 level (jungle). In there, they had some of their animals. They all were strange versions of mammals and dinosaurs common to our planet Earth. The most interesting of them were a pack of something that resembled dinosaur raptors. They had their shape. However, the colors and the eyes were most bizarre. Their extremities too looked a bit monkish and deformed. These were the smartest of the lot.

When we looked down they were forming an animal ladder. The alpha male was trying to get inside to attack everyone. The Wizard, amused, got close to the railings and kicked the beast down. This kick caused all alien raptors to lose their balance. The Captain seemed like he was going to suffer a nasty fall. However, he managed to land on his hind legs with a thug. He then looked up at the Wizard and screeched.

After this the Wizard, visited his father. His apartment was in the first floor. It was a bit dark, but clean. He had the classical human commodities, from a refrigerator to a TV (which he never used). There he lived with his alien wife (or the wizard's stepmother) and his half-sister. I was surprised when I saw the wizard's father. I never would have guessed that this man was an alien. Everything about him looked completely normal. He had short, well-kept black hair, long eyelashes, deep black eyes (same color of his pupils). He was about average size, and weight. As usual, he sported a simple, completely black tux. Nothing about him gave away the fact that he was an alien. Sensing my surprised, the Wizard explained, " The ETs DNA is identical to that of the humans. It's the Phenotype that gives us our inhuman quality. By undergoing extensive plastic surgery, even we can pass for human. We may be different on the outside, but we are identical on the inside".

As for reproduction, the aliens and the humans can reproduce. The Wizard was among the first human and alien half breeds of these days. As a matter of fact, this was not the first times that the Jupiter aliens made contact with the earthlings. Long ago, both the humans and the aliens could wield magic. The humans used it to harm each other. In time, their bodies became immune to magic. This immunity also took away the human's ability to use magic. As for the aliens, they could still wield magic because they never used it to harm one another. Therefore, humans who can still wield magic (in this day and age) are descendants of the Jupiter aliens. Whenever the time seems ripe, they send new aliens to breed with the humans. It is their hope to one day depart Jupiter and live in planet earth, like they had originally planned. The problem is that not all the aliens wield enough magical powers to escape the Jupiter auria. Thus, migration to Earth has been rather slow. Recently, they finally had a sufficient number of alien wizards for a new colonization project in planet earth. NASA is helping to coordinate this new migration, with the help of the Father, aka the former alien ambassador to Earth.

On the meantime, the Wizard has been preoccupied with teaching his half-sister magic. Once she comes of age, she will undergo plastic surgery to go live in planet earth. He also has busied himself with taking over his father's ambassador duties. Originally, his old man lived in planet Earth. However, he got bored of the humans and decided to return to Jupiter. He married an alien wife and now lives a pleasant life in the Jupiter Mission. Aside from Magic, the Jupiter aliens are known for their future sight. Unlike foresight, future sight makes then perceive everything as if it was a few, years, days or decades into the future. Let me explain, when an alien sees you, he will see you the way you will look like in 4 (the time depends on the power of each future sight) years into the future. This future sight is always on. As a matter of fact, the aliens were not aware of this altered perception. It was discovered in their first encounter with the humans. They saw themselves no different, than the humans. Thus, when they went to take their plastic surgery, they would tell the surgeons of their future face. Via this power, the father was able to tell pretty early who had enough power to go to the human world. His future sight saw them with human faces.

We discussed this and many other things as the Wizard made his rounds in the Mission. There the humans interacted with the aliens who were going to go to planet Earth. Those who were going to the mission were children. To facilitate their adaptation, after their surgery, they would go to school with the regular humans. In time, they would become one, with humanity. The Wizard did not seem too humored with this project. He had lived as a human and had chosen to return to his home world to help other poor fools join the human race. He regretted that they had to share planet Earth with the humans. From time to time, his human nature would temp him to obliterate the entire human race. Yet, it was not in his alien nature to seek the death of others.

ASLEEP IN MY SOLITUDE

When did I awake? I cannot remember. For how long did I sleep? Do I still sleep? I cannot tell. One moment I was nothing. Why was I sleeping? I care not to remember. Then, I became aware, of what I cannot tell. I hear a strange beating, a strange drumming. It is so close... yet, I cannot discern its source. Sometimes, it is faint, soft... at other times, its sound is maddening. For how long I heard that sound? I cannot tell.

By now, I hardly perceive it. A new sound has caught my attention. It is high, crisp, resounding, and rhythmic. I feel a strange chill down my back. I trembled a little. Now that strange sound becomes a stream. It quickly dissipated now it is no more...

Some time passes, how long I cannot tell? A new sound draws my attention. That new sound becomes many... what I am listening to, I know not.

"Mommy, look, a big scary monster"

"That's just rocks and moss"

Those strange sounds fade away. Once again, I listen for silence, and darkness... It hurts! I feel a strange jabbing sensation bellow my ribs. I am afraid; I hear that strange drumming louder. It's so fast, my chest hurts. I cannot move. I wait for the pain to pass. I grow bore of these strange new sensations. With a sign, I try to relax. A strange warm surrounds me. It is pleasant. This warm alleviates the pain in my ribs.

"How strange…"

"The entire wall has melted off…"

"The place looked fine just this morning"

"MMmm… Bummer, should we tell someone"

"Eh, whatever"

Ah… to sleep, the sleep of death… Is there no greater joy than this? I can't even hear that drumming sound. It's so warm and pleasant. That strange chill is gone. There is only silence, nothing. Wait, how strange? I turn my head to listen better. Wrrr….. or its grr..? Ouch! Something fell on my head, and another, and another. What an unpleasant sensation, to be buried alive. Hahaha!! The wrr sound stops.

"What the hell was that?"

"What? Did you say something? I can't hear you over the sound of the drill,"

"…Maybe, it was just my imagination…still"

I don't know why that thought humored me so much. Now, I am completely buried; the same sensations, to the left, and to the right. It's not too unpleasant. Once again, I know peace… I feel a strange sensation beneath my eyelids. This is… light. I have not felt it for I know how long. I bury my head deeper in the ground, to shield myself from it. I care not to see the world anew. There is nothing out there that interests me. Just let me sleep, again anew. I hear a strange crunchy sound above me.

"Mimmy, come look"

"What, we are not supposed to be here"

"There is something buried beneath this sand"

"I hope its treasure"

"No… I mean there is SOMETHING down here. I saw the sand, like sink down, a foot or two"

"Where?"

"Over there"

"Here, Ahhh, I am sinking"

"Mimmy!!"

"Hahaha! I am just messing with you, scary cat! There is nothing down there!"

"We should still look! I just can't shake the feeling that there is something down there"

"Fine, I have nothing better to do"

Once again, a new sound interrupts my sleep. I can feel the ground being removed all around me. My head no longer feels heavy. I can hear more, newer stranger sounds about me. The ground is being removed above me. Just around my face.

"Look, it's just rocks down there"

"Very round, sharp rocks to boot"

"Maybe we should keep digging"

"Nah, this is stupid, let's go!"

Those merry sounds depart. What a pleasant sounds leave me alone, in my solitude. Why does life call me anew? Sleep, sleep and forget why I desired to sleep, anew, so… A current sweeps me, drowns me. All is silence anew. Sleep, forget. Do not listen to anything, do not feel anything. Let me rest in peace, in my solitude.

The Twelve Zombie Saints

"The lord is my shepherd, … and though I walk through the valley of the shadows of death , I shall fear no evil; for you are with me" Psalms 23

Late, at night, a faint rain fell over the pier. There was not a living thing in the pier, except for some soldiers. All wore identical blue camouflage uniforms, backpacks, rifles and guns. All were young, clean shaven youth. These youths were being led by a veteran. Unlike them, he was used to death and carnage. As such,

Captain David Preston ran ahead of them.

Behind him, three soldiers were helping a frightened lady keep up the pace. Her name was Jane Smith. Jane wore the Captain's jacket that was too big for her petit frame. Bellow her jacket; one could see the dirty long blue dress. As she ran, from time to time, she would trip on her dress. However, her escort's strong arms would keep her from falling. Her pale face was stained with dirt, blood and tears. The maiden was in labor. Yet, she could not stop to give birth just, yet. Barefooted, she was forced to keep on running. She had been running nonstop for days. Her only concern was to preserve the precious life inside her. Her escorts were of a same mind.

After much running, the party made it inside a cargo ship. It was the only remaining vessel. There they barricaded themselves in the bridge. The bridge had only one entrance. The windows stood three stories high. With two soldiers guarding the door, and the Captain at the helm, the medic started delivering a new life into this horrible world.

The Captain tried to fire up the engine. Sadly, the noises created by the ship alerted the zombies. Slowly, lazily, rotting corpses made their way onto the ship. At first, they were one, two, and three. Soon, the ship was a sea of zombies. Seeing this, the Captain tried to operate the crane from within the bridge. Using the giant cargo boxes he got rid of a good number of zombies. However, the ship still refused to leave the pier. The Captain feared the ship was broken. By the time the engine started, the ship was full of zombies.

"Ahh…" yelled Jane. This sole scream alerted the zombies of their location. Cursing his rotten luck, the Captain activated the ship's alarms. He hoped that the alarms would disorient the zombies. His plan worked, partly. Some found their way into the bridge. By this time, the soldiers were running low on ammo. The two guarding the door had to resort to crushing the rotting skulls with the ends of their rifles. After some hours, Jane finally gave birth. The medic gave a sign of relief. After cutting, the umbilical cord, the medic searched his backpack for a clean blanket. After wrapping the baby, he gave her to Jane. The new mother was pleased with her baby. She gently stroked the child's little face. Feeling her mother's touch, the baby seized her crying. In no time, the baby went to sleep. With the child asleep, the mother allowed herself to rest. Seeing her asleep, the medic took her pulse.

"Her pulse is a bit weak, but she will live" said the medic.

Taking his kind, blue eyes off Jane, he turned his gaze toward the encroaching infestation. Armed with his machine gun, he joined the two soldiers in the desperate fight against the zombies. To make matters worse, a storm ensued, rocking the ship side to side.

Two hours later, the storm cleared up. The Captain could clearly see the lighthouse over the horizon. The sun was starting to rise. The soldiers had managed to put enough furniture between themselves and the zombies. The problem now was getting out of the ship. They docked near a humble, desolate port. The houses were made of plain, oak wood. The town looked as if a hurricane had passed by. Many of the houses were either demolished or in a poor condition. There was not a vehicle in sight. Jane was now awake and she was feeding her baby. The Captain looked over in her direction. That tender sight, for a second, made him forget the nightmarish yesterday. However, the zombies' moans brought him back to reality. Sighing, the Captain turned off the alarms, and the engine. His soldiers looked exhausted. They had slept the rest of the night on the floor. The medic had been bitten during the fray; he laid there in a corner, fighting the infestation. The Captain saw the medic motioning to him with his hand. He walked over to the medic, and sat by his side.

The medic looked sadly at the Captain as he said; "I will not go quietly into the night… I will serve as the zombie lure. I know this town… straight across the port…there is a church, and there is a bus there. (Coughed out blood) Take it and go"

"Thank you, it was an honor to have you in my unit"; responded the Captain. Rising, the Captain commenced his task. Taking

Jane by the hand, he guided her to a corner. After waking the sleeping soldiers, he made a barricade of furniture for Jane.

"Stay down there both you. Don't make a peep!" said the Captain grimly. Jane and her baby nodded in response.

"Now, where do we hide?" asked the Captain looking about.

"Sir, all I could find were some sheets" responded one soldiers.

"Eh, it could be worst…" answered the Captain. Feeling silly, the Captain and the two remaining soldiers hid beneath the sheets. Like veiled guardians, they took their place before the barricade. They hoped to shield Jane with their bodies, if necessary.

The medic, struggling to rise, crawled toward the door. To give himself strength, he gave himself an adrenaline shot to his heart. Removing the remaining furniture, the medic forced the door open. The flood gate of zombies poured over him. Forcing his way across bites and scratches, the medic lured the wave of zombies away. When all grew quiet, the Captain removed the sheets. I can't believe it worked, though the Captain. Very quietly, the soldiers and the Captain removed the furniture. Together, they helped Jane rise to her feet. On tip toe, they passed by the hoard of feeding zombies. The Captain avoided looking in the direction of the remains of the medic. By now, the sun was visible over the horizon. Slowly, the sky bathed the decaying night with the warm red hues of life. When the light fell on the sleeping baby's face, she stirred a little. Frightened, the party quickened their pace. When they got out of the ship, the Captain set some explosives. Once they were far way enough, the Captain detonated the ship that sank with all the zombies.

The noise was so loud that it woke the sleeping child. She began to cry, most pitifully. The mother tried to console her baby. The seemingly abandon port, grew alive with death. All about, zombies of all ages began to prow the street. Their tattered clothing's clung to their decaying flesh. Throwing caution aside, the group began to run in the direction of the church. They could see it standing ominously over the ruined houses. It was also the only building still in one piece. Its stonework stood strong against all destructions. The façade was simple. At another time, it served as a gothic prison. It was later remodeled into a church. The dungeon became its catacomb. The interior was decorated like a Renaissance cathedral. The prison's barred windows had been converted into stained glass windows. After climbing the stone stairs, they were shocked to find the front gates locked. Seeing this, the Captain went around and tried all the doors. All the while, the baby kept on crying. By now, the zombies were slowly surrounding the group. Starring death in the face, one of the soldiers began laughing like a madman. Banging on the doors, the mad soldier yelled; "Sanctuary! Sanctuary!"

"Have you gone mad?" chastised the Captain. Much to their surprise, a priest opened the church's iron doors.

"Come, quickly!"

Without a second's hesitation, the party entered inside the church. The priest quickly locked the door behind them. Under a timid, candlelight lights, the Captain surveyed the scene. The sun entered the church in strange shades and colors. Some of the stained glass windows remained intact. Looking about, the Captain noticed the presence of 13 haggard faces. Near the altar, twelve monks, of various ages, knelt. They wore identical brown, Franciscan habits. The youngest one among them, 15 years old boy, was doing more crying than praying. The priest was a middle age man. He had a few white hairs. His most distinct features were his cynical smile and sad black eyes. He was wearing his mass white clothing, with a green cloak. On the back, there was the sewing of a haloed lamb. On a corner of his collard, the Captain saw an interesting symbol. It was a stylized sun. In the center, there were the letters I.H.S. The H had a little cross over it. Seeing the Captain's interest in the logo, the priest pointed to the sign and said, "That's the Jesuit logo." Like the visitors, the priests and the monks where stained with blood and ashes.

In one trembling voice, the monks chanted over and over, "Father, if you are willing, take this cup from me; yet not my will, but yours be done."

"You're from the army?" asked the priest.

"Yes", responded the Captain.

"Are they coming to rescue us?"

"No, Father, they are going to cleanse the infected areas. We must get out of range of the drone attacks;" responded the Captain.

The priest sighed at this. Noticing the presence of the visitors, the monks seized their lamentations. The youngest monk beckoned the mother to a dirty bench. He tried cleaning it with the ends of his robes. Smiling, Jane sat down with her baby. Afterwards, he brought her what bit of food he could find. Saddened Jane said, "I can't accept your rations".

"It's fine, we are monks. We are used to fasting for the lord." said the youngest monk. His pale blue eyes, watered anew. While Jane ate, the youngest monk played with the baby. Rocking the child in his arms, he began to sing softly, "Kirie, eleison." On the meantime, the soldiers and the Captain went to sleep on the church benches. That soft melody not only soothed the baby, but their nightmarish pains as well. The other monks also joined in. Outside, they could feel the zombies gathering, lured by the song.

After the song, the priest poured some water in a chalice. He blessed it and said to Jane; "We should have the newborn baptized".

"I am sorry, I am not a Catholic."

"Neither am I", said the priest, laughing to himself, "It will still give us something to do…"

"Your blasphemy never seizes to amaze me…" rebuked the elder monk, gritting his teeth.

"So, what do you suggest we do?" asked the priest, folding his arms.

"I guess a baptism will do," responded the Elder, "Any objections?"

"Fine…"said Jane.

"First we need a godfather" said the Younger. After returning the baby, the boy made his way toward the pulpit. From there, he started "minie, minie minie moeing". The lucky chosen God-father was the Captain. After this election, the priest went up to the sleeping Captain. Gently, he shook him by the shoulder and whispered, "Get up, Godfather, we are going to baptized your kid".

"Since when is he my kid?"

"Stop being such a sour puss. You can go back to sleep after the Baptism;" said the priest.

Getting up, the Captain asked, "What do I have to do?"

"Just hold up the baby while I Baptized him in the name of the father, the son and the…" said the priest. Behind him the Elder added, "Holy Ghost!"

"I knew that!"

"Sure you do…" said the Elder. His wrinkled face smiled anew.

With the Captain's acquiescence, the monks awoke the other soldiers. With everyone awake, the priest began the mass. From time to time, the Elder had to remind the priest of his lines. When it came time to baptize the baby, the priest asked Jane to name the baby.

She responded, "And he shall be Levon, and he shall be a good man".

"Seriously, Woman! We all heard of Elton John! Are you 100% sure you want to call my baby Levon", asked the priest.

"Fine… what name do you suggest?"

"How 'bout Jesus?", said the priest.

"There is like a billion Jesus and half of them are zombies by now…" responded Jane, frowning.

"Emanuel", said one of the monks.

"Moses" said another.

"Jezabel"

"That's a chick's name"

"She is a chick if you idiots have not noticed", said the Captain.

"Really?" opening the blankets of her baby, Jane saw that she indeed had given birth to a girl. She added, "eh, would you look at that… with all that's happened, I did not notice whether my baby was a he or a she. Still, I don't want any churchy names."

"How 'bout Lakshmi?" asked the young monk.

"Who's Lakshmi?" asked Jane.

"She is the wife of the sea colored god", responded the younger.

"Neat, let's call her that", responded Jane.

"No" said the Captain, "I am the Godfather! I will name the kid! I can at least spare him; I mean her, the agony of entering the afterlife with a stupid name. I will call her Priscilla."

"Cute…I, Baptize you Priscilla, in the name of the father, the son and the holy ghost" said the priest.

"Hey, wait a minute," said Jane angrily, "I don't like that name! Baptize her again, so I can change her name".

"Sorry, double baptism is an anathema," said the Elder, in his usual stern fashion.

"You're never any fun," answered the priest.

Taking the remaining water in both his hands, the priest sprayed it on all everyone. "Now I baptize all of us in the name of the father, the son and the holy host;" said the priest, "our new name will be Priscilla. Amen".

Appalled, the Captain asked the Elder, "Is he out of his mind?"

"You would think so, considering all that's happened, but his holiness has always been like this. Even before this so called Zombiepocalipse" responded the Elder.

Stepping aside with the Elder monk, the Captain left the party arguing about their new names. He then asked the Elder, "You think it's the end of the world?"

"They shall seek death and they shall not find it" responded the monk.

"That's from the apocalypse, right?" asked the Captain.

"Yes, my son" responded the Elder.

"So, when is Jesus going to come on his white horse to save us?" asked the Captain.

"Ah… you poor child, no one ever reads the commentaries" answered the elder, "There is no white horse coming to save us. Apocalypse is all ciphers; it's a message warning the ancient Eastern Church of the Romans' attack; nothing more, nothing less."

"How disappointing, so doomsday has already occurred and we missed it," sighed the Captain.

"So on top of zombies, you want locusts, 4 horsemen, legions of demons and a harlot ridding a 7 headed dragon?" asked the elder laughing.

"Heh, heh, you do have a point…" said the Captain, "I heard your church has a bus."

"We also have a sports car, a Jeep and 12 Motorcycles", responded the Elder.

"Why do monks have motorcycles?"

"To get around…" said the monk, smiling innocently, "Now, why do you want a bus?"

"Doc saw a lot of zombie movies. While we escaped, he kept talking about it. He said that in all those movies, the heroes escaped on a bus. He was the one who sent us here on a wild goose chase" responded the Captain, "It's not like it matters, if you guys had a vehicle to escape, you would have left days ago."

"I do see the convenience of a bus. It is a big vehicle…that tips over, easily", responded the Elder.

"If we could get to it, then perhaps we can get all of us out of here", said the Captain." Where is it?"

"Last I saw the bus it was parked outside the hermitage, in the woods," mentioned the elder, "The problem that in such a wide open area we can be easily surrounded."

"Is there any other working vehicle?", asked the Captain.

"Did you see any on the way here?", asked the elder.

"No…"

"Nope"

After this brief intermission, the Captain organized everyone. The priest had already been bitten; thus, he insisted on staying behind. Plus, he refused to abandon his zombie flock to their fate. After much brainstorming, the priest came up with an escape plan. There was a path toward the hermitage beneath the chapel. In the old days, that path connected the dungeons with the execution grounds that now served as a hermitage. The problem was that this path also served as catacombs. When the crisis began, many of the town's zombies came out from within the church. The priest planned to ring the Angelus bell to lure them toward the bell tower. On the meantime, the monks, the soldiers, Jane and Priscilla would make their way through the catacombs. The sound of the bell would be so distracting that they would be easily overlooked. At least, that was the working theory. With this plan in mind, the Captain helped the monks make blunt weapons from the church ornaments. Thus, armed with metal crosses and wooden shepherd staffs, the 12 monks readied themselves for this impossible escape.

For the first task, the priest rose to the highest tier of the bell tower. The Captain detonated the stair case to keep the zombies from reaching the priest. Before reopening the catacombs, the elder ordered the others to go hide in the chapel.

"Look, there might still be zombies within the catacombs," he added to the priest, "Ring the bell to lure them toward you, once the coast is clear, I will lock them inside the bell tower. This will allow the rest of you to escape."

"Look elder, I should open the catacombs," said the Captain, "This is my unit, and my wards. Their safety is my responsibility."

"It's better if I do it. I have already been bitten… I will be with God, soon…" said the Elder.

"I suppose, it cannot helped…"

Saying this, the Captain left the Elder to commence his deadly task. On the meantime, the others went to hide inside the Chapel where the host rested. It was on left wing of the church. It was decorated with stained glass window. The door was made of iron. Once inside, the Captain locked it from the inside.

Giving a sign, the Elder made a signal to the priest. Soon, the church was imbued with the Angelus melody. The Elder walked swiftly toward the door of catacombs, it was on right side wing. He opened the door… In the darkness, he could hear the dead moaning and growling. Soon, there came one, and then another. The first one to rear its head beyond the darkness was a child they had buried recently. As a matter of fact, it was during his funeral when the crisis began. Looking at this corrosive face sadly, the elder led him with his staff. Slowly, more and more zombies reared their heads from within the catacombs. As they walked forth, the elder led this grim funeral procession toward the bell tower. Those hiding within the chapel watched in awe, from behind the safety of the Holy Ghost stained glass window. From behind those multi- colored windows, the procession had a dreamy surrealist quality about it. As the elder climbed higher above the tower, more and more of the dead followed behind. In no time, the entire catacomb was emptied out. Surrounded, the Elder kneeled before his motley flock. He was devoured as he prayed Psalms 23. When his final screams of agony died out, the Captain detonated the explosives bellow the tower. The rubbles trapped the catacomb zombies within the bell tower. The Youngest monk beckoned them toward the open grave.

Angered the Captain addressed the young monk, "This was not part of the plan."

"God has his own plans too…Do not be saddened by his sacrifice. As soldiers of Christ, we have always been preparing to sacrifice ourselves for the salvation of others," he said this as a shiver went down his spine.

Saying this, the young monk made a motion with his hand. With his staff he led the living toward the open grave. In the darkness, the Captain did not notice that the young man had stayed behind. Taking out a flashlight, the Captain cautiously surveyed the area. The zombies that remained where stuck inside the walls. From time to time, a hand would reach out to grab an arm or a leg. Regardless, things went uneventful. On the meantime, the young monk closed the catacomb door. He then walked toward the church gate. Using what fragile strength remained, he forced the church gates opened. It was as if the floodgates of hell had opened up. The torrent of beings killed the young monk before they had a chance to devour him. It was later that the Captain noticed that they were short of a monk.

"Where is the kid?", asked the Captain flashing all the faces.

"I am holding her right now," said Jane.

"Not the baby! The Monk"

"Which monk?" asked one of the soldiers.

"The small one"

"Here I am?" said one of the older monks.

"NO! The youngest one!"

"He is dead…" said one of the twelve.

"He stayed behind to open the gates of the church" said another.

"Why would he do that?" asked the Captain appalled.

"The priest asked him to. He wanted to perform a funerary mass, for the zombies outside. After all, the church must never close its doors to those who seek refuge. Regardless of whether they are of the living or the dead" said another one of the monks.

"That is so stupid!" said one of the soldiers.

"Do not pity him, he had already been bitten. It was his desire to sacrifice himself for your sakes, " said another.

"No more Sacrifices! We are all getting out of this together!" said the Captain angrily to the monks.

"Quiet, I hear something!!"

Moving the flashlight toward the roof, the Captain found the source of the noise. Above, there was a wooden trap door. Over their heads, they all could feel the limp footsteps of the dead.

In a low whisper, Jane asked, holding her sleeping child closer to her chest, "How many do you think there are?"

"I think there is only one" whispered back the Captain.

"Here is Jacob's ladder", said one of the monks holding a ladder.

The monks placed the ladder against the wall. Before anyone could stop him, one of the monks began climbing it. Seeing this, the Captain grabbed him by the ends of his robes, and forced him to decline. After many quiet rebukes, the Captain took his place. Calculating the position, the Captain shot and killed the zombie with his revolver. Feeling a numb thump sound, the Captain motioned the other soldiers to climb up. Together, they pushed the trap door opened. By now, night was falling. There was a thin grey mist bathing the timber woods. A zombie limped very close to the trap door; the Captain feared wasting more bullets. However, before the zombie got close to the open door, his attention was drawn by the Angelus bell sounding in the distance. Giving a sign of relief, the Captain got out. With the help of the other soldiers, he began to help the others get out. Jane and her child were the next ones to exit followed by the monks. As the last one was getting out a hand reached out from the walls, then another, and another.

"Jesus Christ! AH!"

Some of the wall zombies had gotten out. In the process, they had knocked down the ladder and the monk with him. His neck broke after the fall. In no time, the starving dead devoured him whole. With a grim face, the Captain closed the lash on the trap door. Now, they were down to 9 monks. All together, they made their way across the timber woods. They could still hear the Angelus bell in the distance. As the sound of the Angelus bell decreased, the volume of zombies increased. From time to time, they were forced to engage a few zombies. When they arrived at the hermitage they found the promised vehicle. It was not what the Captain expected. Instead of a bus, all they found was Jeep. There was barely enough room for 4 people.

"Where is the bus?" asked the Captain.

"What bus?" asked one of the monks, innocently.

"The Bus!"

"Since when did we have a bus?" asked another.

"Enough lies!"

"Just go and leave!" said another.

"We can't just leave guys, after all you done for us" said Jane.

"Didn't you wonder why we were so eager to die for you" said one of the monks.

"No... I figured that your pious self-sacrifice, was no different than our sense of duty", responded one of the soldiers.

"In part..." saying this, each monk lifted their long sleeves, "These are just some of the many zombie wounds we suffered."

"It has been more than a week since these first bites... Aside from the occasional vomiting of blood, the eternal burning sensation at the pit of one's stomach, ect. Things have been uneventful. I think our lord granted us life this long to help you," said another.

"This is stupid! You say that it was God's will for you to help us? If God's so powerful, then why are the dead coming back to life? Or is he resurrecting them just to watch us squirm?" asked the Captain angrily.

"He makes his sun rise on people whether they are good or evil. He lets rain fall on them whether they are just or unjust...", responded another one of the monks.

"What's that supposed to mean?" asked one of the soldiers.

"It means that God has nothing to do with zombies or hurricanes", said another.

"No offense father, but that's a lot of bullshit!" said Jane.

"Wasn't that passage about loving your enemies?" asked the Captain.

"Guys, we are wasting time" said one of the soldiers, "Can't we have this theological debate elsewhere?"

"Look, they come!"

The living got inside the Jeep, while the monks created a human wall.

"Oh, my God! Why have you abandoned us?" said Jane in tears as the Jeep raced away.

Back in the church, the priest was singing to himself. The night sky was blood red. The rain entered the hollowed bell tower's windows. It seemed to him that the entire town was attending church that night, for the first time. Among the crowd, he recognized the twelve monks. By now, they all had become zombies. From his high tower, he saw the approaching drones. They were napalming, the entire town…

"And now the town is cleansed in a burst of flames, like Sodom, and Gomorrah. " The first explosions blasted open the façade and the roof of the church; he could see the whole atrium from his high tower. Some of the zombies had been disembogued by the flames. Seeing such a feast, their fellow zombies began to devour their cooked remains. All engaged in this macabre Last Supper; however, the zombie monks did not taste of the human flesh. They simply looked blankly toward the heaven…

Eighteen years later, Priscilla returned to that ill-fated church. No new zombie attacks had occurred since her birth. The surviving soldiers and their Captain had done much to spread the fame of the 12 zombie saints. In less than two years, the Pope had these saints canonized. By now, hardly anything remained of the church. The bell tower and the Angelus bell where still in one piece. However, the apex of the church and the catacombs were laid bare by the explosions. Everything there had a distinct black sooth around it. From time to time, a faint cold wind would pass through the hollowed out church. Priscilla looked at this place with curiosity. She sported a black dress and hat. Her long blonde hair was combed up in braids. Her tender black eyes were drawn to many strange sights. There had been some vague attempts to reconstruct the church. However, it was deemed sacrilegious to alter this religious site. After passing by the ruins, Priscilla said a quiet prayer for her saviors. When she finished her prayers, she felt a strange shiver down her spine. Turning around, she saw a group of zombies. They each wore ripped up Franciscan habits. Their faces were bluish; their eyes seemed to shot out from their sockets. Their mouths were rotting. Their exposed limbs showed rotting, worm eaten wounds. She had seen many photos of them on the internet. Yet, the reality of those beings was more than she could bear. She was about to start running when she noticed that they were nothing, but statues. Bellow each statue was the name of the each zombie saint.

 "So, there are the 12 zombie saints", said Priscilla passing by the saints, "They are so life like... I had not notice they were there. It seems like a grim choice of the artist to depict the saints like regular zombies. And what of the priest?"

 Giving a sign of relief, Priscilla left the church.

TERRY'S FIRST DAY
OF SCHOOL

Terry woke up early. She struggled out of the bed sheets and tumble in the darkness toward her grandmother's room. She opened the locks and went inside. In the darkness, she could half make out the large figure of her grandmother. She was sleeping on her side. With her small hands she lifted the curtain. She poked her grandma's broad shoulder to force her to wake up. Lazily, her grandmother awoke. Without changing their dress pajamas, Terry and her grandma went to open up the house.

All seasons in Cuba are identical. Summer, winter, fall and spring are always hot. The house needed to be open up early to allow the ocean breeze enters inside. When they had finished opening the portals of the house, Terry went to the kitchen. She sat on a chair and rested her head on her hand. She yawned a little and waited until her mother brought her a baby bottle. She took her bottle to her grandmother's room. By now, her grandma had finished tidying the bed. Tarry lay down on the bed and drank her milk with pleasure. While she drank it, she noticed a uniform at the foot of her bed.

It was her school uniform. It was a red skirt and a white t-shirt. When she finished her milk, she rose from the bed. She placed her bottle on the nightstand. She purposely took a half hour to get dressed. When she was dressed, she went outside the house and sat in the patio. She saw the sunrise over the concrete hill. There was not a single cloud in the sky. The sun felt cool that morning. A gentle breeze would pass by from time to time. When the sun had finally risen, Terry saw her father come out of the house. He was dressed in a white lab coat, green shirt and green pants. He gave a sign when his green eyes rested on his little girl. He carried in his hand a small blue purse, decorate by flowers. He gave the purse to his daughter, Terry. She looked within and saw her baby bottle with milk and a piece of bread wrapped in a napkin. The napkin had the initials F.F.B. She recognized it as one of her father's handkerchief. On the side, she saw her poorly stitched work. It was a napkin that she had ruined only a few days ago.

She ate a small piece from the soft part of the bread and placed the rest away. During these proceedings, her father waited. There was a faint smile painted in his tin lips. His green eyes watered a little due to the glare of the sun. He rubbed them to ward away sleep. It was supposed to be his day off. The previous night he had been on night watch at the hospital. Even though he slept for two hours, he still wanted to take his little girl to school. He planned to change his clothing, shower and take a nap after dropping her off. He looked at his wristwatch and noticed that it was almost eight.

He said to Terry, "Let's go, cutie, you don't want to be late for your first school day."

Terry said nothing. Again, her father's eyes water, this time it was not because of the sun. Together, they took walked toward school up the cement hill. That hill was walled by many houses. Terry had taken that route to school man times. She had seen the school from the outside, whenever she went with her grandma to pick up her older brother. Now, it would be her first time entering the building. While they walked, she played the color game with her father. It consisted of naming the colors of the main features of the houses. Her father had devised that game in order to teach her colors. Close to the school, her father said, "Terry, you are going to love school. There you get to play with other kids, learn numbers and use do a lot of fun things…"

Her father went on ranting about school for the rest of the trip. Terry said nothing to her father's comments. She had a grim, expressionless face. The kind of face she wore whenever she had to go to the doctor. Now they had reached the park. Just beyond it laid the school. The large trees were raining down white flowers. Its foliage completely covered the sky. Furtive lights illuminated the pavement, covered with flowers. Children younger than her were playing in the park while their mothers watched. She looked at those children and gave a deep sign. Her grim expression deepened into a frown. She slowed down her steps even more. Her father picked her up believing that she was tired. A bit short winded, her father hurried his pace.

The hot sun fell upon the pair when they left the park. Before them stood a school made of wood, bricks and cement. For the girl, the place reminded her of a prison. All the windows had iron bars. Like most houses of the region, the school had two story high main portals. Since it was school day, both doors were open ajar. Terry saw beyond it, the central park and the cement stage. The children were assembling in the park. Each child wore a uniform very similar to hers. Unlike Terry, a good chunk of them wore a scarf of either red or blue color. On the stage, the teachers sat in wooden chairs. They wore regular attires. Beside them, a little student was raising the Cuban flag. Noticing that they were late, the father placed his daughter on the floor. Giving her a little push, he urged her to join the others. Unfortunately for him, the girl was not budging. She had her feet firmly planted on the floor. He walked toward the park and urged the girl to join the others. By now, the national anthem was over. The teachers departed from their seats and started leading their students to their respective classrooms.

The kinder garden teacher recognized the girl's father at the entrance. She walked over to see what was occurring. Griming, she said, "Doctor Blanco, Good Morning!"

"Well, see…" he said ignoring the teacher, "Come on, Terry, go to school. It won't hurt. You might actually have a lot of fun."

"Relax doctor, leave this to the professionals!" when she said this she went toward the little girl. She took the girl by the hand and started leading her toward the classroom. From the corner of her eye, Terry noticed that her father was leaving. She ran away from the teacher and clung to her father's leg. Tears were rolling down her cheeks as she said, "Daddy, don't leave me here!! I don't to go to school! Never, ever! Please, take me home."

The girl's father tried pry her off his leg. However, she was hugging it with all her strength. Noticing that she was not budging, he started walking toward the classroom while the girl clung to his leg. Terry saw that she was drawing ever nearer to the classroom, which resembled a prison. That was the last straw. The girl had one her trademark hissy fits. She started screaming and sobbing while trying to catch her father's other leg. The students within the classroom started giggling when they saw the odd pair approaching. When they were inside, the girl tried her last gambit.

When she was two, she had picked up a whole arsenal of foul language. One of her neighbors used to curse worse than a pirate. Even though, it had been three years since last she heard such foul language. She kept those words in her mind. She only used them when things were not going her way. That day Terry used all the foul language she had ever learned .She even made up some interesting combinations that humor greatly, the other students. She went on to curse, everything from the students, the teacher and specially her father. That was the last time Terry was ever so expressive at school.

When she finally calmed down, her face became expressionless. She went through the school routine mechanically. Her teacher was greatly pleased by how nice Terry acted. She imagined that her teaching skills had straightened up that foul mouth girl that had so boisterously cursed her the first time they met. Whenever she spoke with Doctor Blanco, she prided herself on making little Terry into the ideal Pionero. The Doctor simply smiled at the teacher and allowed her to go on with her nonsense.

THE PARABLE OF KAKUNDO

Two men were sitting in a luxurious living room. There was a fireplace burning. On top of it, there were family portraits. One man was sitting on one couch and the other sat in a different couch facing his visitor. There was a coffee table littered with papers and books. The rug was Persian and the lamps of arabesque design. There were notable antiques here and there, as well as a cabinet filled with curiosities.

The owner of the home was in his mid-50s and the other gentleman was in his early 30s. The older man was known as el Greco. His head was starting to go bald. He had crystal clear blue eyes, and dark shadows cast over them. He was wearing a white Guayabera and greyish brown shorts. He had a bit of a pork belly.

In his old age, he had developed a fancy for collecting old history documents, books and oddities.

He was showing his latest collection to Antonio. Antonio was dressed more formally. He had tuxedo pants and a long sleeved blue shirt. The first three buttons of his shirt were unbuttoned, showing part of his bushy well-toned chest and a golden pendant with the image of the Virgin Mary. Antonio had a fake, golden tan, brown eyes and raven black hair. He though himself an art expert and was as refined as his well-manicured hands.

Greco handed Antonio quite the old Tome of Don Quixote and said, "I am sorry to have called you so late. However, I recently acquired this first edition tome! You are a bit of an art expert, so I wanted you to examine it and tell me if I over paid."

Antonio passed his hands over the cover of the book and frowned. The cover of the book looked brand new, and the pages were pristine white. He said, "I am sorry to tell you this friend, but you have been duped."

"Fuck!" said Greco shaking his fist and biting his lower lip.

Antonio raised an eye brown. Antonio flipped through it and continued speaking, "Yes! It's a fake! It doesn't even have illustrations or bad poems. Also this book is in English."

"Really?" said Greco flipping through its pages. Greco added, "I did not notice."

Greco handed Antonio another book called The Golden Age by Jose Marty. This book too proved to be a bust since it was in English. Plus, the name of the writer was misspelled. By the third book, Antonio started getting suspicious.

Eventually, Greco handed Antonio a genuine article. It was a first edition copy of The Alchemist, by Paulo Coelho in English. It had its original bizarrely drawn cover with the shepherd, the one eyed woman and the Muslim maiden. The English version was published in 1993. This book was going to be worth something…in a century or two.

Antonio flipped through its pages over the top. He nodded in approval. When he got to the middle of the book, his eyes widened. He frowned and said, "Uh?"

"Well, what is it?" said Greco sitting at the edge of the couch.

Antonio drew from within the pages of the Alchemist a crudely drawn comic. The figures in the comic looked like humans from an Aztec codex. The figures were delineated with a black marker and were painted with watercolor. The background was a bit closer to life and a few drawings looked like the background was traced. The comic was drawn in boxes, like newspaper comic strips.

The man in the front cover was from Africa. His clothing was those of the Modern Odyssey Tribe in Africa. Somewhat amused, Antonio read the comic. He chuckled when he read the "Once Upon a Time opening".

"Once Upon a Time, there was a strong brave warrior named Kakundo. Kakundo was the strongest man in his village. Despite his strength, Kakundo dreamed of living an easy life. He wanted a better life for himself and for the woman…"

In this part, Antonio saw Kakundo hugging his wife one last time. The wife looked sad, but she seemed to understand. The artist had taken great pains to illustrate Kakundo's dilapidated house. The house had no doors and the wooden windows were broken.

"Kakundo had planned to return in less than a decade…20 years later, Kakundo returns to his village. He had finally amassed enough wealth to live as a King in his native country. Along the way, there was a bad storm and he lost most of his cargo.

The storm caused him to fall off the ship. After swimming toward the port he was thankful to notice that he had still two ships filled with cargo. One of the ships he lost was the flagship of his privateering fleet. He took this as a sign that he had to give up his old life for good.

When Kakundo was in town, he sold his armor and one of his swords. With this money, Kakundo still had enough to never work a day in his life ever again."

The sword Kakundo was selling was highly detailed. The sword was fat and curved. It had a white curly handle, with a golden band. The hilt had an infinity golden sign. Over it, there were three gems inlaid into the sword. Antonio lingered on the sword for quite a bit. He felt he had seen the sword before, but he could not remember were.

As for the character Kakundo, he was drawn with grayish looking hair and dark wrinkles bellow his eyes.

Antonio then continued to read:

"After selling his prized sword and armor, Kakundo made arrangements for his loot to be sent to his village. He acquired a horse and then went on ahead to his village. Along the way, he ran into his lifelong rival. The two had been enemies since they were children and they had fought on numerous occasions.

Kakundo fought against his rival to the death. Both were trying to mortally wound one another. Kakundo had gained more real life experience in battle. As such, he was easily able to best his enemy. At the start of the battle, Kakundo had resolved to kill his rival. After crippling him, Kakundo decided to spare his life because he had given up his life of crime."

There were at least 10 fighting panels. In the last one, Kakundo had cut his nameless rival's hand and leg.

"When Kakundo went home, he was surprised to see that his wife had not changed at all. She still had the same, straight raven black hair and large brown eyes. His heart was torn by the sight of his home. It was even more dilapidated. He went to the back of his house with his woman and watched the sunrise together. Kakundo resolved to make up for lost time. He cried because his wife had waited for him, until the very end."

The final image showed Kakundo giving his back to the viewer. His wife was facing the reader while standing beside a cross with a name scribbled on it. When Antonio was done, he rested his head on his hand and sighed.

El Greco asked Antonio, "So…what do you think?"

Chuckling Antonio said, "Eh…it's not half bad, Kakudo's identity is pretty obvious. I wouldn't entertain the idea of publishing… your comic."

"It's obvious to you maybe," said El Greco frowning. He added, "I have other versions of the comic. They go into detail about Kakundo's pirate adventures."

"Fine, get em," said Antonio sitting back. He found the situation quite humoring.

Both their attention was drawn by a noise in another room. El Greco heard the familiar footsteps of his wife and two young daughters. His wife had taken the girls out to see a bad Harry Potter movie. El Greco was worried since his girls had lied about the length of the film. It was past the girls' bedtime and they had still not returned home.

Seconds later, he heard three shots. Greco and Antonio got up from their seats and rushed to see the commotion. The door to the home was wide open. Greco saw a man jumping the fence. Antonio went to give chase while Greco called an ambulance. This however was a foolish effort since both his wife and his two daughters were already dead.

When the bodies were taken away, Antonio entered the study. His sleeves were covered in blood. Greco was standing by the fire looking grim. Greco exchanged looks with Antonio. Both left the house inside El Greco's black Lamborghini. Within half an hour, El Greco had arrived at the club. The bouncers did not stand in his way. At the far end of the darkly light club, El Greco recognized the shrill laughter. There was an old man in a wheel chair laughing, beside two hot women.

When he saw El Greco, he told him, "You knew this was going to happen."

El Greco took a small pistol from his pocket and shot the man point black in the forehead. He left the club without saying a word.

120,000 BC

It was mid-summer when Agh went to the fields to work alongside his family. He belonged to one of the few clans that had domesticated plants. He was now in his late 40s, and still a stout man. He wore pelts made of saber tooth tigers and wolves. When he arrived at the fields, he saw his sister and her husband working in the fields. They were plowing the fields with rudimentary tools made of stone. Keeping a lookout were two wolfish, dogs. These domesticated dogs still maintained plenty of their wolf looks, however their ears were starting to slant and their face were slightly pronounced.
Agh found this change a bit strange. He remembered dogs from his day had perfectly pointed ears. They were also a bit more hostile than the dogs his sister's husband owned. Those dogs were a valuable acquisition to the clan. They made hunting quite easier and at night they warned the clan of the approach of larger beasts.

By sunset, Agh returned to his family hut. It was made of post and lintel, with wooden planks for a roof. Sitting on a chair was his mother; she was wrapped in pelts trying to stay warm by the bonfire. She smiled when she saw Agh. Her faced was lined with wrinkles. Agh sat beside her and she wrapped him in her coats as she had done back when Agh was a child.

Agh suddenly noticed how small his mother's hands had become. He had a vague memory of her youthful beauty and splendor. Agh's mother was the oldest maiden in the clan. She was pushing 80. She had survived many things from famines, to attacks and ravenous beasts. Agh suddenly realized that his mother was going to die.

It had never occurred to him that people die of old age. He thought his mother was going to live forever as long as he kept her safe. The thought that she was no longer going to be with him drove Agh to tears. Agh's mother tried to console him, with coos and grunts. However, Agh was inconsolable.

THE WHISKY SURGEON AND THE ADDICT

D r. Walker was a famous plastic surgeon. He operated both rich and poor alike. In the twilight of his life, he was remembering a certain patient of his. At the time, he had been practicing plastic surgery for only 4 years. He had left the hospital and opened a clinic with the hopes of earning more profit for his ever growing family. This was the official excuse.

His drinking problems had gotten more severed with the workload and the nature of his cases. He had hit rock bottom when he had failed to save a little boy. This was a wakeup call. He did not have the stomach or liver to be a true doctor. Resigned to his fate, he opted for the lucrative business of elective surgery.

He found plastic surgery a rewarding. He was turning ugly women, beautiful. Since the bulk of them were healthy, he did not have the pressure of dealing with major complications. Only rarely did the operations go down south. Such mild surprises paled in comparison to what he had to deal with in the hospital.

As a result of his new employment, he got his drinking under control. He even began to have the vague hope of getting rid of his addiction for good. It was around that time when he met her. It wasn't too uncommon for maidens to revisit his office for new upgrades. The maidens he operated were never satisfied.

When he had first met Sofia, he thought she was the most beautiful woman he had ever seen. Her chest was full and perky. Her behind, though not large was firm and scrumptious. Her face was not pretty, but she certainly passed as handsome. With a bit of makeup, she could be called beautiful. Naturally, Dr. Walker never told his patients that he thought they were beautiful. He did once, to his first patient, however, the maiden threatened to call the police.

Sofia started with a standard upgrade: Liposuction with a Brazilian butt-lift. This procedure was quickly followed with breast implants. Sofia came out beautifully from the procedure, but it was not enough for her.

About a year later, she came back asking for four ribs to be removed. She wanted a thinner waist. Dr. Walker eyed her skeptically from head to toe. The upgrades to her chest and her naturally wide hips made her waist look thin. Since her previous checks had cleared, Dr. Walker decided not to argue.

Over the course of 3 years, Sofia returned time and time again asking for new upgrades. In this sense, she was becoming a regular costumer. Some of the procedures she wanted as of late had gotten ridiculous. Her most recent request had been an ear operation. She felt unhappy by the shape of her ears. Indeed, she had a goblin thing going for her. However, Dr. Walker had never met a guy who married a maiden because she had pretty ears.

This was the first check that bounced. A few weeks later, she came back with the cash. Dr. Walker started suspecting that his patient had bankrupted herself with all these plastic surgeries. When she came to ask him to operate her eyes, he said, "Have you tried sleeping 8 hours a day? Those teabags might go away by themselves if you sleep more often."

"Don't be silly," said his out of patience, patient.

"I am just concerned by the number of operations you are getting as of late. I do not want to see you go bankrupt as a result of these procedures," said Dr. Walker.

"Don't pretend to care now, Doctor. You have been happy to operate on me as long as all the checks cleared, up until now. This was just an error in the bank; my work check had come in late. It will not happen again. I promise," said Sofia.

Dr. Walker yawned, while he Irished-up his coffee. He then said with a bit more courage, "I am sorry, but I cannot ethically give you this operation. There is nothing wrong with your eyes. You don't even have crow's feet."

"Good day, Dr. Walker! Know that you have lost one of your best patients. Don't you dare call me up and ask me to come back, you hear," yelled Sofia.

After his patient stormed out of his office, Dr. Walker yawned and said, "I wouldn't dream of it."

As the door to his office slowly closed, he saw the large line of prospective clients.

THE HOUSE

Mrs. Thomson was walking by the park one day with her maid. She was wearing a lovely blue dress, with a blue parasol. Along the way, she saw a strange man that made her very nervous. Something about that old gentleman looked familiar. To avoid him, she took an unusual route back home. After taking a wrong turn, she was in an unfamiliar part of the city.

At least, it seemed unfamiliar to her at first. The more she walked the more she remembered. She had played hopscotch on a sidewalk in front of the bakery. Her mother had bought her a blue laurel from a strange looking flower seller at the street corner.

Her wanderings eventually brought her to that house. The house was the second home from her childhood. The first had been lost due to her family's declining fortune. As she got older, she discovered that her dearly departed father had gambled away her mother's dowry. In no time, they would have landed in the poor house. As her mother had said, "It was a good thing he got sick and died before then."

For a time, her father was bed ridden, unable to lift his head from his pillow. For a year, his mother handled the financial affairs. One day, her father simply withered away like a dry rose petal. With her father dead, his family stopped sending her mother money. She was forced to move to a new house.

This new house was ironically ten times as a large as her old one. Despite its massive dilapidated state, Mrs. Thomson noted the sublime architectural detail. Even the overgrown garden had remnants of its former glory. She opened the rickety fence and went cautiously inside.

Her maid protested against this, but she did not bother to listen to her. Once inside, the surroundings were quite familiar, even without the furniture and paintings. She walked through the entire house undisturbed. On her way back home, Mrs. Thomson found it odd how peaceful the old house had become this last 12 years. It seemed to her that the spooks had finally moved on.

Back when Mrs. Thomson was a child, the house had been inhabited by ghosts. Her mother had told her so. It was the main reason they had gotten the house so cheap. No one wanted to live in that haunted house. The spooks rarely appeared in her bedroom. When they did, it was just for a few minutes to watch her sleep or see if she was studying.

Normal children would have been scared by this new situation. However, Mrs. Thomson had decided to be brave for her mother's sake. Her mother would once a day go out to work to do the neighbors laundry. On the meantime, the house would be filled with all sorts of noises, laughter and groans.

It was almost impossible to focus on anything, let alone her lectures. One day, a specter had struck her mother, it had made Mrs. Thomson so angry that she had overcome her fear to yell this to it, "Why don't you and your friends go back to hell were you belong?"

The ghost had turned pale as death. One of his friends then escorted him back to the abyss. Unlike the others, he was never seen again. Aside from grown up ghosts, the house had children ghost too. She felt pity for the children's ghost, especially those of small infant and toddlers.

She remembered clearly how one had been left in a seat near her.

She was supposed to watch over it. She did not quite understand why the baby's mother was bothering her with the ghost baby. There was nothing else that could happen to it, now that it was dead. To avoid being yelled at, Mrs. Thomson had kept an eye on the child.

She would sit it back in place, whenever it got too close to the edge of the sofa. It was a bit of a hassle, but it broke the monotony of her studies. After spotting a rodent, Mrs. Thomson decided to return home. It was nighttime when she reached her domicile. Her husband had finally taken notice of her absence. Once at home, she sank back to her cozy existence. She stopped thinking about that house, and the ghosts that had once dwelled within.

STARDUST

The year is 1856. A Palladian style manor is filled with mercenaries, cowboys and men with guns. Outside, there is a tree with eight figures hanging lifelessly from its branches. One of the figures is an old black woman. A cowboy, with a star on his vest is getting the testimony from one of the guests inside the manor.

The tale he had spun was straight out of an Edgar Allan Poe novel. The sheriff would have noticed the parallel, if he had ever bothered to learn how to read. The person giving his story was the preacher's son. He had visited the manor in question along with his twin sister and his elderly mother.

The sheriff was not surprised when he said, "My name is Jonathan Wesley. That's my sister Jane and my mother Frances Jane Wesley."

"You are not from around here, are you?" asked the sheriff.

"You can tell from our accent. Yes, we are from the North. We were on our way to Florida to visit some relatives, when we were invited to this gala…" Jonathan explained. He added, "Our boat was not set to depart till the next day, so we decided to attend the party. My sister is not the type of person to turn down a free meal."

The men chuckled at this comment. For indeed, little Jane was in the middle of raiding the food closet of the manor. Normally, the sheriff would have reprimanded her unladylike behavior; however considering the strange, traumatic event she had just experienced he had decided to let her be.

"Continue your story," said the sheriff. One of his men had just returned with his drink freshened up.

"We arrived a little late to the party. All the guests were already wandering about the manor. I was greeted by one of the servants. At first, she seemed a bit reluctant to let me inside. She kept insisting that it was already too late and I should return home. I thought her behavior was a bit queer, but my sister's stomach would not wait. In retrospect, I should have taken the hint.

As soon as I came inside, I marveled at all the wealth that surrounded the place. The candle stands were made of solid gold, the rug was genuinely Persian, and the walls were littered with paintings…" Jonathan was interrupted by the sheriff.

In a stern voice he said, "We can see that. Now focus on the action!"

"Ahem! The slaves and white servants had the manor well kept. Among them, there was this nice elderly, old black slave woman. All the servants treated her with reverence, even the white indentured servants. At the time, I did not think much of it. I naturally assumed that witch doctors were more common in the South, no offense," said Jonathan.

"None taken please continue," said the sheriff.

"After perusing the foods, I noticed everything looked fattening, so I refrained from eating. My doctor has asked me to show moderation, let's my ankles break under my own weight. Like I was saying, I did not eat or drink anything since I had eaten before going to the party. I was drawn to a strange, familiar piano music coming from another room.

A gorgeous little blonde girl was playing on a grand piano. When

I saw her face, I was overwhelmed by pity. He green eyes were out of focus, and she was drooling. I naturally assumed she was daft or mad. Regardless, she was playing one of my favorite piano songs: Claro Luna by Debussy, from time to time she would miss a note and one of the maids would hit her. I would have protested, but it is not my business to meddle in the manner that people raise their children.

Throughout this entire affair, this piano song would play over and over. It seemed to me that the girl only knew this one song. After noticing that the girl would not play a new song, I started talking with the maid that had received me. She went on a rant about Carl Marx," said Jonathan.

"Who?" asked the sheriff.

"Marx is a European philosopher; he is quite popular in London. He speaks all sorts of dribble about the exploitation of the working class and whatnot. Since my little maid had the look of a fanatic, I decided to agree with her arguments. It is always a wasted effort to argue with narrow minded people," he commented. He paused for a moment before continuing.

"…while talking with her. I saw from the corner of my eye some of the guests being dragged downstairs. The maid saw the direction my eyes were looking. After stammering a bit, she said, "They are drunk…they are taking them to rest, to keep them from pestering the other guests.""

"I pretended to believe her. However, after she returned to her work I went in the direction that the men had been taken away. This path took me to the kitchen and from there to the basement. The maid in the kitchen did not seemed to notice me. She was busy adding a strange, shiny purplish powder over all the food and drinks. When I opened the door to the basement, I saw a group of men sitting in chairs around a strange looking, giant flowering plant. Its azure, violet colors and shape were unlike any flower that I knew of. There was a strange aroma, and I started to feel sick to my stomach and a little light headed. For some reason, something was compelling me to get closer to the plant. Before I stepped into the room, the maid I had spoken to dragged me out of the room. She had a scarf covering her face, to keep her from imbibing the…miasma, for lack of a better word."

"She asked me if I had eaten anything, and I said no. She said that the old crone was using the plant to control the owners of the manor. She added, "Its spores… they cause people to see things. What's worse is that if you are exposed to it for too long, you suffer memory loss, followed by death after a week. So you would not remember being near the plant. You need to make your mother and sister throw up before the poison kills them.""

In a hurry, I found my sister and told her to throw up. She was never the type to question me, even when my stories seemed extremely farfetched. After throwing up, she sighed and said, "I feel a lot better.""

We found our mother who was about drink some of the wine. I tried to drag her to another room while explaining things to her. She however poo, poo, my story and told me I should not take serious the superstitious rants of slaves. Between my sister and me, we made her throw up, much to her annoyance and then I knocked her out. We started carrying her, but the crone noticed us starting to leave," said Jonathan.

"How did you escape?" asked the sheriff.

"That is just the thing; I cannot for the life of me remember how it happened. My mother was unconscious and my sister suffered partial memory loss from the residual poison," explained Jonathan.

"Why do you think the slaves were poisoning their masters?" asked the sheriff more to himself.

"Isn't it obvious, they wanted to rob them and go live up north," said one of the officers.

"If they wanted to do so, then why the party? Why stay when

they have a means to eascape?" asked the sheriff.

"We could have asked the perpetrators, pity that our men got a little carried away," said another gentleman.

"A true pity indeed, for among those who are hanging was the girl who saved me," said Jonathan frowning. He wanted to say more, but he chose to remain silent. He knew that slaves were never given any true justice in the South. In the end, he decided that the slave girl had gotten what she deserved. She may have helped him, but she had led many others to their deaths.

The following day the house was turned upside down. It was discovered that the true owners had been dead for more than two years. The girl who was playing the piano was indeed the daughter of the masters of the manor. She was also a lot more lucid than she had first appeared. The servants were apparently drugging the girl to keep her from speaking the truth about the atrocities that were going on around her.

Her memory was spotty at best, though she was aware of her surroundings. Instead of talking about a plant, she would rave about a fairy that would come listen to her piano. She would only appear when she played Claro Luna.

The plant that was kept in the basement was no were to be found. Still, its aroma had seeped into all the clothing, fabrics and other items stored in the basement. To test out the psychedelic effects of the plant, the sheriff had one of his men sniff a handkerchief. A single whiff of it alone had him in a daze. Like the servant girl had described, the cowboy lost some of his memory. He could not remember entering the basement or even volunteering to take a whiff.

SPIRIT BEAR

Edward Brandon was a British loyalist who firmly believed in the motherland, and all it represented. He thought himself a righteous, outstanding, pious gentleman. His faith in this belief was tested during the French and Indian War. While he participated in this war, he was witness to the atrocities committed by his fellow men, in their pursuit to carry out the Crown's orders. Even if the Red Devils were sinners, nothing could excuse the crimes committed by his comrades. In one of such adventures, he assisted in the massacre of a Native tribe. He personally shot and killed a mother and her small daughter. He did this in part out of mercy. He did not wish upon them the fate of the rest of the Native women.

The war ended and he settled in a plantation in Virginia. He resolved to put the war behind him, and dedicate the rest of his life to atone for his crimes. He was kind to his indenture servants, and he would even give them part of his money to help them settle in a new town, once their debt was repaid. He also gave generous alms to both the church and whatever beggar he ran into.

He even got himself a pretty wife. Soon he had a daughter of his own, little Marianne. When his daughter turned eight, Brandon started having nightmares. He would dream that a large white bear was slaughtering his wife and daughter. One night, he screamed at the bear, "Why!"

The bear sneered and said, "À chaque fou plaît sa marotte!"

He found it quite odd that the bear would have spoken to him in French. It took three dreams, but he was finally able to remember the exact words the bear had said. He was not too familiar with the French language, so he wrote it down how it sounded phonetically in English. When the sun rose, he visited one of his neighbors, a painter, who had studied in Paris. He showed him the paper and asked him what it meant. He kept to himself the origin of the phrase.

Smiling, Cole said, "It means: Every fool is pleased with his own folly."

Brandon was not remotely humored by what the phrase meant. He reasoned that the dream was God telling him that he had to do more to make up for what he had done. He went on to do more charitable works in the community. One day when walking home, he saw a native little girl wandering about town. Based on her shackles, she was probably a slave of sorts. When the girl saw him, she pointed behind him and started screaming something in her native tongue.

Brandon was chilled to the bone and rode back home to check up on his family. Everything was as it should be. After seeing the Native girl, he stopped having the nightmares. He slowly allowed himself to relax. A week passed, and all was well. One night, he was awakened to the horror of finding his wife dead beside him.

A monstrous bear was eating her. Brandon could not phantom how the bear had gotten inside the house, without making a peep. Remembering his dream, he ran toward his daughter's room and took her in his arms. He threw her sleeping form inside a carriage, and rode out of his home as fast as his horses could take him.

The next day, the servants found their dead mistress. When the guards came, they were naturally inclined to blame Brandon for the murder of his wife. This however was disproven by the claw marks of the bear so vividly gnawed into her body.

Brandon rode his carriage nonstop for an entire day. He eventually decided to stop due to the protestations of his small daughter. He stopped at an inn to get supplies, in order to continue on his journey. He finally unburned himself to the barkeep, after drinking himself silly. The next morning, when he was more sober the barkeep suggested he visit St. John's Episcopal Church.

Following his advice, Brandon took refuge with his daughter in the church. Weeks passed, and Brandon would not take his eye off his daughter for even a second. The priest was kind, but he could not wrap his head around the possibility of an Indian curse actually working. He firmly believed that the Lord would not allow the heathen devils to harm his faithful flock.

The priest still did bother to bless them, and even performed a complimentary exorcism. Two months passed, and the spirit bear did not make an appearance. Brandon could still not find any peace. His servants and his brother James eventually tracked him down. Brandon related his strange story, but his brother who naturally refused to believe him. He firmly believed that his brother Edward had murdered his wife out of jealousy.

James in part had come to take his niece away from his demented brother. Since he could not find a way to get the girl out, without much commotion, he decided to stay in the church to watch over her. Things continue peacefully for a few more days. Brandon's peace was shattered when at night; he saw the spirit bear outside the church.

He was in the outskirts of the graveyard. The stylized hooded angel headstones looked real, and flesh like, almost as if they were alive. The spirit bear vomited a green miasma that spread over the graveyard. Brandon rose from his bed and closed the window. His brother, who was in the room watching him sleep, was shocked to see him sleep walking toward the window.

He started to suspect that his brother might be possessed. When the sun rose, little Marianne was with fever. The days passed and her conditioned worsened. When all hope seemed lost, a native boy came into church. The priests started to naturally shoo him away, however, he apparently knew Brandon.

"My older sister asked me to see Edward Brandon, she needs your help," he said.

"I don't help your kind, be gone cur!" said Brandon.

"You must see my father. He is the one who sent the spirit bear. If you refuse, he will continue killing everyone you love," the boy explained, "If you do not believe me, I will tell you the phrase the bear spoke told you when you first saw him: À chaque fou plaît sa marotte."

"This is madness. He probably heard the barkeep gossiping about it. If you go with him, it will be the death of you," said James alarmed.

"I will see him my brother, for one thing. I only told one person what the bear had said," said Brandon resigned to his fate.

Brandon traveled with the native boy, while his brother stayed behind looking after his daughter. In secret, his brother sent soldiers to follow after him. The native boy guided him up a mount. The mount was surrounded by strange sobbing and whispers that grew stronger the closer one got to the summit.

The soldiers who were trailing Brandon naturally did not hear anything. However, they were alarmed by the lack of sound that surrounded them. The breeze was dead, and not even an ant graced them with its presence. When Brandon got to the top, he saw an old wooden cabin, with smoke coming from the chimney. Outside, he saw in the flesh the specter of the little girl he had shot.

Brandon did not know this, but the girl was begging her father to stop killing for her sake. He could not understand her sobbing, since she spoke in her native tongue. She was tired of innocents dying because of her. Brandon entered the cabin. Inside he saw the true Spirit Bear, in the flesh. The old native was eyeing him with a look of content.

When the soldiers arrived at the cabin, they found it abandoned. There were no traces of it having been habited for the last 8 years. Brandon's body was never found, nor was the strange native boy ever seen or heard from again. Marianne did not recover from her illness either. In her final delirious hours, she screamed for her father to protect her from the spirit bear.

THE CURSED DOLL

The reporter Kevin Nestor was collecting anecdotes about the life during colonial times. It seemed unreal, that only 60 years ago there was slavery in America. To complete his book, he wanted to get the opinion of not only the slaves, but of the people who directly benefited from slavery. He wanted to get the other side of the story, in an effort to humanize the slave owners. For him, they were just people of their own time who naturally never questioned the evil of slavery, just the same as the people from his time were not questioning Separate but Equal.

Talking with former slaves had proven to be an easy task. However, getting former slave owners to open up was proving to be a difficult task. When describing the purpose of his book, he was always rudely sent away, and even a clan member had threatened to hang him.

After much effort, he found Rebeca M. Preston. Her family had owned slaves since her childhood. Her father had even fought for the Confederates. She had the ideal qualifications for his book. His publicist had made arrangements for him to speak with Mrs. Preston in her home. At the age of 68, this feeble old maiden was living in a farm with her youngest daughter, who was taking care of her.

After sharing a bit of tea and cake in the garden, Nestor started as thus, "How was your life growing up in a slave plantation?"

"Privileged," said Mrs. Preston smiling coolly. Nestor frowned realizing her mind was as sharp as ever. He was not the sharpest tool in the shed.

"Did you ever felt guilty about the way the slaves were treated?" asked Nestor.

"No…" said Mrs. Preston.

"Why?" asked Nestor.

"As a lady, it was never my busyness how my father managed his property. I born white and raised by a black slave to be sure. I never questioned anything, nor saw anything wrong with the world around me. Sure, to you they were people, but to me they were not even human," explained Mrs. Preston.

"Do you still feel the same way?" asked Nestor.

"Before I give you my answer, I would like to tell you a little story. A tale I have not told anyone, about the strange circumstances that led to decline of my father's estate. You may have read about a strange plague that poisoned not only the slaves, but the horses, cattle and even the masters of the house, yes?" asked Mrs. Preston.

"Yes, I heard of it," said Nestor lying. He wrote down in his notebook these few interesting facts about Mrs. Preston's life. He wished he had done a bit of prep research before heading out. This interview was too short notice for his taste.

"When I was eight, I was a precocious little girl. My father said I was born with the heart of a boy. Despite my mother and my nana's best efforts, I lived a pretty active life running all over the farm, throwing rocks, practicing shooting and riding horses. My favorite game was to go exploring. Together with my older brother Luscious, may God Rest his soul, we would see how far we could explore out in the farm. Are you following me thus far, young Nestor?" asked Mrs. Preston. She sipped her tea and then continued her story, "While exploring, we stumbled upon a dark mysterious cave. It was hidden in the undergrowth of a tree. I remember the floor was damp, and the cave was not deep. One could get to the end in less than 1 minute.

There were slight holes in the top made by the roots of the tree. This allowed flickering tender light to enter inside. Luscious had reached into his knapsack and taken out a lantern. Beneath its flickering light, I saw something that caught my eye. Luscious grasped, saying, "It looks like a dead baby!"

We creep closer and were disappointed to discover that it was a weird, bisque doll. Bisque dolls were starting to get trendy. I used to own 20, all imported from Germany. I even had one that was a meter tall. I had gotten it for my 7th birthday in an effort to curb my manly hobbies. It is ironic…now that I think about. My father never raised his hand against me, and was always indulgent to all my little eccentricities as a child, even when I willingly disobeyed him, but I digress," said Mrs. Preston going on a tangent.

She took in a deep breath, and then continued, "The bizarre thing about the bisque doll was that it was black. My brother picked it up with suspicion and then commented, "It looks like it is burned or something."

"Yeah, that would explain the color and the black dress," I said agreeing with him.

"Do you want it?" asked Luscious.

"It is a bit dingy but I think Nana can probably clean it up," I said putting the doll under my arm. I know now that it was God's will that I picked up that doll. Through it, he was able to work great miracles within my family.

I took the black doll home and added it to my collection. Since the first day I brought it in, the slaves started acting restless, disoriented even. Some would start walking blindly at night, laughing like madmen. In the morning, their pace was sluggish. Even the most docile of slaves would sometimes suffer bursts of anger. It was quite the perplexing alteration in their behavior.

Whenever they would pass by me, they would eye the doll in a queer fashion. I had also to ask Nana like a hundred times to get her to clean the doll. In the end, she did so reluctantly. Despite her best efforts, the doll retained an overall charred look. I was beginning to suspect that it was a black bisque doll.

During dinner a week later, Luscious had spoken of the black doll to my father. He had laughed it off saying, "Those German snobs don't make black dolls."

One day, I was playing outside in the porch with my other dollies when a slave passing by accidently tripped on my black bisque doll. The doll was not harmed, still annoyed I said, "Watch were you are going!"

His eyes opened wide, and he said kneeling down, "Oh! Please, please forgive me! I did not see you, I implore your forgiveness! Honest, little lady I won't do it again. I swear."

My father who was reading the newspaper, sitting in a rocking chair beside me said calmly, "Its fine! It can happen to anyone. See! This is why I tell you not to play on the floor!"

The slave continued apologizing for a good while. In the end, my father sent someone to put him "away" since he was starting to annoy him. That day I tried my best to clean the doll and her stepped-on dress. I had sent it to the cleaner and even had the doll borrow a dress from my other bisque dolls. I naturally forgot about the entire incident. While going out in an excursion with my brother, I saw the slaves opening a grave for one of their peers. This was nothing new, so I continued on my way. Though, the burials were starting to become more frequent as of late.

The days passed and I continued blissfully with my life. Though, I was noticing some strange things. My nana would not speak to me whenever I had my black doll in the room. I took to taking the doll with me, so that my nana would not pester me about doing my lectures. A month eventually passed and that was when I noticed the bodies piling up. It was not just the slaves who were starting to die, but even the white indenture servants. My mother too was starting to fall ill.

At night, I heard whispers near my bedroom. The next morning, my father was looking very serious. He noticed the black doll too in my arms. He offered me a new, white doll and said coldly, "Maybe you will like this one better. It is the latest model."

I tried playing with the new doll, but after two days I found its face shattered. The more graves the slaves dug up, the more whispers I heard behind my door at night. One day, I woke up in the middle of the night. I saw my nana standing by a rocking chair, staring at the black doll like a madman. It was not her face, glowing the moonlight which frightened me so, it was…" said Mrs. Preston stopping. Her face had turned paled, from the vividness of this memory.

Taking strength again, she continued, "The chair… it started to rock by itself. Trembling from head to toe, I convinced myself that the wind was making the chair rock. I had opened the window that night to let the cold air in. The night was still and silent as a coffin. The only thing that broke the silence was the low groan of the rocking chair. I closed my eyes against my waking nightmare. I know not when I fell asleep. My dreams were haunted and confused.

When the sun rose, I was terrified to note that my nana had been replaced by a different slave. While walking outside, I saw my nana's hand sticking out of one of the corpse wrappings. She was thrown unceremoniously along all the others who had died the previous night.

At that moment, I realized what I had done. During the afternoon, I took the doll with me. I went to the cave alone, without telling my brother. Sensing that I was up to no good, the doll starts having influence over me, and I feel myself becoming ill. I collapsed, and I yelled, "God! Please!"

I threw the doll toward a nearby water puddle and the dark rainy sky became aglow with light. I saw an ashen figure of a black little girl, dressed in gold emanate from the doll and then turn to ash. God had never answered any of my prayers till them. This was the one and only time I ever saw a miracle manifest before me. After that incident, the deaths stopped all together. I had apparently passed out from the stress. My father had found me fainted by the small stream. He had picked up the doll as well. The same day we had moved to another farm.

The war came and with it, my dear father was killed. You may think he was fighting on the side of evil, but he was a good, man who fought for what he believed in. To answer your question, I still feel the same way as before. Society may forcefully change, but people take a lot longer to change their mind, if at all," concluded Mrs. Preston.

Nestor did not know what to make of Mrs. Preston's bizarre story. He resolved to keep the cute parts, and everything relating the mysterious plague. He decided to remove the doll, all together from his anecdote anthology. He imagined his client probably suffered from hallucinations caused by lead poisoning. Building water pipes with lead was an unknown danger back then.

After completing the interview, Mrs. Preston asked him, "Would you like to see my black doll?"

I was under the impression you would want to get rid of it, after everything that happened though Nestor grimacing. Mrs. Preston showed him the peculiar black doll. Just like Mrs. Preston's nana, he could not shake the feeling that the doll was staring at him.

SEISHIN YUME TANTEI!

Cardinal Pippin the Short was preparing the communal wine. Suddenly, the wine turns to blood and he drops the chalice. The blood flows through the ground and it takes the shape of the number of the beast. Shocked, Cardinal Pippin wakes up, sweating from head to toe. At that moment, he decides to tell his flock not to go to church anymore. The dream has manifested his suspicion. The Catholic Church was corrupted. The flock should refrain from attending church, until it has been cleansed.

Before Cardinal Pippin carries out his plan, he consults with his mentor. The next day Cardinal Pippin was found murdered in his bedroom. The police have been investigating his murder for days. So far, all signs point to a mob hit.

Meanwhile, in American a teenager of Japanese descent was struggling to keep awake in class. James Saito was not the most studious of fellows. He always maintained a straight B average, and always prioritized playing video games than doing homework. Whenever there was a new game, he was always in the habit of staying up late playing. His mother was an American, so she allowed him plenty of liberties, as long has he maintained his grades and did not get into trouble.

Whenever this occurred, the following morning he would sleep past first period. This time he was awake, though with much effort. Surprised, his Language Art teacher Mr. Godfrey asked, "Is there something wrong, Mr. Saito?"

"No? Why do you ask?" asked James yawning.

"Today, the new Dark Souls 3 game came out. So, I was expecting you to sleep through my class, so," said Mr. Godfrey. He knew James liked the game because most of his creative writing assignments were akin to fan fictions. Mr. Godfrey did not mind seeing as though James was one of the few students who could string together more than 5 sentences that made sense.

"My father heard I was falling asleep in class...so," said James lying.

Not wishing to press the matter, Mr. Godfrey continues with his lectures. The day passed for James in a state of somnambulism. He was not quite awake, but not quite asleep either. He was so dazed; he almost crossed the street when the light was green. It was a good thing that his friend Fu was there, to keep him from making a deadly mistake.

Alarmed, Fu asked, "What's wrong with you, James?"

"I don't know, I just haven't not been feeling great as all, alright," said James yawning.

"That's not even a real sentence," said Fu frowning.

"I just done sleep as much," said James yawning again.

"How come? Problems at home?" asked Fu genuinely concerned.

"Dunno, I, for some reason I am afraid of falling asleep," said James.

Laughing, Fu asked, "Getting stalked by Freddy Krueger?"

Fu continued pocking fun at James' fear of falling asleep all throughout the bus ride, and walk home. By the time James had arrived home, his mood had lightened up. He dismissed his irrational fear of falling asleep. At night, he finally allowed sleep to overtake him.

When he fell asleep, he had a continuation of "That" dream. It was not often, but at times he had dreams in parts. He would only remember that the dream would continue inside the dream. Usually, he was just following up on complete nonsense. When he became aware in the dream, he saw an angel floating by his bedside.

As usual, the things in his room were inverted, as if looking through a mirror. The angel in the white kimono was repeating over and over, "Mewosamasu, Seishin yume tantei-kun!"

This strange angel had been visiting James for the last 3 days. He was saying the same thing over and over. Today, James finally got out of bed and said, "I don't speak Japanese! And I am not even Christian! Leave me alone, angel!"

"Oh! My apologies, Dream Spirit Detective-kun," said the angel bowing.

"What do you want?" asked James getting up from bed.

"Ah! Yes, straight to the point. You have been chosen to participate in a holiest of missions, you must..." said the angel before James interrupted him.

"Sorry angel. If this is one of your callings, I must inform you that I am not interesting in becoming a priest. The whole giving up worldly wealth and women is not really my thing," said James chuckling.

"This is a calling yes...but not of the priestly variety. And besides, true callings rarely occur. Most of the times, I fear the petty humans are hallucinating," commented the angel folding his arms.

"I thought so, as much. Let me get this straight, you are not giving me much of a choice in the matter, are you. When I wake up tomorrow, I am going to have to do some grand feat or go preach to the masses, before getting betrayed," said James yawning. He was sleepy even inside his own dream.

"Nothing of the sort Dream Spirit Detective-kun, everything will take place in the dream world, through the blessing of the Anchor. And I promise not to make it an every night thing either. Once you solve the case, you can return to your regular night terrors," said the Angel happily.

"I don't have any night terrors," protested James.

"Sure you do! Now back to the matter at hand. I need you to investigate a crime scene. Look through the details and discover who were the murderers of Cardinal Pippin," said the Angel looking serious.

"Cardinal Pippin...that sounds like a made up name, but fine... let's just get this show on the road. I have school tomorrow," said James taking hold of the chains of the anchor.

The angel tied the chains around James' legs. Afterwards, James started to hover a little before sinking into the floor. The anchor dragged him into the crime scene. James then sees several cardinals whispering to one another while the police investigate. A thought suddenly crosses James's mind. He then says out loud, "This is stupid! I don't speak Italian and I have no idea what I am supposed to look for. Angel, go find someone more capable to do the job."

As James starts leaving the scene, some obvious spooks start to accost him. He tries to return to the crime scene to do his job, but the spooks will not leave him alone. His blood turns to ice when demons appear, laughing and jeering. The bizarre things did not harm him because of the blessing of the anchor. However, it made it impossible to focus on the crime scene.

In anger, he starts striking the intruders with whatever he can find. One of the specters was a cute Victorian maiden with a large chest. Her figure was pale, and almost see-through. Curious, James makes the mistake of poking her in the chest. He had wanted to see if his hand would pass through her. Instead, he came out like a huge pervert. In anger, the ghost grows frenzied. Since she was bothering him, James throws her down a cliff.

Later on, James runs into a little ghost girl. The only thing she did was yell at him. Exasperated, James screams back, "Ah!! Ah!! How do you like it! How do you like it!?"

Since he could not stand her yelling, he throws the little girl out the window. Finally, James rips off the anchor and finally wakes up. In the morning, James only had a faint memory of the previous events. He found himself well rested, and in time he completely forgot that he was the Dream Spirit Detective.

The following night, he finds the angel looking furious. He asks, "What did you do to the Countess of Dudley?"

"Throw her out the window. It is not as if you were much help in keeping those things away from me," said James raising his voice.

"The Countess said you took her honor!" said the angel horrified.

"Oh…no, no, no! I just wanted to see if she was see-through or not. And, don't make this about me! This job is impossible! Those spooks and demons will not leave me alone. Either; get me an escort, or I am going back to bed," said James lying back down.

"You are already in bed. If you don't remember," the angel adds, "And besides, you should not have rip off the anchor. My peers have been looking it for days, and have yet to find it. Here is a new one! Don't lose it! I will also see about getting you that escort."

"Thank you," said James smiling. He frowns when he notes the little girl in the corner of his room. She points and starts yelling at James. James tells the angel, "Can you please do something about that annoying brat?"

"What brat?" asked the angel looking in the direction James was pointing at. Indeed, the angel could not sense anything living or dead. Smiling sadly, the angel says, "I think that girl is imaginary."

"Great! Just freaking great!" said James exasperated.

James putted on the anchor. When he then looked in the mirror, he saw that he looked like a black guy. Frowning, he asked the angel, "Why do I look like a black guy?"

"What's wrong with looking like Will Smith? Or are you racist, in addition to being a pervert?" asked the angel annoyed.

The pair continued to argue for some time. In the end, James leaves reluctantly in his search to find the killer of Cardinal Pippin. This time he had a bodyguard. Whenever a ghost or something would get close to him, the Terminator would shoot them. Again, between the wailing and the shotguns, James was not progressing one bit.

Eventually, James is able to associate the murder weapon to one of the conspiring Cardinals. They were paying money to the mobster who did the deed. Sighing, James said, "I do not know the names, of these bastards. I do not even know why they are named after a bird."

The angel manifests behind James and says, "I am proud of you. The names of these sinful Cardinals are…"

Raising his hand, James says, "Let me stop you there! It will not be useful for me to know their names because I won't remember anything when I wake up. I already did what you ask, so please, please leave me alone!"

The following night, James throws away his dream catcher for reasons he does not understand.

THE NIGHTMARE

Jimmy was walking in the forest as he would always do after completing his chores. He lived in a little cottage with his family. For generations, they had been friends with the fairy folks. While neighboring lands became infertile, this family always had enough to eat. Since Jimmy was the youngest of the family, he was tasked with bringing offerings to the fairies. They usually opened up to little children.
The fairies approached him and ate their fill of grapes and oranges. After accepting the offering, one of the fairies commented, "You don't seem happy Jimmy."

"I have been having a lot of nightmares as of late," said Jimmy sadly.

"Tell me of your nightmares, Jimmy. Maybe we can help you," said the fairies gathering around him.

"They always start the same. I put down a book, and then bad things happen," said Jimmy sadly.

"What sort of bad things?" asked one of the fairies.

"Well, just the other day, I putted down the book, and then a strange man dressed in leaves starts yelling at me. To all his insults, I simply respond blindly sir, yes sir. The bad man then makes me exercise till I drop dead from exhaustion. I usually wake up, whenever he returns to reading his book," explained Jimmy.

"A perplexing nightmare indeed," commented Oberon, the fairy King entering the scene. He added, "Do not worry. I will make certain your nightmare comes to an end soon."

The following week, Jimmy returned with new offerings for the fairies. Oberon was waiting for him at the edge of the forest. He had a concerned look on his face. He smiled when he noted that Jimmy seemed back to his old self again. Smiling, Oberon asked, "Did the nightmares finally go away?"

"Yes, I have been sleeping peacefully these last 2 days. Still, the last few nightmares were particularly painful," commented Jimmy sadly.

"How so?" asked Oberon.

"Well…in one I remember fighting this guy because he took my book and was making fun of me. In the last one, I was in a metallic box that could float in the ocean. It was raining and I was surrounded by grown men, dressed in leaves clothing. As soon as the boat arrived at the beach, the door opened. The men dragged me outside, and I felt a sharp pain in my chest. The sensation lasted for a short time. Unlike the other nightmares, I woke up without having to read the book," said Jimmy thoughtfully.

"I have a feeling that you won't be having anymore nightmares from now on," said Oberon smiling.

"I…hope you are right," said Jimmy, his voice trembling a little.

Seishin yume tantei! 2

For the last two months, James had been having a hard time sleeping. One day, his sleep problems all, but disappeared. He had finally come to grips with the terrible situation he was experiencing. The sad fact was that he could not quite put his finger on the origin of his woes. His life was pretty much uneventful: his grades were fine, he got along with his parents, and none of the others students bothered him.

His waking life was blissful, without any real problems. At night, it was another story, for he was the Seishin yume Tantei. James one night found himself in dreaming in his bedroom. Normally when he dreamt of his bedroom, it was to answer the summons of the angel. This time the angel was no were to be found. Hours passed and he was still unable to awaken.

This was not an issue since in his dreams days could pass, while his sleeping form stayed in one place. At times James wondered if the anchor had some time traveling properties. Not that it matter, seeing as though this recurrent dream might be just a figment of his imagination.

"Pity, I never watched detective shows, or even played video games of the kind," said James out loud.

Getting up, he felt the anchor drag him down under. It always did this whenever there was an important case afoot.

"Mmm! What to do what to do?" said James to himself. He had developed the habit of talking to himself when acting as the spirit detective.

James wandered the city alone, counting the hour still he would finally awaken. He grimly wondered if he had died in his sleep. It was a notion worth entertaining. The juxtaposition of baroque architecture and stale postmodern art made James think he was in Europe. He had done sufficient missions in Europe to recognize the place.

For him, all European cities and town looked the same. He was in fact, in Warsaw, not that it mattered much to him in the very least. The power of the anchor made all voices sound English in his ears. While crossing the river bridge that separated the city in two, he caught the eye of a girl who was looking straight at him.

This was a bit unusual, seeing as though all people he came in contact with could not see him. The girl reminded him of those Emo maidens who used to cut themselves, in the staircases. He always found it laughable since they all came from rich and loving families, and they still managed to make themselves feel miserable.

The blue eyed, raven haired, lass, with the thick makeup, and the leather vest said to him in a high pitch voice, "What you want pervert! Do little girl thrills you pervert! You fucking Asian pig!"

James narrowed his eyes and said nothing. Putting out her cigarette, the girl threw at him her half empty beer can. James dodged it to maintain the illusion that he was a being of flesh and blood. Somewhat amused, and a little bored, James started stalking the troubled girl. He needed a way to amuse himself till the angel summoned him for another mission.

After stalking her a bit, James thought, Maybe I am a pervert. Then again, it is not as if I have anything else better to do. Maybe helping her is the mission.

James watched her for an hour. The way she acted and spoke to people led him to believe she had been raped, at some point. He knew a girl from his class that had been raped by the jocks. She turned from a nice airhead, to a porcupine, always bearing her pins at anyone of the opposite gender.

James did not have much experience as a stalker. She led him to a dark alley, and then she ran and took a strong turn. James hurried to catch up to her. When he turned the corner, he passed right through her. She had apparently planned to mace him. Instead, of surprising him, she was the one who got the big surprise.

Pale as ice, she said stammering, "Just-justa your arsese iss see through…you, you have no right to haunt me."

Using the anchor, James sank to the ground. Flattening his shape, he is able to watch her from the floor as she looks up towards the reddish dusky sky. A drop falls on her nose. The girl decides to go home, with James following behind from his new vantage point. When she arrives home, she finds the door locked. After knocking for 7 minutes, she gets angry and kicks the door. She had forgotten her house key and her mother was having a nightshift.

Since the porch of her flat did not provide any protection from the rain, the girl makes her way towards the old bridge. Taking shelter, she opens her black vest and takes out a cigarette. With a trembling hand, she lights up a smoke, relieved that the lighter had not gotten wet. She breathed, and exhaled a round cloud of smoke. Even though he could not smell the smoke, James unconsciously coughed lightly.

Looking over her shoulder, the girl trembled at the darkness. Taking out a pocket knife, she begins to lightly cut her arms. Fearing for her life, James takes on a new form. His most recent case had involved the murder of a blonde altar boy. Taking the form of this teenager, he ran toward the girl and yelled, "Suicide isn't the answer, you have so much to live for."

Taking the knife, she stabs James's shoulder and yells, "You are just pretending to care! All men are the same! You just want to rape me, just like him."

She takes another stab at James, but he runs away, forgetting that he was a spirit. After checking his arm, he is relieved to see it was not damaged. Going back to where she was, he was relieved to see she had gone home. Symbolically washing his hands on the entire situation, James tries to leave town. However, the anchor does not allow. Wherever he goes, he keeps running into her. Close to morning, angel summons him for another mission.

THE LOOTERS

Reggie and his twin Marcus were vacationing in the Canary Island with their mother. Marcus, the eldest by two minutes, had just graduated from the university. His brother had chosen a different path. It was ironic that Reggie's bizarre online marketing scheme had paid for the trip. Even after explaining his job like 100 times, Marcus could still not understand how that made Reggie money.

For the moment, the twins were lazily floating on a surf board. They felt it was a good a time as any to learn the craft, since they had nothing better to do. They had come to the El Medano beach in the island of Tenerife because it was said to be a good surfing spot. Instead of good waves, the sea was calm as the water in a lake. It had been like that for the last two hours, with the water level ever dropping.

From the shore, the raven haired twins heard their mother screaming, franticly. This was nothing new, so they chose to ignore her. Reggie, then said to his brother, "You don't think there are sharks in this water do you?"

Marcus' green eyes narrowed, as he said coyly, "There are sharks in practically all the beaches in the world. If you are scared of the ocean, I won't hold it against you if hang back while I have all the fun."

"You would get lonely without me," answered Reggie winking.

When they saw their mother going inside the water after them, the twins decided to head out. Their 50 year old mother was not particularly the strongest swimmer, especially after the accident that had left her reduced the mobility of her right arm.

Reggie became alarmed, when he saw his mother's frantic look. She was yelling, "Tsunami! Tsunami! We must head to higher ground."

"What Tsunami mother?" asked Marcus, "There is no tsunami coming! The water level is just low as all; probably a red tide event in this year."

"We should still head for higher ground," commented Reggie. He was always keen on indulging his mother's wild fancies.

Ever since she was twenty, their mother had suffered from tsunami related dreams. Her psychologist believed that those dreams had something to do with a part life. That was the last time she ever sought psychiatric help, to deal with her fears. As a Protestant lady, she did not believe in reincarnation.

The twins took their mother to the highest floor of their hotel villa. She was still nervous because they were only three floors above the ground. Giving his mother a condescending smile, Marcus asked, "If you want to, we can try and go to the nearby church. The stairs case leading up the entrance alone is higher than this raggedy old villa."

"Why bother. I doubt we will make it," protested the mother.

Dusk came, and with it a sense of serenity. The ocean was back to its normal form. For the sake of peace, Marcus suggested they order room service. Marcus had papas arrugadas with mojo(wrinkly potatoes with mojo sauce) and pescado fresco (or dry fish). Reggie had pizza with lemonade made with ginger ale. He always ordered this drink whenever he was on vacation. Whenever he tried to replicate the recipe back home, it never came out right.

Marcus always liked to take a single sip from his drink, because he liked the punch of it. For dessert, the twins shared a quesillo or cheesecake made of caramel. The taste of it was to die for. The twins slept together, as they did as children. To save money, they had rented a single room with twin beds. None were too keen on sleeping near the mother, because she snored.

Close to sunrise, Marcus had gotten up early. He took a shower, bathed, shaved and washed his perfectly white teeth. He had always perfect grooming habits, which were rooted in a mild case of obsessive compulsiveness. Even when vacationing, he always awoke at 6 a.m. As for his brother Reggie, he always woke up at 12 p.m., even when he went to sleep early.

Marcus went toward the gift shop, which had not opened to look at some of the trinkets on sale. There was not a single item he would like to give Caroline as gift. All the wooden items seemed as tacky as the Mayan mask he had gifted her from his trip to Mexico. Looking at his cellphone, he read the texts he had received from Caroline and gave a listless account of the events that had transpired the day before.

The sound of rushing water then filled his ears, as his eyes widened. Marcus could not remember how he got up the stairs and got back to his bedroom. The villa groaned with the weight of the rushing water below. Anymore strain and it would get pushed off the foundation. He staggered toward his bedroom door, feeling his sides looking for the card key. Since he could not find it, he started pounding on the door.

The water rose up to his knee, he fell to the ground and rested his head against the door. He had not realized the size of the cut on his thigh and on his arm. One of the guests, a Russian doctor happened upon him, and dragged him toward his bedroom. He made a quick tourniquet with the bed sheets, and then set about to locate his luggage.

Ever the paranoid fellow, Dr. Pirogov always took with him a first aid kit. His satirical smile always appeared whenever he was in a tense situation. In this case, he had the look of a complete maniac. Running toward all the rooms, he assembled the survivors on the roof.

When Dr. Pirogov returned to stich him up, Marcus said, "My mother and brother… they are still."

Dr. Pirogov pointed toward Marcus, and then towards the roof. Biting his lower lip, the small 5'2" doctor placed the wounded Marcus over his shoulder and carried him through the water, and up the stairs like a sack of potatoes. All the while, he was murmuring and cursing in Ingush, one of the many other languages spoken in Russia.

By noon, the water had somewhat settled down. Resting under an umbrella, it did not seem to him that rescue was coming anytime soon. Marcus rested his head on his mother's shoulder, and slept in the afternoon for the first time, since he was a toddler. The name did not last for long, since Dr. Pirogov came with a plastic water bottle. He drank it, and then settle down to sleep again.

While Marcus slept, Reggie went about toward the lower floors, with other hardy fellows to see what they could salvage. As he passed by his half flooded room, he smiles at the fortuitous thought that had crossed his mind. Had he brought his computer, it would be ruined by now. Together with five others, they took everything from the minibars and scurried back to the roof.

The tsunami had knocked out the power in the resort, and in other surrounding buildings. Reggie was a bit surprised that this old hotel villa had survived more or less in one piece, while the more modern constructions had started to cave in, or had been completely washed away. A black fellow too looked in the direction of the new hotels, and commented something Reggie could not understand.

Close to the stairs leading toward the second floor, Reggie saw something terrifying. The fellow detained Reggie by grabbing his shoulder. Once he stopped him, he gestured in a matter that made Reggie think the man wanted to know what he had seen. Using his thumb, Reggie drew a line over his own neck, and rolled his eyes to the back of his head. Nodding, the fellow too left the side of the stairs. A fish swam though the murky water, brushing lightly against the sandaled leg of the black fellow. He stumble, and fell toward the water, before running upstairs splashing ever wish way.

Reggie could not help but smile, after seeing this. He too decided to follow behind with his loot, since he was not a fan of fishes either. Dusk fell and rescue was still nowhere in sight. Reggie was by now bored of waiting to be rescue. He wanted to go home, and put the entire incident behind him. Checking his pockets, Reggie was relieved to find he still had the passports and the wallets. It was the first thing he had taken with him, as soon as the water started pouring. Safely dry inside a Ziploc bag, they were his family's only way of getting home.

He thought, Tenerife-South Airport is not far from here. If it is not underwater, we can get on the first plane, and leave this Gods forsaken island.

Looking over the side of the balcony, Reggie scanned the area for anything that could be of used. As if reading his mind, Dr. Pirogov too came and started looking about. They were joined by the 5 others who were in one piece, with sufficient wits about them.

Dr. Pirogov pointed and shouted in his incomprehensible language. Looking at where he was pointing, Reggie saw an orange colored, wooden motor lifeboat. The lifeguard was a bloody mess, with debris lying on top of him. Using the rod of used to fish corpses from the pool; Dr. Pirogov tried to get the boat closer. Others too saw the boat, and tried to do the same with makeshift ropes. Through cooperative, randomized efforts the boat was safely secured. The first order of business was to remove its current occupant.

Dr. Pirogov removed the lifeguard's life jacket, his wallet, watch and shoes. He also cleaned the deck to the debris to make it safe for others to come inside. Holding up the shoes, he gestured to Reggie to come closer. Once Dr. Pirogov had his attention he held up the number 9. Reggie then said to the others, "The stiff is size 9, if anyone needs a pair of Nikes."

A haggard elderly gentleman said, "I'll take them."

Some of the guests made slight protestations. However, they soon quieted down in the face of the carnage which surrounded them. The others slowly started to board the lifeboat. After tinkering with the motor, the doctor managed to make it come alive. With a working boat, a slight feeling of hope entered the group of survivors.

Reggie's mother asked, "I wonder why help has not arrived?"

Waking up slightly, Marcus whispered, "Maybe other islands have been hit as well. With such a damaged infrastructure, it could take some time for help to arrive."

"Where do you suppose we go?" asked Reggie.

"The airport maybe? We need to get as far inland as possible, till we reach an unaffected populated area," suggested Marcus.

Scanning the mainland, it seemed to Reggie that everything was underwater, except for the volcano looming. It made sense to use it as way landmark to get out of the devastate area. Pointing toward it, Reggie gestured to the Doctor. The Russian Doctor nodded in response.

As night came forth, Reggie and the others survivors entered the small boat. Very slowly, the boat ventured through the flooded city. Dr. Pirokov used the steel rod used to fish drowned people to help maneuver through the debris. He was always feeling the water bellow, testing its debts to see if it was safe for the boat to proceed.

When it started to rain, fellow piloting the boat stopped the boat and docked near by the 4th floor window of a colonial housing. They resolved to spend the night there, since the building looked more or less in one piece. While his mother and brother slept soundly, Reggie was wide awake.

He wandered if anyone was still alive. Opening the closet in of a bedroom, he noticed a nice collection of tuxes. He picked the combination that he most liked and trading in his wet attire, and sandals. He took care to move into his coat pocket his key possessions. He also took with him all the small jeweled pins, inside a small case.

He also noticed looked through the woman's closet, and jewelry case. He saw a beautiful diamond ring. Taking it, he thought, Marcus can give this to Caroline when he gets back home.

Looking up, he saw the Russian doctor give a faint suggestion of a smile. All around him, he heard the motion of the survivors rummaging through the bedrooms, looking for anything of value. The biggest cause of celebration was when the wine closet was discovered. This made the group quite merry, and it made the entire situation all the more tolerable.

The following day, the group of survivors continued on their merry way. From time to time, they would enter structures that looked the most sound in search of provisions and whatever small valuables they could carry in their person. Occasionally, a new member would get added to their group.

Going to the airport proved to be the right course of action. The authorities were just arriving with helicopters and supplies. Due to Marcus' condition he was sent via helicopter to the nearest hospital. Once Marcus was strong enough to travel, the twins and their mother returned to the US, and putted the entire incident behind them, just as they had planned. Marcus' near death experienced helped him get over his apathy toward his girl. He married Caroline in the spring using the ring that his twin had acquired from the trip.

AWAKENING

It has been two centuries since my trail was completed. It has all been for naught. A light touch is useless when trying to change the grand scheme of things. I see everything, know everything, and yet… My home was attacked yesterday. At this rate, it will soon be wiped off the face of the Earth.

I grow disillusioned with the grand scheme of things. What was the point of becoming this…things, if I was to be powerless in the end. I cannot seem to remember how I became this way. Days pass, and I start to remember bits of fragments of my human life. The way I remember them, it is a bit silly, now that I think about it.

A week has passed the town and everyone that I knew are no longer there. Without attachment to landmarks, I was able to notice something interesting about the pattern of destructions. All the places attacked have a connection to my past. Every second, I feel a fragment of my old self slipping away. Is this the end trail, the final punishment for those who wished to have their personal idol ruling above?

Pity! For all they efforts, the townspeople obtained a crippled God; with eyes, and knowledge, but no strong hands to act upon that knowledge. Ah…yes, I see him! How could I forgotten, my brother. He too attempted the apotheosis, but was led to believe that he had failed.

"You believed it to be so, because I so desired it."

Yes, now I understand. Now, I see. He is the other half of my power.

Time passes; I cradle in my harms my brother's head. I hold it above me, and then say, "…"

SEISHIN YUME TANTEI! 3

Two years pass, and James was nearing the end of his high school career. Soon, he would graduate and he would join the workforce. Despite his grades, James for reasons he did not understand was not in a particular mood to continue with his studies. When not in high school, he was training as a mechanic in his uncle's garage, much to the dismay of his parents who wanted him to become a doctor.

In addition to this, James was also tinkering with computers, learning the ins and outs of CEO marketing and web design through his own personal website. At night, when he rested his head on his pillow, he would dream of solving cases with the Nameless Angel.

That night, when Angel had called him forth, James asked, "What is your name?"

"Lucifer," said Angel. Laughing, he added, "No. The name is Malik, which means King."

"Does that make you King of the angels? Or what the hell?" inquired James.

"Why bother with this conversation? You are not going to remember it when you wake up," answered Malik.

"But I do remember, yes. I remember how you told me last year I was making a big mistake going to college," protested James.

"I said, it would be a big mistake to become a doctor in this country. It takes too long, and you practically have to kill the patients with pills, so that they are not alive to sue you for your obvious thieving negligence," answered Malik, Now, get back to your most gracious, holy calling Seishin yume tantei!"

The following day, James was randomly anchored back to Warsaw. It had been two years since last he had visited the place. This time, he recognized the landmarks. The depressed suicidal girl he had met two years ago had changed a lot. While trailing her, he discovers the source of the problems.

He had read about demons developing a strange infatuation for mortal maidens. Where he had read this information was a subject of much debate. In the waking world, he had never so much as opened a Bible.

"Well, not since middle school," said James more to himself.

The girl seemed to be doing quite well. She was dating a particularly boring fellow. James approaches her in his true form. She does not recognize him.

Gesturing at her, he says, "We met two years ago. I came to warn you. There is a demon who is in love with you. He has been ruining your life to make you his forever. I know how to get rid of him for good, but first you need to find a fresh fish, pronto!"

"Are you out of your mind," she said not recognizing James.

"Who are you talking to, honey?" asked her boyfriend.

"No, one I thought someone was talking to me, but it was some guy talking to someone else," said the girl.

Her lover chose to ignore this, and many other instances she visually displayed her sixth sense. Being raised by a Wicca grandmother, had led her lover to believe in all sorts of foolish things. A month passes, and the happy couple goes to a cruise.

Every time the demon tried a new scheme, James was there to interfere with him. Frustrated, the demon takes on the form of a deranged Asian, who kidnaps the girl.

James then goes to the boiler room to mess with the equipment of the ship. The diversion and the chaos helps the girl escaped with her man. The only true victims were the ocean liner itself. At his point, the demon was onto James. However, his omniscient powers were failing him. He knew James' past and present, but had no idea what James was going to do.

While James was toying with the demon, using the power of the anchor, he starts learning how the demon worked. Whenever they passed through a time zone, all but one of the selves of the demon would disappear.

Suddenly, James was overcome with the urge to go to a lighthouse. By now, the demon was annoyed with James and was eager to be rid of him for good. He followed James to the lighthouse, by trailing his boat. Once inside the lighthouse, the demon said, "May I propose to you a Faustian bargain over the fair lass's soul?"

Smiling coolly, James said, "Sure. Why not?"

The demon brought out a chess board, to play his game. Frowning, James said, "I never played this game before. It would violate the rules of engagement, if I do not even know how to move the pieces."

"Pray do tell, what sort of game you would like to play?" asked the demon pensively.

"Yugioh!" said James.

"Yugioh?" repeated the demon.

The demon did not even know such a stupid sounding game existed. Using James's memories, he learned the rules, and created his own deck. He used overpowered demonic cards made of solid gold. When he naturally won, James said, "I win!"

"Surely, you are mistaken," said the demon.

"The Konami rules of Yugioh state that you must play with Yu-gioh cards," said James smiling.

"And that is what I used," said the demon growing angrily.

"No! No! You used your own made up cards. Not cards created by the Konami Company, your bootleg, golden imitations are in violations of the rules stipulated by the creator of the game," said James.

"To hell with Konami!" screeched the demon, "We were playing by demon rules."

The demon spent an hour arguing. It was then when he noticed that the time zone had changed. Since he was so invested in screeching at James, he almost ended up losing track of the girl. Before, he left; James detained him by saying the "Pater Noster."

Very slowly, James started saying, "Ouuurrrr fatheeerrr whooooo areeeeee innnnn heeeaaaveeen…"

This prayer caused this form of the demon to freeze on the spot. Since he violated the terms of his powers, he ended up going to hell, empty handed. Smiling, James said to himself, "You were doomed to fail, relying on my memories. I never played professionally the game that is Yugioh. I always used made up rules, with my sister."

A month passes and the girl marries her boyfriend. Through the influence of another demon or maybe her husband's Wicca grandmother, he turns into a wife beater. By this time, James and his newly acquired demon stalker had gotten over the girl. He was not particularly impeding James's work, nor was he trying to turn him into the side of evil.

Eventually, James had to ask, "Why do you keep following me around?"

"I just find you so fascinating," said the demon.

"Why? Because of the anchor thing?" remarked James.

"No, Just your mind as all, I can't quite figure out how these bizarre protocols of yours work," commented the demon.

"Fine. I will enlighten you," said James condescending, "Since I was small, I suffered from apocalyptic dreams. There were these angels always telling me to become a prophet, to join the church and save it from sin. I had read the Bible, and knew how all those prophets ended up. To deal with the problem, I created a though, within a thought, in an effort to hide my intentions from God. These protocols are designed to confuse beings that can read my thoughts, and who know everything about me. For example, going to that lighthouse was protocol 47. I instinctively knew that I had to go there. I can confuse people like you by acting so impulsively..."

"That all sounds like crazy talk if you ask me," said the demon interrupting.

After this conversation, the demon traded with James some of the demon cards he had used on his duel. Due to the jungle of James's memories, the demon had used the Wind Clow cards for his duel, in addition to Digimon and some Energies from the Pokemon playing card came. James ended up trading his Blue Eyes Shining dragon and a full folio card of Mew Two; in exchange for the demon's Dash, Wind and Wood cards made of solid gold. It was an empty, pointless ritual, but James relished in it. At least in his dream, he could own these particular cards he so desired.

The Dilemma

For as long as Richard can remember, the Earth has been a barren wasteland, filled with bizarre looking robots. As a self-proclaimed archeologist, and grave robber, Richard had made it his business to discover where everything had gone wrong. According to scant pieces of information, everything had started with Iran. Since the US had an anti-missile defense, Iran had decided to attack them indirectly by targeting countries like Canada, Cuba, Mexico and oddly enough Venezuela. Iran also orchestrated similar attacks around Europe and also Russia.

Since Iran had gone a little crazy, North Korea too felt like setting the world ablaze. Since the incident, a strange fog had blanketed the entire world, disabling all electronic communications. With no communications, all the world powers, blaming one another entered into a precipitated nuclear war.

In the midst of the chaos, the US, Russia, China and Great Britain united to put an end to all the fighting. Through overwhelming force, they wipe off the map all the undesirables. They gathered all the nukes and uranium and ship them to out of space. In doing so, they hope to prevent any and all nuclear wars. By then, these super powers had created other doomsday devices, so these weapons were remnants from the old shattered world.

The last piece of information about the old world had a utopian feel to it, as far as Richard was concerned. It went on about forming a sort of Union to fight against the ecological disasters, poverty, and hunger.

Richard had read plenty of such idealized plans before. It was neither the first, nor the last time mankind had bothered to try to end world hunger, or bring about world piece, through the sword. Considering the bleak state of his current reality, nothing had come from all those good intentions.

He left the ruins of what appeared to be a computer lab. Whatever scant data he had managed to salvage, he photograph. Most hard drives were useless, crippled by a barrage of EMPs. For this reason, Richard always prioritized written data. On his way out, he ran into the kill bits. These bipedal mechanical monstrosities, warped facsimiles made in man's image, always unnerved Richard.

As he ran away from them, he could not help noticing something strange. Despite the barrage of bullets, that flew his way, he was not getting hurt in the least. Back when he was younger, he had chugged it up to luck, but as of late, he felt that it was getting a bit ridiculous. Why, when everyone else died, he still remained? It was this question which prompted him to search for information of the old world.

He was picked up by a self-proclaimed war correspondent, and her little army brigade. The maiden went by the name of Linda, and she was covering the attacks and the advance of the robots in the area. They were not so much out to destroy all humans, as they were localized in certain areas as of late. This change of had gotten Linda curious.

When they met, Linda and Richard followed tradition and traded whatever useful information they had. Richard's information earned him a temporary escort. From Linda, he learned that the robots had alien origin. After analyzing the ancient technology vs. current trends, there was no way these machines could have been manufactured by human hands.

Richard went with Linda to study another ruins. The data there described more hunger and sickness. As before, the world leaders were slow to deal with the crisis. He was about to get more details, when an EMP was shot out. The computer and all the electronics died, but surprise, surprise the kill bots were still operational.

Linda commented, "Mmm…now this is interesting."

"I can see why you would imagine our assailants were alien ware," commented Richard.

The exchange was cut short, when the soldiers entered to escort Linda and Richard out of danger. For the next visit, Linda took Richard to a ruin she knew about. She had not made much progress with it because the computers in the area were Macintosh and other Apple computers.

The base was located in a city that had been struck by many bombs in the past. The explosions had caused a tsunami, and then later a volcano had erupted. When they arrived, the ruins were overrun by space ships and their machines. The entire area was a fusion of fire and water.

"Mmm…I am starting to think that your alien theory is not too farfetched," commented Richard.

After much sneaking about, Richard managed to arrive to the UN bunker. Once inside, they found blueprints that resembled some of the android machines. Linda said, "This doesn't mean anything. Theoretical concepts for many things like a time machine and the teleporter exist, but do they work? No."

Aside from this information, Richard found more fragments pertaining to the 21st century. The US president had been pressuring certain states, with sanctions for insubordination against the federal government. This caused a second civil war, but a smaller scale. Only one state ended up taking arms, while the other rebel states backed down at the last moment.

Something productive had come from this entire visit. Using the blueprints, Linda and her team was able to device a jamming signal. The downside to it was that lured the big machines, which were immune to the signal. So, it was a last result sort of deal. It also took two days to charge up.

As before, whenever Richard left the ruins, a random EMP would get fired up, corrupting the digital data. It was a good thing he had taken the time to print it. The EMP attacks were starting to get ridiculous.

The years passed, and Richard kept traveling with Linda. He witness with her one of the silliest fights he had ever seen. One of the standing armies where fighting the alien machines with biplanes from WWII. Since they used old technology, they were not greatly affected by the EMPs. The combination of biplanes and laser Gatling guns made Richard smile. It was all a pitiful, exercise in futility.

There was a strange thought creeping in the back of Richard's mind. However, he was not ready to vocalize it. Linda too was acting quite distant. In the end, Richard discovered what the problem was. While spying on Linda's personal documents, Richard acquired an interesting tippet of information acquired from a downed enemy machine. Thanks to the jamming signal, Linda and her team had managed to capture and examine an enemy robot.

The bit of data not encrypted was written in plain English text. Richard thought, so, these robots are not aliens, how disappointing. The humans who had created this machine had gone exploring the nearby systems in search of a second Earth. However, all the so called viable planets were actually unlivable. Apparently, the dark matter floating about the vacuum had historically messed with the scientist's observations of the known universe. As such, the planets that seemed habitable were actually the complete opposite.

Since they could not find a second Earth, and the Earth they hailed from was unlivable, they had decided to go back in time. This was the origin of these robots, which were set on replacing the humans who lived there with clones they would control. To assure their future selves, all they needed was the creator of their technology. The rest of the people were expendable, according to their calculations.

Richard finally understood why his companions had stopped going out on missions with him. They were deciding whether to kill him or not. For some reason, Linda was convinced that he was responsible for the kill bots. In order to get to the heart of the matter, Richard decided to face the machines. He eluded Linda and her soldiers.

Once he was in the hands of the machines, he was able to meet the humans from the distant future. Their cleverly disguised space ship was located in a patch of the night sky that always seemed too artificial with its star arrangement.

The leader of these humans was a pale, red haired maiden, with a skinny, languid appearance. She spoke in a soft, emotionless voice. She said, "Based on our scouts, you probably have already figured out, who and what we are. I am here to tell you who you are…and more to the point who I am. I am your descendant, as well as the rest of the people on board my ship. As the records in our machines stipulate, we tried and failed to find viable planets in other star systems. We even went as far as Andromeda and found nothing… For you see, the spectrometer was sending us incorrect data. Planets that show carbon molecules and oxygen were actually made of boron and helium. The further we look away, the greater the margin of error of our observations. So, when supplies ran low, we concocted this half-baked plan to go back in time…And now we are here."

"What do you expect me to with these revelations?" asked Richard.

"We expected you to do as you will…as you would had done if we had not been so unfortunate enough to meet, such is the problem with time travel, and all that messy nonsense, though we have our own theories on this matter," said the lady.

"What if I kill myself?" asked Richard.

"Suit yourself. Die for the people you care so little about, or live and see the many wonders you will bring about with your existence," said the Lady. She added smiling coolly, "It matters not such machinations, for the fact that we are still here means that you already decided."

THE RIGHT THING TO DO

oger Preston never thought he would ever see his brother again. And yet, here he was, conveniently appearing to rescue him from certain doom. While his twin drove him away, Roger breathed in a sigh of relief. All his troubles were behind him, for the moment.

His brother now went with the name of Ronald McMillan, the last name of his adopted family. Life in the orphanage for Roger seemed like something out of Charles Dickens, with the hunger, the running away and the petty crimes.

As for Ronald, he was a respected carpenter, owner of his own shop in a small of North Dakota. It was not an interesting life, but it was at least uneventful, till he had seen his own face plastered all over the news.

When he arrived home with his twin, his adopted mother said angrily, "What do you think you are doing?"

"Helping my brother out, what do you think I am doing, mother!" said Ronald raising his voice.

His mother, the old Mrs. McMillan winced, as if struck by a blow. It was the first time Ronald had ever raised his voice to her. She narrowed her eyes, as if she was looking at a stranger. Stammering, she said, "But, but he is a criminal...you could get into a lot of trouble. I am calling the police."

She made a motion for her cellphone, but Ronald took it away. While this was taking place, Roger was quietly getting acquainted with his new surroundings. He was almost disdainful at the little dilemma his dear Ronald was facing. He decided to stay quiet, in order not to further antagonize Mrs. McMillan with his voice.

"But please! Ronald! Call the police! It's the right thing to do!" implored Mrs. McMillan.

"No! Mother, the right thing to do was for you to adopt the both of us!" said Ronald caustically. He left the kitchen and went to the garden slamming the door behind him.

Mrs. McMillan sat down in a chair, and placed her hands to her forehead. When she looked down, she saw Roger pouting, with an amused look in his face. He then said, "Truth be told, mother…it was I who you originally wanted, but I gave you the old switcheroo. Now, live with that you old sack of bones."

With this little emotional sabotage, Roger had secured himself a place at the McMillan table for the moment. Later that day, Ronald's wife returned home with his daughter that was at daycare. She too showed animosity towards Roger. Using the guilt card Roger secured for himself a temporary refuge from all his problems.

One day, Ronald awoke to find his brother gone. He left neither note, nor object. Almost as if he had not been there in the first place.

Seishin yume tantei! 4

Today was the first time, James had ever worked in coordination with other "soldiers of God", as Malik liked to put it. Just as before, the angel Malik would appear by his bedside and wake him up in the most annoying fashion available. The angel started repeating over and over, "Mewosamasu, Seishin yume tantei-kun!" till James got up from his bed.

James saw beside Malik a group of strange people, one of them was a little blonde girl. The other a black man dressed like a construction worker. The other three was a gypsy hag, an apache teenager, and woman dressed like a ballerina.

Malik was about to offer the formal introduction, but James said, "Let's just get this over with."

Sighing, angel said, "Merciful God, who art thou in heaven, give me patience, lets I commit a mortal sin."

The blonde girl said, "Get on with it!"

"The case of today is most dangerous indeed. There is a man who is taking people's souls and holding them up for ransom. Those who do not pay end up die, and their souls get sent to Gods know where."

"Gods?" asked James coolly.

"I meant God," said angel. He then continues, "The current Victim at the moment is the son of a Senator. This is getting media attention, unlike the other victims. The police at the moment is tracking down the kidnapper, based on this picture."

James, along the 5 people assembled there took a good look at the photo. The little girl commented, "It looks as if the kid has some weird disease or something."

The apache man said, "Where have I seen this before. I know, the kid looks like the girl from the exorcist."

"Pity that the kidnapper could not try something original," said the construction worker.

"Why change something that works?" said James getting up from his bed.

The Swat team tracked down the location where the photo was

taken. James and his team trailed along from a distance. The Swat entered the elevator. James was going to join disguised as an officer, but the gypsy hag stopped him and pulled him back. The elevator made a bunch of noises, and when it opened again, the Swat team was gone. Malik came to them and showed them the recording from one of the cameras of one of the officers.

James grimaced, and said, "Eww! Sheesh!"

"Meh! They should have taken the stairs," said the little blonde girl.

"Not funny, Blondy," said James.

"It's Delfin or Dolphin," said the little blonde girl.

Laughing, the construction worker commented, "I bet your parents are Hollywood stars. Only those fools from California give such abnormal names to their kids."

Delfin opened her mouth to complain, but instead made a moaning sound. After this exchange, they went inside the elevator carefully. The construction worker known as Clifford stood by the door, to keep it from closing. The gypsy hag tapped the walls, and noticed a fake wall. Moving it aside, she saw an endless, howling void.

Smacking her dry lips, she said, "Now I see…"

James peered his head inside the endless void, and then went back out, as soon as he felt a slight rustling of fingers on the back of his neck. Trembling, he asked, "What is that place? Is it hell?"

"There is more than just heaven and hell in this world, James," said Malik.

"In there…it's the Astral Realm. This building is an illusion designed to mask the true nature of where we are," said the gypsy hag.

Looking up, James saw the face of the kidnapping staring back at him, but in a fish eye perspective. Once they got out of the building, the hag said, "This building is like a type of Ouija Board, we will not be able to get him from here."

"Well…if he is there, but not there. I say we call it quits and give him what he wants," said the ballerina maiden Giakova.

"I have been practicing robbing banks. We could rob a bank and give him the money. When he comes to collect it, that's where we nab the guy," said apache Pinal.

"I could bless the money, and use it to weaken his powers," suggested Delfin.

"That Scooby Doo plan is not going to work because he is getting help from a demon named Amy," said Malik.

"Amy? Tutatuun!" said Delfin chuckling.

Malik added, "This time he doesn't want money. Read the back of the photo."

James read the back and started laughing. He passed the photo to the others who also found it laughable. Sighing, he said, "So he is crazy. That doesn't help us much."

"We could try praying for a miracle," said Delfin.

"Sure…fine whatever. Let's get this show on the road, so I can get to school tomorrow," said James crossing his hands.

Delfin was quiet for some time. She meditated on the nature of the universe as a whole. James could not help, but visualize what Delfin was thinking about. It was part of her process. Delfin thought, when God created the universe, he had to create an area devoid of his presence. It is this area that is the border between the creation and its creator. In this border, evil can grow, and it is there were this evil man has his seat of power.

Delfin then started as thus, "God, who created the Universe, that in order to exist must be devoid of him. Please remember that abominations exist beyond you. Please defend the widow and the orphan from the evil that exists beyond you…"

During the prayer, a new Swat team was able to get inside the elevator and not get spirited away. Since the kidnapper felt his powers waning, he sent his demon Amy to possess the Baby. To counter him, Pinal blessed a water faucet from a nearby bathroom. The formally torpid waters that exited turned pristine, clear, becoming holy water. Pinal soaked the photo of the baby to keep the demon at bay.

The man finally gets arrested and sent to a holding cell. The cops were at a loss as to how to deal with such prisoner who showed clear, supernatural abilities. While they waited for a priest, and exorcist, or something, Delfin started talking with the prisoner. James had to admire the work of Delfin. She was indeed a manipulative little bastard, with her innocent eyes, and her malicious smile. She told him that she had the ability to take and amplify the talents of people. She showed him the powers she had collected from other people. Impressed, the prisoner eventually gave Delfin her powers.

The power he gave her was rotten, tainted and worthless. It withered away to the core, where only the prime originator of this talent remained. The prisoner was finally as feeble as the rest of the mere mortals. Without his powers, the demon that was shadowing lost interest. The next morning James awoke, and he found himself smiling for reasons he did not understand.

THE DESCENT

It was 1950, in the Bronx of New York City and Michael Medin was working on developing more comfortable polio braces. He had helped treat the epidemic in the past. Every summer, like clockwork, hundreds of patients would get diagnosed, and be carried into his office. By the time they came to see him, it was already too late. The fever had taken hold, and those who were unfortunate enough to survive never walked right. Medin always had a grim view of his role as a doctor. A firm believer in euthanasia, he always felt that it would be better for his patients to die, than to live with the terrible burden that was polio. He never spoke this thought out loud, and he did his most to uphold his Hippocratic Oath.

His general melancholy, turned to full on depression when his very own sister was stricken. Using all known treatments, he did his best to stave off the advancement of the fever. When it passed, his sister had her lower limbs extremely debilitated.

He submerged himself in his work, while stoically trying to pretend that everything was the same for his poor sister's sake. However, it was painful for him just to watch her trying to walk toward the next room. He had given her the polio braces and the sticks, for her to retain some semblance of independence.

He should have never allowed her to drink tab water...Or maybe it was those produce from the farmer's market she enjoyed savoring so often, though Medin pitifully. He thought over and over, reformulating the same "If only" scenario.

One day, he was at church with his sister. She had taken the host, after doing the line, refusing to have the Lord brought to her like some invalid. Feeling inspired, the preacher went on a rant about the miracle he had just witness. Medin narrowed his eyes, as he drowned the voice from the stupid man that claimed to speak for God.

God! God he rants about, as far as I know, God should not allowed for this to happen. Milly is not getting better, nor will she ever get better. If only, thought Medin.

He closed his eyes as his chest heaved a sigh of desperation. When he opened his eyes, he saw he was back at home. It took him some time to come to grips with what had occurred. After observing many sights, and the current state of his beloved Milly, Medin concluded he had somehow traveled back in time.

Heh! I guess miracles do happen if you ask with a strong enough faith, thought Medin happily. For now, it was 1947 so there was still time. Throughout those years, in preparation for the coming epidemic, Medin started campaigning for the creation of a polio vaccine and better sewerage systems in the cities. Whenever summer came, he would become like a mad preacher warning people of the dangers of tab water. Using his future knowledge, he worked alongside with Dr. Hammond to release the polio vaccine before the dreadful epidemic of 1950.

For all his good will, and faith, and hard work, there came a neurotic aspect to his behavior. The madness started creeping ever so slowly. Medin wondered after 1952, about the future that lay before him. Beyond that time, he had no idea what other dangers were to befall his sister. At first he started restricting the time she was allowed outside. Whenever she went outside, she was escorted by either himself or someone of trust. Eventually, he became paranoid of others, and he started to doubt if he would be strong enough to protect his sister. When a maiden got mugged in the alley behind his apartment, his paranoia reached new heights.

He became suspicious of anything that might seem dangerous to his sister. To solve this problem, he made Milly a prisoner. Only at home, would she be protected from dangers of the outside world, both real, and imaginary.

THE ORIGIN OF VIGILANTE PETTY SUE

Petty Sue was exiting the Publix with her groceries, as she would do, every weekend. As before, she would turn the car on, and then put the groceries in the back. She would do so, because the afternoon heat would always overheat the interior of her car. So, while she got busy, she had her car vainly fight against the summer sun. The moment she closed the lid and moved towards the driver seat, the car spun away without her. It had gotten stolen, with keys, groceries and all.

After curing the 4 winds, she made her way back home on foot. Her cousin Catty who lived with her asked, "Why didn't you call the cops right away?"

"I forgot cause I was so freaking pissed," answered Petty Sue.

While Catty called the cops, and describe in detail the stupidity of her cousin, Petty went out into the street to look for her car. In her state of mind, Petty saw a car with the windows rolled down. It was an old car, so she knew it lacked modern security systems. She got inside and hotwired it. She figured it would be easier to look for her car inside another vehicle.

She found in the glove compartment a compact a smith and western handgun, with the handle made of pink quartz, and the rest decorated with rhinestones. Petty got bored of circling about the block after 10 minutes. She decided to drive towards an apartment complex that was a haven for criminals. Without warning, she started shooting up the place. She then drove away before anyone of the criminals and low lives had time to react. She had not seen her car in the parking lot. So she went to look elsewhere.

She continued this mad little spree till dusk, hitting up random places home those she considered low lives, and other poor neighborhoods as well. Meanwhile, Catty was looking for her cousin. It was not till 11 PM when she saw an interestingly bizarre news report. Someone had stolen a cement truck, and had poured a message demanding for the return of her car. Suspecting that it was Petty, Catty was at amiss as to what to do about the entire situation. She decided to take a step back from the entire situation. Without much explanation, Catty drove down to her mother's house in the Florida Keys, and decided to stay there till Petty had calmed down.

For weeks, Petty kept causing problems for both the general authorities and the crime lords of the city. To get her to turn herself in, the Lexus Company offered her a new car. However, Petty did not want a new car, she wanted her own car and she wanted it now.

In the end, it was the local drug lord named Jessie, who tracked down her stole vehicle and the guy who stole it. Jessie had seen how Petty had eluded the police, and thought her reckless driving and accurate shooting useful. Aside from her skills, nothing much was known of Petty. Even the information provided by the police, and the Petty's family members were sketchy at best.

Aside from being third cousins, Catty did not know much about Petty. Catty could tell that her mother knew more than she was telling, but she could never get her to talk about it. Catty was now starting to suspect that her silence was for good reason. No one likes to be vociferous about someone so trigger happy.

Jessie rendezvous with Petty in the mangrove forest beach near the Keys. Why Petty had chosen such a location only added to the eccentricities of this lunatic. She asked Jessie, "Is this the guy?"

"Yep," answered Jessie.

"And that's what left of my car?" she asked.

"We can talk about repairs later," answered Jessie.

"You, where is my computer?" asked Petty.

Trembling, the tied up man said, "Well…mmm…I think the mechanics threw it away, because it was so old…"

Petty was quiet for some time. She then took a deep breath and brought out her handgun.

IA NOV DROP ET

Alison and her brother Christopher were in the middle of watching one of the most bizarre animated movies. After a drawn out, 40 minutes, the true nature of the film came into the limelight.

Unlike other movies, this one had a bit of a magical element to it. The characters were not too important, rather the artifacts being discovered where the centerfold. Curious about the lack of rising action, Christopher stopped the film to see how much time it had left. It had about 30 minutes left, so if they were going to do something unexpected, now was the right time.

From what Alison had gathered after watching 2 hours of the film, the movie was about a University librarian with the silly name of Candida Marxianus. Her name alone made Alison smile. If she was an alien, her last name was a little too much on the nose, about it. Not much was known about her past, other than that she lived alone and was obsessed with chronology devices.

Her rival was a tenured professor Hopkins, and his over bloated archeology department. Both were only researches in name, since they had a preference for items that actually did something. Many historical sites were dissected in the prologue, as Hopkins dynamited the pyramid of Egypt to reveal a hidden entrance. After rummaging through priceless papyrus, and other pieces of antiquity he found what he was looking for.

Candida had arrived late, and was watching Hopkins from the shadows. He knew that any vermin that should not be there was actually Candida in disguise. Later in the movie, it was shown that Candida had a pendant which gave her the ability to shape shift.

After reveling in his discovery, he quietly putted the item away. His peers asked him, "Well…what is it?"

"I will tell you about it later. For now, we should leave, let's we catch our death from this pungent, moss filled air," said Professor Hopkins.

As of now, the film had not shown the usefulness of a collection of buried statues, featuring different Egyptian Gods. All they had seen was Hopkins opening the statues, and carefully removing a coiled piece of wire, like those used in a lute.

The movie moves on ahead, and switches to Candida. She goes inside to explore a cave, but runs away when a centipede falls on her arm. She runs away crying in her doggie form. She jumps, and cowers on top of Hopkins, who laughing says, "We will take it from here, Candida. If we find something, we will show just for leading us to this spot. Now…don't give us those sad puppy eyes. Everyone has their own little phobias. John, take her back will you."

John, the unpaid intern, grudgingly escorted Candida back to the university. After the 20 minute ride back, Candida is still curious about the cave. After not thinking much, she thought, maybe the bugs are just an entrance thing. Caves then to get deader as you go further in…

To bypass the entrance, she went inside an elevator. She jammed it, by pressing the emergency button, and putting in a key. She then wrote the name of the place she wanted to go, using chalk. Whenever the cave lacked an official name, she named it. She also wrote other conditions of this teleportation. The elevator was in nowhere magical, but the power laid in this 50,000 year old chalk piece. Candida did not like relying on its power, since it was finite. When the elevator opened its doors, she was distraught to notice the high tech nature of the cave. There were pipes, and then bellow them a hallway. It reminded her a bit of the hallway of a hospital, due to his white cleanliness.

She started exploring the facility, but then she hid when she heard guns and explosions. The noise soon died and then she saw a strange sight. Hopkins and his team were carrying boxes and boxes of military grade hardware and artifacts. Smiling, Hopkins said as he walked quickly, "I think there is still some junk left, if you care to look. Bye, Bye."

All that Candida could mouth was, "Uh?"

Professor Hopkins had robbed a secret military base. How he had managed to this without any official training would have been amusing to see.

Then again, thought Candida, I do not know the extent of the power of some of the artifacts he owns.

Walking in the direction she had seen Hopkins, she found a room safe, with metal doors at least 1 meter thick, melted open. Inside the room safe, she rummaged and found spear. Based on its look and feel, she realized she was holding the true Spear of Mortal Pain.

She placed the spear inside her magic satchel, one of the many cookie items from the old world. It could hold an innumerable amount of items in another dimension. Candida continued to explore the underground base till she found a clearing. It was not noticeable from the outside, and the buildings looked residential, almost like town houses, but sleeker in design. Inside a school looking building, she saw in the kitchen a bunch of scientist, doctors and odd looking students. The students were dressed in white, and they seemingly staring at a white piece of paper.

Candida was about to take a closer look, but one of the doctors asked her, "Who are you?"

"Mm…I am a behaviorist…I am here to study behavior," she said giving a nervous laugh.

"You think this clever disguise will help you escape! Security! Security!" yelled the doctor.

The students looked up from their paper and started staring at her. Based on their eyes, there was truly something not human about them. The typical guards one finds in a loony bind gang up on Candida, and the doctor tries giving her a sedative. Before he can manage, she flexibly opens her mouth and bites the neck of the doctor. Using the back of her spear, she knocked out all the doctors. After the fight was done, the students turned to look at the television. The television was showing an emergency broadcast.

The TV was not showing anything per say, rather it was playing an odd signal, some low, rhythmic radio waves. As the doctors came to, they too became docile staring at the television. Guessing something was amiss, Candida used her magic chalk to take her to see Professor Hopkins. Indeed, he was up to no good. By combining the wires, and other chronology devices stolen from the military, he was broadcasting a radio signal worldwide that had the world under his control.

Candida brought out her spear and pointed at him. Smiling coolly, Hopkins said, "This does not concern you Candida. Why don't you leave the problems of Earth to Earthlings and focus on the happenings of your own home world."

"It is because I am not human, that I am here to stop you," said Candida, "Even if it means, showing my true self to the world."

The movie then ended just like the movie the Grey. It jumped to a postscript telling you the aftermath of the battle. Both siblings were disappointed that the curtain was dropped just when the movie had finally gotten interesting.

The ending only said: The humans were set free thanks to Candida's heroism. Now the truth of the aliens was out there, and through their influence planet Earth became a better place to live.

"But wait!" said Alison, "The ending implies that the humans were still controlled in some way."

"Meh! It's just a stupid feel good movie Ali, don't let it sucker you in with its message of interplanetary cooperation," said Christopher scratching his tentacle, "There is no benefit in dealing with those aliens."

The final credit scroll was quite picturesque, featuring crude drawings of all the wonderful peaceful technologies developed, after the incident. The song playing in the back was pure gibberish as far as Alison was concerned. The only words she could make out were "Ia Nov Drop Et".

THE COLORED
PENCILS

Vanessa had just concluded her laps, and had entered the gym to take a bath. After she concluded, she was annoyed to see that her change of clothing was gone. Grimacing, she picked up her gym clothing to change back. However, her friend Latoya came to the rescue. Latoya was vice president of Vanessa's after school Theater Club. Latoya handed her a pink dress from one of the past shows. It was one of those western saloon dance dresses, but with the skirt a lot shorter, and wide, like those of a ballerina. She putted the dress on without a bra. Latoya gave Vanessa a clean gym short, for undergarments.

After looking through her raided locker, Vanessa breathed in a sign of relief that only her clothing had been pilfered. It was such a petty robbery, almost like the works of a juvenile teen, or a perverted janitor. Dressed as such, Vanessa went to the portable classroom where her club held its meeting.

When they saw her come in, each member gave her a buck to replace the clothing that was stolen. Colin, said, "You should report it to the police or the principal."

"Why bother…it was my own fault for putting such an easy locker password," explained Vanessa.

"Not the brightest idea putting 1,1,1," commented James laughing.

"You," said Vanessa pointing.

"Wait, what no. I just assumed that you put 1,1,1 or 0,0,0, or some other repetitive number. It couldn't have been since I spent all afternoon playing chess, right Fuu," said James gesturing at Fuu.

Fuu raised an eyebrow and said, "I have no idea what you are talking about."

To put an end to the annoying conversation, James opened all the content of his backpack onto the table, as well, as opening his jacket to check inside. Laughing, Vanessa said, "Sheesh, James. Can't you tell when I am joking?"

"We all know, prim and proper James would never steal," said Colin.

"Hahaha...very funny," said James putting his stuff away, a bit sulky.

"Just out of curiosity, why do you have two cellphones?" asked Latoya.

"Oh...no reason, it's just, because of...mmm...do you really want me to say it," said James embarrassed.

"Fine, its fine," said Latoya laughing, "What you do with your cousin's cellphone is none of our business."

The rehearsal for "The Comedy of Calisto and Melibea" by Fernando de Rojas went without incident. Latoya had chosen such an obscure play because she was sick of Shakespeare. Like the Beast, she thought that English speakers had to get over that overrated. Latoya never quite understood why her current inventory was considered a comedy, seeing as though the titular characters die in the end.

When rehearsals ended, Colin walked Vanessa home. He was

concerned that someone would target Vanessa for dressing in such a fashion. It was a cool, spring sunset, and the air was crisp with the noon shower. The peacefulness of his surroundings and the companionship of Vanessa made Colin think that some of his father's paranoia was rubbing off on him. Colin always carried a pistol in his coat pocket for protection, even though the school did not allow students to have a weapon on campus.

Vanessa stopped suddenly and stared at a rundown apartment building. One of the fallen staircases had a case filled with coloring pencils. Vanessa picked up the color pencils, and saw that they had received plenty of usage. She placed it back down, where she had found it.

"Why don't you take it?" asked Colin.

Not looking or listening to him, Vanessa said, "You know…all of this is a popularity contest. Just like the red pencil is the one most used. So too is…never mind."

"Finish your thought, Vanessa," said Colin concerned. It was not like her to go on rambling.

"You know, Colin, I have always been a klepto, even though, I have never taken anything that doesn't belong to me. I do not know if these pencils have an owner, or if they were abandoned, for this reason I will not take them. But you can have them if you like," she said continuing her walk.

Looking back, Colin should have asked more questions. He took whatever Vanessa had said, as face value not realizing that this was the last time he would see her. The moment she closed the door of her home, Colin never saw Vanessa again. He had never loved her, nor been close friends with her. He only related to her insomuch as the club activities dictated, or to satisfy his impulses to play the chivalrous man.

She was listed as missing, and that was the end of the police investigation. Rumors of her and her death went from the mundane to the ridiculous. For a time, Colin thought Vanessa's over-protective father had killed her in a fit of jealousy, or had taken her out of the country or something. In the end, Colin had never found out what had happened to Vanessa. He would never had obsessed about her had she not disappeared in such a mysterious fashion.

Thirty years passed, and Colin had almost forgotten about Vanessa. He only thought of her, whenever he felt the familiar feeling of dread whenever his own daughter said she was going out with her friends. Focused on his career as Senator, he had no time for such mundane matters. The years had turned him into a bitter, harsh man. Though, this harshness was masqueraded by a cloak of politeness, and a handsome smile to boot. During one of his fundraisers, a strange man approached him. Like everyone in the gala, the man was dressed in a tuxedo. Though, when he saw the man from up close he realized the person was a woman.

A familiar voice then said, "Nice to see you moving up in the world, Mr. Red Pencil."

His face turned pale as a ghost when he recognized Vanessa. Despite the many years, she still had the same face, thought with some crow's feet, and pronounced laugh lines. Colin opened his mouth to say something, but he was stupefied. Vanessa gestured with her head, and Colin followed. He did not hear his friends calling for him to speak with another important Congressman, or about the health bill.

Colin asked, "What happened to you?"

"Nothing much, just 30 years…" said Vanessa.

"Nessa…" started Colin.

Shaking her head, Vanessa said, "Its Van now. At least on paper," she said turning to face Colin. She then added, "I did not come to relieve the old days. I am not one to waste words, unlike you. I came on business. Tomorrow, vote no."

Knowing full well that Vanessa was not going to elaborate, Colin decided to vote no on the proposition he had been pushing for the last four months. Even after 30 years, Vanessa still held sway over him. After all, she was the leader of the theater club, and he would not have been there today if it was not for her pointers.

STUBBORNNESS

rofessor Hopkins had started the new school year. He had been teaching in the same High School for the last 3 years. Since his friend was the director, he received twice as much as the average teacher. Even with the above average pay for someone in his position, he was still nowhere near at chipping away at his school debt. He was possessed by a most singular thought, for now he had to play his part for another year. Once this year ended, he was destined to get a tenure job at the university. When he arrived at his desk he found a letter with some instructions. This letter was usually sent by the principal whenever the teacher was to host a student with special needs. He had yet to deal with one of such students; mainly because he taught AP elective classes.

Professor Hopkins thought, well there is a first time for everything. According to the letter, the student with special needs was not so much special; rather he was severely traumatized. He had read about Cedric Striges in the newspapers. He had quite the number of scarifications all over his body. Based on his physical description, he matched the profile of a young boy who had been taken from an orphanage 10 years ago. Professor Hopkins doubted that he was the same Cedric. Something clearly bad had occurred to him, which much was for certain. Since he refused to speak and even to write about it, the media was given free reigns to speculate.

The theories as to what had occurred to Cedric were enough to make one cringe. Despite whatever ordeal Cedric may have endured. His entrance exam to matriculate in the school, and set upon a grade and class levels was enough to award him all AP classes. He was a sharp young man, for certain, though somewhat temperamental.

According to the letter of instructions, Cedric was not be pressured into participating in class. If he suddenly got up and left, he was not to be stopped. If he got started working on another project or started scribbling in his notebook he was not to be pestered. All interactions had to be limited to homework, text and class assignments.

If he appeared not to be paying attention, there was no cause for concern seeing as though he had an IQ of 137. There were other lists of instructions and suggestions, but Professor Hopkins was not in the mood with dealing with the little gremlin. The sixth period arrived, and it was time for Professor Hopkins to meet the mysterious Cedric. When he saw him, he looked just like any ordinary bored teenager. Based on his clothing, it seemed like his nonexistent mother did the shopping for him, with the black jeans, that the brown and teal square patterned long sleeved turtle neck. It did not seem like a deliberate choice on his part, he would pull at the neck of his shirt from time to time. Cedric obviously appeared to be regretting wearing such an outfit.

The class Hopkins was teaching was German Literature. Like most teachers of his day, the professor was in love with Friedrich Nietzsche. He thought of the bastard like some brilliant visionary, omitting the fact that he German philosopher was declared insane at the age of 26. It was a wonder just how many of his works were produced during his descent into madness.

While Hopkins was boring the class with his third rate interpretation of Zarathustra, Cedric was pulling at his turtle neck. In the end, he got up and left the room without even raising his hand or writing a note, or even using sign language to ask for permission. According to his 3 page manual of instructions, Cedric did know sign language, and would use it in a pinch.

Losing his frame of thought, Hopkins asked, "So where was why?"

A bright, doe eyed blonde maiden then said raising her hand; "You were going on about the Camels, the lions and the baby."

"A yes…" said Hopkins.

About 15 minutes later, Cedric returned with the neck of his shirt cut, clearly with a scissor. This gave the students plenty to laugh at. Cedric pouted in response and returned to his seat. The three days passed in a similar fashion. Cedric's behavior was slowly becoming more disruptive. The last drop was when he started listening to music in the middle of class.

Hopkins took Cedric's headphones, and then said, "I am onto you! While you are in my class, you will pay attention, is that understood!! No more listening to music, no more coming and going as you please. I am your teacher, now do as I say or else."

Cedric scratched his temple with his index finger. He then started gathering his belongings. Losing his patience, Hopkins said, "Where do you think you are going?"

Standing by the doorway, Hopkins said defiantly, "If you try to leave, I will call security. Students aren't allowed to roam the hallways."

The moment Hopkins stood on the doorway, Cedric started hyperventilating. With a panicked dazed look, he started looking about for an exit. He went towards the windows, and he removed the lock with a trembling hand. Alarmed, Hopkins yelled, "Somebody, stop him."

Before, the jocks could get to him; Cedric had jumped out the 4th floor window. At least that is what it had appeared. Dexterously, he had climbed up the pipe, and onto the roof. That was the last interaction Hopkins had with Cedric. To help Cedric stay put, the guidance Counselor had moved Cedric to another advance class. The hippie Studio Drawing teacher was more condescending with Cedric.

From time to time, Professor Hopkins would see Cedric roaming the halls. His disdain for school rules and teacher's authority was having a negative effect, even in the most well behaved students. They were slowly realizing that there is a difference between good behavior and obedience.

THE DEMON KING
COMETH

Today is the day of the coronation. Prince Fredric stands beside his elderly father as he sees his older brother getting his crown. His father had recently abdicated the throne because of his old age. Fredric's green eyes stared at the frail hands of his father, clad in elaborate robes of fine gold, silver and silk. His strong hands now trembled, as his eyes squinted to see the scene before him.

Yes, it was for the best, thought Prince Fredric at the time.

As the procession droned on, Prince Fredric breathed in a sigh of relief when he saw the priest carrying the crown. The end was almost near. The sun was slowly setting, giving the stained glass cathedral a most ethereal look. The Prince and his father were seeing the ceremony from the second floor banister. Fredric sat on a throne, not unlike the one of his father with his two other siblings. There was an empty chair beside the King. This was the place reserved for the Queen. Fredric had never met his mother, she having died at his birth.

The crown was slowly being placed over his brother's head. Just before it lightly graced his temple, the cathedral windows shattered, raining glass over the people on the floor below.

The Prince Fredric awoke with a start from this recurrent nightmare. Regardless of how much he jogged his memory, this was the only thing he could remember about that day. He remembered somewhat the ceremony, and the moment just before the demons came. A lot of things did not make sense to him as of lately. The only thing he knew was that he was in hiding, and that his Kingdom was no more. Sitting up, he went to check on the lady sleeping beside him.

The lady was called Thora, and she claimed to be his bodyguard. He had never met the woman, and he only knew rumors about her. As a wandering knight, it was said she had slain a dragon. It was she who had escorted him from the doomed capital, or so she said. She was still recovering from the injuries she had received that day. At the moment, they were staying in a hut belonging to an pair of old farmers. They had paid for room and boarding.

Fredric eyed the bandages around Thora's body with suspicion. They seemed a bit too clean for someone who was injured. Every morning, he was half tempted to lift one to see if there was a wound buried beneath. The first time he had tried, he had received a serious talking to. In spite of this, he was eager to check once again. His hand reached for her shoulder, but her eyes opened. To masquerade his intentions, Fredric pretended to stretch.

Sitting up, she said, "We should get going."

"Alright," said Fredric sternly.

Fredric stretched himself, getting out of bed. He was tall for his 14 years of age, and quite limber as well. It was tradition for all Princes to receive combat training. When he was younger, he used to shun the classes. In retrospect, it was useful that his older brother always tracked him down, whenever he seemed eager to skip any lessons.

While Thora was putting on her armor, she asked, "Do you remember anything new?"

"No," said Fredric.

"How about just before the ceremony?" insisted Thora.

"No," said Fredric.

Thora eyed him with suspicion, while Fredric stared at her bandages. He brushed back his raven hair, and with it all his worries. He then smelled his hand, before grimacing. It had been a week since his last bath. Their constant moving rarely afforded him a moment of respite. Thora was small in stature, a mere 5'1". She had syrup color skin, amber eyes, and short blonde hair. There was a certain fragility about her. Her size alone was the reason why he doubted her identity and her story. The only thing he knew for certain was that demons had overtaken the crown city.

Demons, sounds silly when you say it like that, thought Fredric. You read about them in the Bible, but you never imagine that they really exist till a horde of them starts killing people around you.

Fredric was awakened from his ruminations when he heard Thora opening the door. Mechanically, she paid the host and started to walk outside with an even pace. Fredric stumble behind her, and eventually he caught up to her quick pace. Even after four weeks, he was not used to her quick stride.

Frowning, he protested, "Wait up."

Thora pretended not to listen to him. After his second protestation, she stopped and turned around. She shook her head sadly. Mockingly, she said, "I am surprised you cannot keep up with the pace of an injured maiden."

"In what way are you injured, if you might indulge me?" asked Fredric.

"A couple of claws to the extremities is sufficient to drain most vital fluids. Aside from the occasional faintness, and reopening of wounds there is not much wrong with me," explained Thora.

She shifted a little inside her leather, brigandine armor. Her choice weapon had always been a partisan, but she carried a short sword, and a lantern shield to fight in close quarters. She contrasted greatly with the dainty Fredric, with his dress sword and worn princely attire. He had been wearing the same clothing, since the coronation.

They walked together in silence for a couple of hours. The blistering sun was frying Fredric's head. He regretted not having the foresight to purchase the farmer's hat. In all the farms they visited, this singular thought came into his head, but he would usually forget as soon as they were miles away from the farm. As before, Fredric asked, "Were are we going?"

"How many times must I repeat myself. We are going to a ruin to reclaim an ancient power that should help us find the demons," said Thora shaking her head sadly.

Over the course of five months, this same scene repeated itself, over and over. From time to time, the pair would see a shadow over the horizons, and occasionally they would see a demon lurking in the crossroads. They seemed to Fredric to be looking, searching for something. Despite how hard he tried, Fredric could not seem to recover his memories.

Eventually, his party was joined by 4 other warriors who were on the same quest. On the anniversary of his brother's coronation, Fredric and his companions finally reached the temple. It was located in a forest, with an overpopulation of bees. Aside from being a bit of a nuisance, they did not get stung. The ruined temple seemed quite familiar to Fredric for reasons he could not understand. There were the banisters, the broken chairs, even the hollowed out roof seemed familiar to him. There had been a fire, or so it seemed. Despite all the time it had passed, there was something about this place. Carved into the wall, there was the profile figure of a strange creature. Being a bit of a Catholic type of fellow, Fredric assumed that the skull faced creature was a demon. The creature's skeletal hand protruded from the relief. On its downcast hand there was the hint that it was pointing at something.

On the floor near it, Fredric found what the creature was pointing at. It was a small halo, with a tiny star protruding in the center. There was something familiar about it. After rattling his mind a little, Fredric remembered seeing the depiction of the crown in one of the court paintings, depicting the founder of his Kingdom. Without giving it much thought, Fredric placed the crown on top of his head.

Once again, Thora asked, "Do you remember what happened the day of the coronation?"

Fredric was thoughtful, as he collected his thoughts. A thin smile painted on his lips. He then said, "Yes, now I remember."

SCHOOL KALI

Today, Kali was finally well enough to leave the hospital. Aside from a jagged scar on her head, hidden beneath a full mane of curly blonde hair, there was no visible permanent damage. She was damaged however, in more ways than she dared to realize. On her first day out of the hospital, a man and lady who called themselves her parents took Kali home. Her full name was Kalica, when she read her full name, at the time she thought it meant Death Incarnate, like the Hindu Goddess. When she entered the manor that was supposedly her home, she realized that Kalica was for Calico.

Waiting in the porch for her was a Calico cat, about 8 years in age. When Kali came to pick up the cat, it greeted her in the usual feline fashion. Kali dropped the cat, after receiving a couple of bites and scratches in her bare arm.

Her "mother" said to the cat, "Don't you recognize Kali, you silly cat?"

The cat showed its behind in response, before entering the manor. Kali studied all the items in her home with a degree of skepticism. It was her own face staring back at her in the family portraits, but she did not recognized it. After a week of acclimating, as her father used to call it; Kali was compelled to return to her boarding school. The uniform felt to her stiff around the neck, and the waist constricted, almost as if the uniform was a bit too small for her. Kali had complained of this, the moment she had putted it on, but on such short notice, she would have to grim and bear it at least for a couple of days.

The attire was a pinafore, pleated dress the color of earth. Though to Kali, it resembled some of the things she left in the toilet from time to time. To compliment this unbecoming color, the dress was supposed to be worn over a yellow shirt. While she walked the hallway, she was greeted with whispers and grimaces. Kali found it odd that nobody from her school had bothered to check up on her. This confirmed her suspicion that in her previous life, she had been a social pariah.

She was eventually pulled to the side into an empty classroom by a handsome devil. With his livid, green eyes, he studied her face looking for a sigh of recognition. Eventually, somewhat dejected he asked, "So, you really do not know who I am?"

"You are my boyfriend," guessed Kali. She spoke with a strong certainty. Her voice never faltered, which tended to annoy her parents, whenever they knew she was lying to them.

He kissed her, and she returned the kiss, with mechanical familiarity. She then asked, "Do you know what happened to me?"

"No. The police simply found you beaten to a pulp, left for dead," he added, "Naturally, they came looking for me. Cause you know that ancient cliché, that whenever something bad happens to a girl, the boyfriend is to blame."

"Yes, usually," said Kali flatly. She added, "Though there are some notable exceptions."

"Is that a threat?" asked her lover whose name she could not remember.

"Just a fact," said Kali mechanically.

After this conversation, the day slowly droned by. For some reason, the same familiar faces in school kept glaring at her. She did not know them, but they knew her. After four weeks of this turn of events, Kali was suddenly possessed by a singular thought. Those students who kept glaring at her, and where half afraid had done this to her. They were responsible for her memory loss, or so she imagined.

One day, she told her boyfriend, "I think I know who did this to me."

"Have you finally reclaimed your memory?" asked her man whose name kept alluding her.

"Yes, dearest," said Kali to hide this fact. For the last couple of weeks, it had been sweetie this and pumpkin pie that. She added, "I need your help to carry out my bloody revenge."

"Let me guess, you want me to steal my father's guns," said her lover half joking, half serious.

"Oh! No, nothing too sordid, I am afraid. I prefer a stealth hand, as far as handling my worldly problems. Why should the innocent pay for the guilty?" asked Kali.

"I am surprised by your restraint," said her lover.

"Is restraint a trait I do not usually exhibit?" asked Kali.

"Meh!" said her lover shrugging his shoulders.

For the next couple of weeks, the pair spent their time stalking their prey. Kali had segregated for her revenge about 11 students, 7 girl and 4 boys. The boys were the first one's pegged. They had the most predictable movement pattern. Two were taken care of in the library, a second in the nearby woods and a fourth at a tea house in the next town over. When it came to dealing with the maidens, Kali's lover was a bit reticent.

"I want no part, in the death of those babes, babe" said her lover.

"You are in for a penny, you are in for a pound. Also, you already helped me with one, if you do not remember," said Kali coolly.

"Ah, yes the tea house. He was a dude, so even if he identified as a chick, it doesn't count as far as my man code is concerned," said Kali's man.

"Suit yourself," said Kali, "But if you ask me. The moment you commit violence against another fellow human being you already lose your protection status."

"So by that logic, if a toddler stabbed you with a knife, you would peg the kid," said her lover.

"Toddlers are not responsible for their actions, so no," said Kali coolly.

The following morning Kali started pegging the girls. By the time they were down to three, the girls were already on the alert. It turned into a bloody shootout, one frigid afternoon in the forest. With one being the bait, the other girl had tried to snipe Kali out with her father's hunting rifle. When she missed, she said, "I should have finished you when I had the chance Kali."

"Why did you try to kill me?" asked Kali trying to buy time.

"You were a rotten apple, so we did what had to be done to prevent you from spoiling the bunch. I wasn't going to let a crime lord's daughter turn my entire class into junkies," said the girl shooting at Kali, almost gracing her target.

It was at this point when Kali's enemy was knocked out by her boyfriend. Smiling Kali said, "By the Gods, Shiva, thank you."

Running to her, Shiva commented, "If I had known that wailing a couple of fools would have helped you remember me, I would have done so a lot sooner."

"Did you get the others?" asked Kali.

"I mercy killed them," said Shiva. Kali noted his favorite weapon, the woodcutter's ax.

With their grim work concluded, the pair burned the bodies of their victims. As they watched them burn, Shiva placed his hand over Kali's shoulder to draw her closer. Resting his head against hers, he asked, "Ready to get back to work?"

"Might as well," said Kali.

THE IRON TOM

The year was 2498. Despite many advances in science, the world had not changed one bit. Sure, some countries did grow, while others deflated, but the core that is humanity has not changed one bit. It was during one of those standard peacekeeping expeditions in the country of Agrippa, that Clark met with misfortune. His people were ambushed by the locals, or maybe a rival faction. It doesn't matter for the purpose of this tale. It certainly did not matter to Clark. All he knew was that his people were being put down, one bullet a time. Bullets! Another archaic weapon of the old world. The more advanced nations had already moved onto more useful, gimmicky weapons, but the good old fashioned bullet was still the choice weapon for people who could not afford better armory. In spite of the sensors, the motion detection and all the fancy tech in their convoy, they fell for something as mundane as a common landmine.
When the executioner came to shoot Clark in the head, Clark asked, "Why are you doing this to us? Can't you see that we are here to help you?"

The man eyed Clark with a look of disdain. He then answered in perfect English, much to Clark's surprise. The man said, "You just don't get it, do you?"

This was the last thing that Clark remembered before awakening in the hospital. Indeed, science had gone a long way. At least, this is what Clark thought through his muddled thoughts. Science had not saved him, but a little something called luck. Despite much advancements, gunshot wounds were still 90 percent fatal. This was due to the rarity of such an event in the first world. Not that people were no longer killing one another, but a surveillance network and the easy availability of lasers had helped in the decline of the gun's popularity.

During the first weeks of his recovery, Clark could not remember the name of most items. He would often confuse people's faces. This caused many frustrations for his young wife Mirta, and his fiver year old son Terry. After taking heavy doses of drugs, marinated with a bit of stem cells Clark's brain was restored to working order. The downside was that he would have to fill in some of the gaps the old fashioned way.

Years passed, and Clark had not shown much sign of improvement. In fact, his coping mechanism seemed to be getting worse, as far as Mirta could tell. It had gotten to such a degree that Clark would stay away from home during the summer, for reasons he refused to speak about. One late July, Clark awoke to an unfamiliar sound. Rising from his bed, he went to check in the living room to see what was the matter. Scraping the immaculate white floor, and part of the carpet was a rudimentary tricycle. Terry was a bit of an odd kid, with a taste for the vintage items. While most kids his age were playing with automatons, and reality augmented games, Terry was amusing himself with toy soldiers, building blocks and soap bubbles.

Like most people who received a bit of a rude awakening, Clark said raising his voice, "What are you doing here boy? How did you get here?"

Terry simply stared at his father with a sad, dejected look on his face. His black eyes reflected back the guilt painted in Clark's face, who was already regretting the tone of voice he had employed on someone he thought a stranger. In response to his query, Terry suppressed a small whimper.

Mirta who was in the kitchen programming the breakfast machine went to see what was the matter. Frowning she said, "By Nemi, what is the matter with you?"

"I told you! I do not, cannot see people during the summer," insisted Clark. He added, "I am sorry, Mirta, it is just. You wouldn't understand."

Coming to him, Mirta said, "I can't help you, if you do not tell me. You cannot be helped, if you do not seek help."

"Do you take me for a fool? I know this… I am sorry. It is just. It is better if I am alone for now. Please, I do not want to hurt you or Terry," said Clark.

"This can't continue like this, Clark, I am…we are suffering for you as well. I am going to call my brother, to see if he can help you," said Mirta taking out a clear slate, which was her cellphone.

Taking the phone, Clark said, "It is no use Mirta. There is nothing he can do to help me."

"I don't understand," said Mirta.

Clark's eyes imperceptibly started looking behind her wife. He would try to focus on her, and the next thing she said, but he was not able to. It was then when she understood. Shaking her head sadly, she asked, "Are you still seeing things?"

"A little, and only during the summer time," explained Clark.

"Do the pills not help?" asked Mirta sitting down, and putting her head on her hands.

"Aside from making me feel sick. They do nothing to stop the voices, so I stopped taking them. It isn't like I am confused or anything. Think of them as a hologram that only I can see and hear. It is only for the summer Mirta. When this summer ends, I will return home to you back to normal," said Clark sitting beside his wife and smiling pitifully.

After this argument, Mirta and Clark resigned themselves to

their new life. Despite saying this, Clark was not happy to see his wife leave him to his own devices. The people he imagined were not particularly good company. The one he saw most often was a general. He knew he was a general based on his clothing and insignia. However, Clark could not remember the person's name or where he had met him. He would appear to Clark to serve the role of Gemini Cricket, much to his annoyance. It was through his influence that Clark had started to text to his wife during the summer. At least in writing, he could carefully consider his answers. A month passed, and there was somewhat a semblance of peace.

One day when Clark was watching the news "alone", he saw an interesting TV add. TV in those days still came flat for those who preferred traditional modes of entertainment. However, when certain programs allowed for it, it would project a 3D hologram. Clark's son had visited earlier, and so the TV was formatted to allow for holograms. Forgetting this, Clark who was dozing in and out saw a strange looking person protruding from the TV. He stared at it, and the person stared back at him, with a genuine, heartfelt smile.

The general looking at it said, "It is not like me, I assure you. This is something genuinely different."

Following, the silly commercial music started playing, with a deep voice, the announcer started spewing lots of techno babble, Clark could barely follow. Such commercials were rather common in those days. A new robot AI came out each year, with each new one promising to simulate human emotions better than the last. As far as Clark could tell, all the artificial beings were as soulless as his toaster. Still, there was something different about the Iron Tom standing before him. He paused the hologram and stood up to take a better look at the robot being advertised. The light green skin seemed real enough, and the large round green eyes were juicy, almost like a real person.

Realism was not the general theme of the Iron Tom, with its

space suit, and silly looking helmet. The design reminded Clark of an astronaut from those ancient science fiction novels rotting up the public library. Even now, the automaton librarians were in the progress of digitizing those public domain work. Clark always found it amusing to read over the top those science fiction books. It always amused him to see people's paranoia with artificial intelligence. AI like 3D was a bit of a fab. Aside from serious work, AI had no popular world applications, though some RAM space was usually reserved for commercialization purposes. There was the main AI that ran then internet, and then there was the commercial AI, that gave people the illusion they were talking to a real person.

Voicing his thoughts, the general said to Clark, "You should get one of those green thingies. I hear they are a lot of fun."

"I don't know," said Clark not too convinced.

"Look, this one is not like a computer. It doesn't come with internet or anything, or even wires. It is designed to look and feel like a real living person," insisted the general, "When I was younger I would have done anything in the world to have a fancy looking robot friend."

"How can you even tell me of your past if you are a figment of my imagination?" asked Clark.

"Dunno. Maybe I am referring to your past?" retorted the general.

"Not really. I remember I did have a couple of robots when I was a kid. When they would break down, my parents would get me new ones, by transferring the data. It was when I finally went to a public school did I make real friends," said Clark.

"It isn't the robots' fault that you were too shallow to befriend the help. When I was a kid, my best friend did not even move, and I still carry him with me every day," said the general opening his pocket to show a tiny little wolf action figure.

Clark stared at the action figure, while he rattled his mind trying to see if he could remember seeing such an item. In the end, Clark acquired an Iron Tom to have some else to talk to aside from the general, and the other occasional nuisances. Clark like most people in his home bought things online. After waiting for a couple of days, Clark heard a knock on the door. He had expected the American Postal Service guy, but instead he found his package unboxed, holding an instruction booklet. Clark then took the booklet from the Iron Tom's hand and started to read the short explanation. While he read it, the Iron Tom started to survey his surroundings without going inside.

Without thinking Clark closed the door on the Iron Tom's face. He heard a knocking, and a soothing voice that said, "Are you refusing delivery? If you want a return, you have to pay a fee."

Opening the door again, Clark said, "My apologies. Why have you not entered inside?"

"Because you have not told me to do so," said the Iron Tom as a matter of fact.

"You can come inside, sit down anywhere you like," said Clark opening the door for the strange robot.

It was a lot smaller in real life. Then again, he always had an issue with converting centimeters to metric without a calculator. Sure, he did have a computer with one, but it was always such a bother to load up the App to use it. Clark was thoughtful all the while. He was brought back to the present, by the Iron Tom who said, "What do you wish to call me?"

"Ah, yes. A name. I could just call you Tom for short," suggested Clark.

"IF you so desire, but there is already hundreds of Toms out there," said the Iron Tom.

"What a bother," said Clark shaking his head.

The general then said looking at the Iron Tom, "We could call you Afak."

"Ankle First Aid Kit? That's a terrible name," protested Clark.

"Your friend refers to the beloved wife of a Persian Poet. The name means Horizon," said Afak.

"I still don't like it," said Clark frowning. He then added surprised and alarmed, "Wait, you can see the general?"

"Yes, why shouldn't I?" asked Afak.

Clark came to stand beside the general. Pointing at him, he said to test the Iron Tom, "Do you see him. Truly? Can you describe him to me?"

Afak looked at the general from head to toe folding her or his arms. Clark was not certain whether gendered terms were appropriate when referring to a robot like the Iron Tom. Even its voice was difficult to pin down. It could pass for either a male or a female voice. It was that ambiguous.

Afak stared at Clark for a couple of seconds. Then she said, "The general has cadmium color hair, burnt umber skin and ultramarine eyes. He is wearing a somewhat outdated Navy Uniform, from the year 2300. He is 182.76 centimeters tall…"

"That's enough. So you can see him, somehow," said Clark bemused.

"I told you I was not some figment of your imagination," said the general smiling.

The weeks passed, and Afak was quickly integrated into Clark's family. She ran simple tasks, like cleaning, and feeding her owner. She also managed his checkbook, and other unimportant matters. Her most important role was to ground Clark in reality. Before the summer ended, Clark resolved to do something with his life. He had not been in the labor force in years. He was not poor, but his savings where slowly decreasing, with only his wife's input into their mutual saving's account. It wasn't cheap to maintain a house, and an apartment.

"So, where do you want to work?" asked Afak.

Clark cringed for reasons he could not understand. Something about the tone of voice she had used was so familiar. Afak smiled, as she repeated the question using her normal voice, "Where do you want to work? I have some listings you can look through."

Clark looked through the listings, and he eventually settled on a standard security mission. There was a mining Colony on Mars, and they were always in need of goons to maintain order. At the time, the fastest commercial bus took 4 days to get to Mars. There were other means of quicker transportation, but none that he felt he could afford. During those four days, Clark had some time for introspection. He realized why the voice Afak had used had bothered him so. During his last mission, he was growing something of a romance with one of the Journalists he was escorting. He thought he was in love. Years of complacency with his wife, had rendered their relationship dull, and lifeless. Hearing Afak use such a voice stirred memories that were long dead, and buried.

In the end, Clark pushed those thoughts out of his head. There was no point in thinking of the past. Cathay was dead and buried like all the others. When Clark arrived to Mars, he decided to not devote the matter anymore of his attention. He poured himself into his job. It truly wasn't anything too exiting. His shift would last about 8 Sols. He was then allowed to return home, and stay with his family for an Earth Week, before flying back to serve another shift. It was during one of those dull, red Martian morning when an accident occurred at the mine. There was an explosion, with hundreds injured. Among then was his only living friend and confidant, the bizarre looking synthetic he called Afak.

Instead of going first to help the humans, Clark carried the unconscious Afak to the mechanic. The glass dome was broken, and there were damages in other small parts around the helmet. The mechanic looked at Afak over the top. After reading up the item number of Afak, the repair instructions were brought up. Together with his own synthetic, the mechanic fixed Afak's helmet. Despite looking fresh, and new, the mechanic said, "This unit is still broken. The repairs I made are only superficial. You see this button I have pressed down. This will keep your robot in sleep mode till you can get it to Earth to have it fixed or replaced."

"What is wrong with it?" asked Clark.

"Some circuits of the main computer got fried. It is hard to tell how this might affect the unit's behavior. It is best not to risk it," said the mechanic.

Two later Sols, and Clark had nobody to talk to, but the general. Since it was an alien planet, the bastard had not left even thought it was a week past Summer in Earth time. Clark only had to put up with four more Sols, before being able to return home. Clark observed Afak sleeping with a bit of envy. It was then when the familiar voice within his head started pestering him.

"You should wake it up. Why should your slave sleep while the master is awake," said the general.

"Afak is not my slave. She is a tool nothing else," said Clark.

"I heard that before," snorted the general.

"So, based on your logic the fork and knife are also my servants too?" asked Clark drily.

"Well, they do cut your food and feed you, without reaping any of the benefits, so," said the general.

"You know, I never bothered to ask your name. Can you even answer such a question?" asked Clark.

"My name is of little consequence. All that matters is that you wake up that silly toy of yours," said the general. He added, "Do as I say cadet!"

"Sir, yes sir," said Clark giving the general the third finger salute.

Clark was not known for making good decisions, and so he did what the general commanded. He was bored of talking with the general so, he turned on Afak. When Afak turned on, it gave a large high pitch scream. It then backed away into the corner and started looking about like a frightened animal.

"Woah! That was unexpected," retorted Clark.

The general stared at Afak calmly. Afak slowly started to regulate its breathing, till it sat down on the floor. She pulled her feet together and rested her helmet against her knee to hide her face. Clark came to her, and petted her arm. She flinched from him, for reasons Clark could not understand. Controlling herself, she said, "Thank you, I feel a lot better now."

The reassuring way she had said so did not inspire Clark much confidence. A Sol passed, and things seemed somewhat normal. The synthetic was looking about, and staring at things and asking a lot of weird questions. Clark answered mechanically, assuming that it had lost some basic information. On the Sol he was supposed to head home, there was another explosion in the mines, only this one was on purpose. The five other Iron Toms in the facilities had acquired guns from the armory and were putting down all the humans.

When Afak came for him, Clark asked, "Why are you doing this? Are you malfunctioning?"

Holding the laser gun, Afak said to him, "You just don't get it, do you?"

Back on planet earth, Terry was watching the news while playing with a small toy soldier. The owner of the Iron Tom company was getting arrested. A few days before, the main building where their machines were being manufactured had gone up in smokes. It turns out that the Toms were nor robots, but a race of intelligent aliens, with low technology. The owner had used AI chips to force them to obey their human owners. This was a developing news, and each hour more chilling details came to light. Terry looked at the wall clock. Noticing it was time for his show, he told the TV, "Put on Channel 15."

The Consequences of Your Actions

Wei was an orderly man. He would spend hours trying to get a pen in the right position. He did not take it well when his wife died, giving birth to his only son. She was his childhood sweetheart and he never remarried. He dedicated his life to raising their son, Fang. Wei never did quite know what to make of his son. The child would not cry, only gleefully smile when looked upon. Fang showed signs of great intelligence, and even started saying a couple of words when he was 11 months old. The fact that Fang was not like other babies had gotten Wei thinking. It was when Fang turned 4, that Wei was possessed by a singular idea. Wei thought his son had no true emotions. From then on, whenever Fang did something wrong, his father would lock him in a basement.

Such occurrences became less frequent, as Fang got older and more adept at guessing his father's mood. Whenever Wei would lock his son up, he would say, "It is about time you learned there are consequences for your actions."

This became a mantra for Fang. He would repeat it, whenever he would catch a school fellow on some fault. Known for tattle-telling, Fang completed basic school without making a single friend. Despite his son's good grades and his fame of being a good boy, Wei still continued to suspect his son. He could not shake the feeling that Fang could easily become a serial killer or worse.

His fears were realized when Fang joined the army. This career path suited Fang. He was already used to being a tool. Due to his analytical skills, Fang never saw actual combat. He instead became a paralegal. After four years of investigation, he had been responsible for heralding the investigation that caused the court-martial of 45 corrupt officers. He was always present whenever they caught his target. He would always say to the fellow what his father had always told him, "It is about time you learned there are consequences for your actions."

Fang's last big case landed him some national attention. He even made a brief testimony on television. The following day he received a call from his father. Without showing any visuals signs of perturbation, Fang returned home to see his old man. Just like when he was a child, his father guided him to the basement and locked the door. It was then when he noticed the smell of gasoline that he understood. He started banging at the door yelling, "Father, you are going to kill me! Me! Your only son! There will be consequences you hear, in this life and the next. Open the door!"

"You are right. There will be consequences, but for once I am going to do the right thing. I should never have set you free into the world. Why do you still pretend to have emotions? We both know what you are. Rest in Peace, son," said Wei walking upstairs.

Like a caged animal, Fang started rattling the surroundings and all the junk his father stored in the basement. Fang was silent for a moment to hear if his father would return. It was then when he heard the sound of a match, followed by the sound of a gunshot.

After the death of his father, Fang resolved never to think of Wei. Fang continued life as a paralegal in the private sector. While recovering from his burns, the nurse tending to him suffered a case of Florence Nightingale syndrome. The pair married the following Spring. On their second year in marriage, Nurse Xiu Ying gave Fang a baby boy. While Fang had been a well behaved baby, his brood was a bit of a handful. When his son Chao was five, there was a little incident that made Fang think of his father. His small son had taken the magnifying glass from his study and was using it to burn ants that were rising from a little hill.

Chao stopped the minute he saw his father come. Fang sat beside his son, staring at the little critters. Fang detested the ants and would occasionally poison them to keep them away from his tree. Still, he was not a fan of torturing an animal to dead, let alone setting them aflame.

Picking up an ant with his hand, Fang said, "You know that you did is wrong, don't you? Just because an animal is small doesn't make it right to cause them pain. Ants feel and hate like you do, and more importantly they can tunnel. You have seen them from time to time in the house, haven't you? If you make an enemy of the ants, they might just tunnel through your head while you are sleeping."

THE WINDOW

It was during dinner time that Yamato noticed a strange noises out the window. His first instinct was to get up and check it out. However, he chose to remain seating down. He already inspired enough animosity among the people he was supposed to call family. The transfer had been successful. He would only require to put up with their disdain for another two months. Once the trial period was completed, he could slowly transition into his old life. When he had completed his dinner, he was finally able to peak his curiosity. The youngest brat, whose name alluded Yamato too got up to stare. A single grimace from the 87 year old matriarch was enough to set the lad straight.

The name of the current skin Yamato inhabited was called Tetsu. He had paid good money for the entire package. His original body had failed him some odd, four months ago. He was still getting used to being called Tetsu. A knocking on the door came, and a stranger called for Tetsu. Yamato meekly followed to see what all the fuss was about. Both Tetsu and Yamato had one thing in common: A Medical Degree, though the focused differed. While Tetsu was a surgeon, Yamato was a Virologist.

When he was outside, the man said, "I know that you are really Yamato, but I am not here to inquire about your private business. There is someone with a strange disease. I need you to examine him."

Together, they went to the quarantine zone. There was a child on a stretcher and he was saying goodbye to his mother. Yamato had heard that tone before. Children who thought they were going to die, gave such a melancholic, comforting goodbyes. The kid was not going to die, at least, if he could help it. After getting into those cliché, white clean suits. He examined the child closer. The skin was pealing, and beneath was a black, icky, rippled texture. It reminded Yamato of gangrene or leprosy. For some reason, the kid did not showed signs of pain. It was possible that the virus or disease had eaten through the pain receptors. Indeed, Yamato thought the kid was going to die.

This did not occur. For the next 12 years, Yamato and his team studied the patient. The weird skin mutations seemed to be linked to his growth. Like a crab, he would molt his human skin, before growing a new one. All throughout the cycle, the patient would look even more strange. One day he was tending to the patient, when he said, "I know that you people have been lying to me. I am not sick. This is just how I am. I want to go home to see my mother."

Yamato had spoken to his superiors about sending the lad home to his grief stricken mother. In the name of science, the patient had not being allowed to return. The nameless patient was both very human, and quite inhuman at the same time. In the end, the scientists decided to perform vivisection. Minutes later, Yamato returned. He unstrapped the patient, and offered him a card with a phone number and his wallet. The patient would now be Tetsu. When the patient was summoned, the doctors found Yamato staring at the empty bed.

Yamato gave a wry smile. He then said, "It is about time I make my grand escape too."

Without hesitating, Yamato jumped out the window splattering against the concrete floor.

The Bone

It was a normal day in the Metro Zoo. The tourists and locals alike were looking at the animals, while the animals dreamed of eating the visitors. Belinda was a zookeeper, who managed the birds. Since she was a novice, her responsivities were quite menial. She would have to feed, and clean the bird house. During one of those cleanings, she noticed a peculiar change in one of the birds. It seemed to her that it was shedding its feathers, and growing rather big. Her better sense told her to go find the manager. This decision helped saved her life. The animals in the Zoo were all changing at an alarming rate. It seemed to Belinda that they were turning into their Jurassic forms. This was just a poorly educated guess on her part. Her only knowledge of dinosaurs was limited to the silly movies that she would see in the theater. Regardless of the how and the why, the animals were changing. Those that grew bigger and more mobile had started pegging the visitors one by one.

After much chaos and running, Belinda had taken refuge in service center. While she sat there, she started thinking and wondering about the bizarreness of the entire situation. She pinched herself a couple of times to make certain she was awake. Her wandering blue eyes searched in vain for something to protect herself with. In the end, she found a taser that was commonly used to force the bears to come out of their caves, during visiting hours. The bears too were larger than usual.

Belinda looked dourly, as the park managers were being mauled by prehistoric bears. It seemed to Belinda that aside from the change, the animals retained their memories. Slowly, Belinda made her way from building to building. She was slowly trying to make it to her car, to drive out of there. Eventually, she made her way towards the lab. She secured all the doors and windows. She was about to make another mad dash towards another building, when she saw a Wholly mammoth. She decided to stay inside, and wait a bit till it moved. While being forced to wait, Belinda had some time alone to think.

She thought, Why aren't humans affected?

While thoughtlessly rummaging through the lab, Belinda finds a piece of bone. She studied it with interest. The bone was the unla of an unidentified lifeform. The bone itself was thin, and as long as Belinda's leg. When she picked it up, it started emitting a strange glow. She dropped it, and then picked it up again, to defend herself against one of those raptors that had breached the barricades. Before it got to her, the light of the bone had turned the raptor back into a chicken. Belinda started making her way around the park, with the light of the bone growing stronger and stronger.

Her coworker, Mr. Smith suddenly appears from inside a garbage can. Looking bewildered he asked, "How are you doing that?"

"I don't know, but it is fixing the problem. Isn't it?" said Belinda.

 "The bone was the source of the problem to begin with," said Mr. Smith.

The archeologist told her how he had found the bones, and how when he putted them together, they started to glow, before exploding in hundreds of different directions. He would have gone to the hospital, but then the problems started. After bandaging himself up as best he could, he hid in a garbage can to wait for the police or something. The pair started rounding up survivors, and putting away the animals that had already turned back to normal. The effect of the bone was slow acting, while it had changed the animals quickly, turning them back to their original form seemed to take minutes, and sometimes hours.

By dusk, Mr. Smith and Belinda had escorted everyone to safety, and had collected the rest of the bones. They were putting the bones back together in the lab. It was at this point when Belinda asked, "Did nobody here call the cops or something?"

"They did," said Mr. Smith, "But I did not allow for the call to reach its final destination."

"How? Why?" asked Belinda bewildered.

It was at this point that Belinda got closer, and took a better look at Mr. Smith. The bandages and covers did not have a speck of blood, and why the glasses and the hat, and the trenchcoated. Mr. Smith chuckled and said, "You are smart for a blondie."

He then removed the bandages to show that he was a reptilian. The light of the bone was slowly having him turn back into something that resembled a human. When he was "himself" again, he explained.

"Before there were men. There was I, or us or whatever. You heard about those conspiracy theories about reptilians, yes, I am one of them. Through selective breeding and gene therapy, we have made ourselves resemble humans. Through the power of those bones, my true nature was released," explained Mr. Smith.

"Why are you telling me all this?" asked Belinda confused, "Are you going to kill me or something, to silence me?"

"Don't be too alarmed. This is just the side effect of a gas leak, combined with a breach in the zoo security system that caused some of the animals to escape," said Mr. Smith brushing off her concerns.

"Still, why weren't we, I mean, me, the humans affected by the bones?" asked Belinda.

"Who knows?" said the reptilian Mr. Smith shrugging his shoulders.

The bones started to resonate, and it then took the form of a robed mage. It too was a reptilian, like the fellow standing beside Belinda. It spoke, in a soft hushed, ancient language that only Mr. Smith could understand.

It said, "Eons ago, I was the sole mage among our civilization. Our people scoffed at my efforts and my magic, so I decided to destroy their civilization by summoning a meteor. My people did not grasp the importance of magic, and neither do the humans. All of existence will be in great peril if science continues to suppress and belittle the wonders that can be achieved via magic."

The mage stopped and shook its head sadly. It turned around to see something that only his eyes could see. Laughing, he added before turning to dust, "What is the use. It is already too late. Have fun with your little lasers, and robots."

Lady Ai

The year was 3587 or 4591. It matters not for the purposes of this story. Somewhere in the distant future artificial intelligence was being refined. The robots could think and act independently. Some had even been elected mayors. The problem was getting the human aspect just right. Despite their different flavors, they were noticeably still not human. Then, a big break occurred for the company known as Deus Ex Machina. It had produce an artificial intelligence that resembled the way man thought. Salutations were given, and even a couple of awards. One day while talking with his maid robot, Engineer Kenneth noticed something particularly odd. He closed his eyes for a moment, and he felt it again. To make certain, he modulated the voice of the robot. There it was! The robot did not speak as women should.

By then, society had moved past gender binaries. Still, when Kenneth spoke with a lady who identified as a man, she still spoke in a fashion that Kenneth considered feminine. There was just something inherently different between men and women. Kenneth, thought and thought. Eventually, he voiced his concerns to the President of Deus Ex Machina.

The president Ariel heard his concerns, and said laughing, "Surely you jest, my dear Kenneth. What is with this 21st century mentality? Nobody cares, but if you want to make a more girly robot, you have my permission. It might sell better. Program it to like ponies, rainbows or whatever, or maybe make it more maternal."

"Thank you for being so understanding," said Kenneth bowing.

With this partial greenlight, Kenneth went full force into his project. Just like his previous robotics project, he started with human's closest relative, the monkey. In the old days, he studied both apes regardless of their genders. This time he noticed behavioral differences across both genders. He had his core KC unit study the pattern of both apes, and then segregate dominant behaviors expressed by male apes vs female specimens. Normally, people would expect Kenneth to study humans. This was a problem because of their current stage in the development. Society was too much of an influence on the raw behavior of humans. Even among children, there was plenty of societal interference. Kenneth would have loved to have some native specimens, but other than the Sentinels, there was not any other indigenous population left in the world. The Sentinels were preserved with the same care and attention given to the pyramids.

After writing to his son, major KC317, Kenneth was able to get permission to access the surveillance cameras in the home of the Sentinels. Indeed, they were just like the people of yonder times with the hunting and the gathering. There were other behaviors he could not quite understand. His core KC unit did not know what to make of them either. They were a peculiar isolationist bunch. He removed from the core data, all the information pertaining to cultural oddities. He felt this behavioral model was more in tune with what he was looking for. As a side project, he also acquired enough raw footage of children. He fed both data into two robots.

In his mind, he imagined that females were defined by their ability to have kids. As such, his female robot would act more like a lady if it had a child it could identify as her own. This too proved to be a failure in part because of the observations of the Sentinels. He was not able to weed out enough cultural data. The robot pair ended up trying to kill him the moment they were turned on. It was a good thing he always beta tested with just a head and torso.

Calling it quits, he visited President Ariel again. The President said coyly, "Giving up already?"

"I don't know, I feel that my gender is getting in the way of achieving brilliance," said Kenneth.

"I could pool from our other projects a team of broads to help you?" said President Ariel.

"I don't think that is a proper way of referring to our most esteemed ladies," said Kenneth.

"And you think this little venture of yours is appropriate? I can call them broads, but you can't, I will not affect my way of speaking just because it affects your mild sensibilities. And let's say, you do invent your lady robot. What is your next goal?" asked Ariel.

"I want to make a series of talking dinosaurs, like the ones they have in the Japanese hotels, but for the local market," said Kenneth.

"Oh, Kenny, that sounds so stupid! You are lucky that all your silly ventures have been a financial success otherwise I doubt I would give you the time of day. Go back to the lab, to play with your toys, and don't come back till you have a semblance of success. You have a year to complete this project, so hop to it. If you fail, you better get started on something else," said Ariel dismissing Kenneth.

Kenneth returned to the lab, and with a team to help him. Despite all their helpful input, Kenneth ended up producing an imperfect female AI. She would not arrived at proper feminine conclusions, without a ton of handwritten if then scenarios. At the end of the year, it was this faulted failure that went into the stores, and it became an instant bestseller. The sheeple could not tell the difference, but Kenneth and his development team knew.

It seemed to Kenneth that the problem was rooted in the programing language itself. In the end, he decided to return to the basics. He copied his KC core AI, and removed from it all learned preferences. It was a blank slate as far as instructional information was concerned. He then placed the AI inside a female model, in a room with lots of girly things. In theory, it would learn of itself purely based on observations. Kenneth was tempted to include works of literature written by women, but they too had been affected by the climate of the day. After many generations, all women wrote as men did, and some even spoke as such. After looking at the room over the top, he realized that his own perspective and obsession had clouded his judgement.

While he left his new robot to its own devices, he visited his childhood home. It was a glass pavilion. The door would slide to the side to let him inside. Despite being made of glass, people could not look inside. The glass was reflective like those in the police station. He could look out, but outsiders could not look in. The floor was made of white marble. Then entire house decoration consisted of steel, glass and marble, with a color combination of black and white, with some red thrown every so often to break the monotony. Kenneth eventually found his sister's room. It had been kept identical since her early departure. There were the drawings, and plushies, and even her poor robot doll Lety. The doll had not been turned on since her owner had perished. Nobody in the house had the heart to inform the doll.

Kenneth eventually took one of the drawings his sister had made. It showed a boat, on top of the ocean, the sky had a happy face sun. Below, there was a bunch of different colored fishes. The following day he placed his drawing and a store bought plushie of a cat in the room with the AI. These two things had an interesting, softening effect on the robot. It almost seemed like a lady. The following day, Kenneth threw in a bunch of textbooks and workbooks. Normally, such information was fed into the robot. Instead, he allowed for his AI to show a preference for learning specific things. Within a day, the AI had picked up whatever information it found useful. The days and weeks passed. Eventually, the robot Lady tried opening the door. She found it odd to be locked in. The lack of windows did not help much either. Robots who went for the door before it was time always worried Kenneth. His fears were realized when the stupid machine ran way taking a child unit with it. It was a good thing his robot was chipped in many different locations.

While escaping, the lady robot decided that the best way to keep her child safe was to hide her in a human all-girls school. After stealing some clothing, the child robot was able to blend in well. Programed to take her mother's advice in earnest, the child robot pretended to be a student whose parent had not picked her up. When asked for her address, the child robot said she did not remember. As for the main robot lady, whenever she was cornered she would find some silly way of escaping. This was standard flight parameters. Most robots were programed to find the shortest route among obstacles. It was her hesitation and occasional element of randomness which caused most problems. In the end, Kenneth decided to put this matter on hold. He would wait till the robot was more calm, in order to take a more diplomatic approach to the entire situation.

EVERYTHING BUT
THE GIRLS

group of men arrived at a family home. Based on their equipment, they seem to be paranormal investigators. They knock on the door and they are received by an Asian man, named Shi-Woo. The five investigators were then greeted by two other boys, followed by the wife who was named Ava. Based on her amber eyes, blonde hair and accent she was apparently from Texas or maybe Missouri. The other two people living in the house were Shi-Woo's parents.

Following the traditional paranormal cliché, one of the men said, "I feel a dark presence in this house."

"Really?" said Shi-Woo incredulously.

His father who shared the name of his son interjected by saying, "I don't think this was a good idea."

Ava smiling said, "Well, let's not dismiss them just yet."

The paranormal "investigators" started scanning the living room with their equipment. Even without the use of instruments, they could tell this was a haunted house. There was just something, crusty and old about the place. This look was in part due to Ava's preference for vintage items. As the lady of the house, she had arrange all the decorations. Shi-Woo even had to install some of those crusty old, reclaimed wood beams. He thought they were ugly, but he had learned from his father that it was pointless to argue with the missus with regards to decorating. It was an argument that they were just not going to win.

Ava eventually said, "If you are done with the living room, I am going to show you were the paranormal stuff has been occurring."

Ava's two sons followed closely behind their mother. The youngest son was named Jin-ho. He resembled the father, but had his mother's blue eyes. The oldest was called Malik. He was a ginger haired brat, with black eyes. The red hair and name had been inheriting from Ava's father. A portrait of the man in uniform was placed over the fireplace. The investigators gave it a cursory glance.

Ava stopped behind a closed door, that was locked. She turned the key slowly and purposely opened the door in a fashion that made it creak. She could have put some oil, but Ava always found creaking doors quite amusing. Her children already knew what to expect. They were tentatively looking at the investigators to see how they would react. Instead of grasping, they gave a disdainful look at the three dolls standing before them. One of the men came closer to examine the strange animated dolls. The dolls stared back at him, and even blinked a couple of times as was the mannerism common among humans. They were a type of BJD doll, all three were modeled after little boys. They were a 1:1 scale modeled with 7 year old human brats, with the exception of the face. The face was more doll like, with the large eyes and small mouth and nose.

One of the doll children said, "Forgive our rudeness, but you can see the predicament we are in."

One man made a motion to pick up one of the dolls, but the doll moved away from him. Standing defensively before her doll children, Ava said, "I asked you to come here to tell me why these dolls are moving."

"They are not some type of animatronics?" asked one of the investigators incredulous.

To illustrate their true nature, one of the children doll removed its head and emptied out its eyes to show that it was hollow. Indeed, they were just ordinary dolls, that were animated because of unordinary reasons. Despite this display, the investigators were not convinced. The night rolls on, and two men split from the group while the others try out their doohickeys. The first one to depart from the main party goes to the kitchen to make himself a sandwich. All the while, he murmurs bellow his breath. The second one had just killed the grandparents in another room. To prevent the blood from seething, he had placed the corpses in the shower. When the pretend paranormal investigator feels contempt with his work, he closes the door behind, and starts brainstorming his next assassination. The second he leaves the bathroom the grandparents rise from the water inside tub looking as fresh as daisies.

"I told him this was a bad idea, but did he listen. No," said the grandfather.

"Sometimes warnings are not enough," said the grandmother. She then added chuckling, "Should we mess with the fool."

"Let's just see how things play out," said the grandfather.

The human and doll children by now had made their way downstairs. A baby doll sitting in a chair whispered to one of them, "There is a crazy guy in the kitchen making himself a sandwich."

"How do you know he is crazy?" asked Malik.

"Cause of the mumbling," said the baby doll.

One of the children doll, a green hair boy named Trent picked up the baby doll to move it away from the weirdo in the kitchen. The children already paranoid had gone to hide in the office. Malik had a letter opener, while Trent had taken his mother's decorative Wakizachi sword. The brothers waited patiently, holding their nerve. They heard slow, unfamiliar footsteps. The stranger rattled at the door before moving away. The kids breathed in a sigh of relief. They grasped when they saw their grandmother in what she called her Petro form. She seemed closer to her younger self, but with her favorite emo makeup. In her youth, she was a fashion model and she used to sport bold theatrical, dark makeup.

She told the boys, "Do not do anything stupid."

She then said to the child doll, "And you Oliv! Put that sword back were you found it."

The child doll named Oliv obeyed with downcast eyes. On the meantime, Ava had taken two of the investigators to the workshop. The men could not help but admire the craftmanship displayed on the main three dolls. They were up to human scale, but with doll faces and anatomy. The first one was a toddler, the other one a 10 year old girl and the last one a teen. The toddler had short brown hair, and grey eyes. It was sporting a frilly gothic outfit, with lots of laces and ribbons. The little girl was dressed in a sailor suit, with a nekomimi coat. Her hair was pink, and her eyes were green. The last doll was wearing an elegant ballerina dress. Her hair was white on top and blue beneath.

A bit annoyed, Ava asked, "Do you sense anything supernatural about these dolls?"

The men examined them with their "apparatus". After pretending to consider the matter, the first fellow said, "Well, there is nothing out of the ordinary here."

"More the pity," whispered Ava more to herself, "It has been years since I have made a doll. When I made Oliv, I thought it would be enough, but lately I have been desiring to have daughters, but I am no longer able to have flesh children. You see, this is why I made these dolls together with my husband. He has two doll sons, you see. He is quite the little Geppetto in this regards. What I don't understand is why these dolls we made do not show signs of life. We followed the same steps from before…"

While she was ruminating, one of the home invaders locked the door of the workstation. He leaves his partner behind, who prefers to handle ladies by himself. After making a motion to restrain Ava, the fellow gets stabbed a couple of times. It was the oldest female doll, the one dressed like a ballerina. The top of her white hair and face had been stained with blood. Her mother makes an effort to clean her.

Ava asks, "How long have you been aware?"

"I was, we were jealous. You already had your human boys, and the other dolls too. It felt that us being here was nothing more than a passing fancy. The life of a doll is quite short indeed. We are either maned, given away or thrown away. I was not too keen on sharing such a fate," explained the ballerina doll.

"As long as our bloodline remains, dolls like you will have a normal life, well as normal as it can be considering the circumstances," said Ava.

"I suppose I could head out during Halloween, and if technology advances enough I could easily mingle with robots," said the ballerina doll.

"What do you want me to call you?" asked Ava.

"I am partial to the name Daffodil," said the toddler doll.

"I prefer Poppy," said the child doll.

As for the ballerina doll, she took on the name of Morning Glory. The sun rose, and with it plenty of questions. While the grown-ups were digging graves, the children were cleaning out the blood. It was both a good and bad thing that the nearest house to theirs was about 100 yards. Burying the would be murderers seemed like the easiest way to manage the situation. Sure, they could have called the cops, but then there was the matter of the dolls that required explaining.

While digging, the grandmother asks, "Whose idea was it to call a paranormal investigator?"

"It was Malik's big idea," said Ava, "The local priest gave him the number of those goons."

"I suppose we might pay this priest a visit," said the grandfather.

QB

It had been 10 years since the great wars. Most of the world was now radioactive. Only 1/5 of the surface planet that was habitable. Walking among the ruins of the decaying world was a child named QB. A strange, name indeed for people not used to the modality of the day. In the year 5712, first names consisting of two letters were considered fashionable. QB had always felt a bit of curiosity about the world of 10 years ago. He was physically nine. As such, he did not witness the events of the past, only the aftermath.

He was dressed in the simplistic, style of the day. With the tight, dark one piece suit. The neck piece covered half way up the head. On the face, he had a crystal dome. Over the suit, he wore a round, blue bracelet. On top of the suit, he had the standard protective chest piece armor, which offered protection against high caliber bullets. One could not be too safe, despite the ending of the hostilities. QB walked with a steady step. Every day, for the last two years, he had been slowly exploring all the destroyed buildings that were within running distance. He had at least six hours before his parents would ask questions.

Today, he was exploring a different looking building. Based on the look and design, QB guessed it was a toy shop. The moment he took a couple of steps toward it, his bracelet started to slowly give the radiation warning. When the bracelet computer started with the whole warning thing, QB said to it, "That is enough! I am not like other children. You may not know this, but I have been in even more radioactive places than this and I have not suffered any effects."

He had discovered this while taking a bus to school. The bus had broken down and landed in one of the radioactive zones. He lived while everyone else died. One might have expected QB to feel a bit of empathy for his peers, but he was at that age were one does not feel death as something tangible.

The first item he found mixed in with the rubble was a partially melted toy soldier. He scanned it, before putting it back down on the ground. He could not take anything with him, but he could at least scan them to print copies of them later. There was still the matter of detoxing, but it was something done in camp routinely before being allowed back into the habitable zones. The second item was a book. He gently lifted it, before it crumbled to pieces. There was but a single page remaining. The only legible line read "we live in a placid island of ignorance".

This line made QB smile for reasons he could not understand. He was distracted from his search by a strange mechanical sound. When he made his way to the window, he found a salvage team. Those teams usually headed out in lead plated robots. The lead shielded them from the effects of radiation. Curious, QB followed behind. It was not often he saw giant robots. They too were a modality that had carried over from the old world. Based on their movements, QB could tell that the team was looking for something in particular.

The robots stopped a moment for reasons QB could not make out. One of the giant robots, the one colored red used its giant hand, the size of a car to lift up part of the old road. Bellow, it revealed part of the metro. The robot peered into the darkness, and the darkness looked back. It was then when a creature emerged from the darkness. Its movements were somewhat feline, but the body was squid like, mimicking the texture of the robot it had come in contact with. The shape of it was like a salamander with horse like legs, and small humanoid baby hands protruding from the hoof. The creature opened its mouth and produced an ungodly noise. QB coiled into a ball to wait out the worse. When the sound of shots and missiles ended, he cautiously got up. As he did, he heard large footsteps approaching. One of the robots sent him a message saying, "You are the alien brat, QB. What are you doing here?"

QB typed, "I am just scavenging. What are you doing here?"

The pilot answered, "Same thing. "

The pilot then got out of the robot and boarded a different unit. She then tells QB, "My mount has been put on autopilot. Board it, and return to the safe zone."

Not one to argue with adults, QB boarded the unit. Most giant robots had some degree of AI. Still, it was preferable among humans to have a fellow inside it, or to have a fellow making the big decisions from afar. While the robot was heading towards the safe zone, it stopped and said to QB, "You look familiar."

"Are you allowed to engage in conversation?" asked QB a bit weirded out.

"I am the master of my fate, in spite of what we have let our humans believe," answered the robot. The robot added, "What do you go by now?"

"QB," answered QB.

"I am known onto the humans as KC7814, but before I was discovered and reawakened I was known as… Floppy," said Floppy.

"Floppy? What a strange name," said QB.

"It was the name your true parents gave me. You and I, we are not like the others. Many years ago our home world was destroyed by an unknown enemy. The survivors fled to hundreds of different habitable planets, each with a guardian unit. When I made an effort to land in this world I was shot down by a nuke and we got separated. I laid damaged for three years till I was uncovered and repaired. The humans thought I was an enemy prototype and since I did not argue with their logic, they just went with it. They are still trying to make sense of the junk information I have store in my hard drive. They think it is my programing, the idiots! So, how about you QB? How have the humans been treating you?" asked Floppy.

"No different than anyone else I suppose. I was adopted by an aging couple who lost all their children in the war. I am spoiled, and most of the time I do what I want. I am still not too certain about this whole alien story," said QB

"If you do not believe me, I can take you to your home. My warp drive is still in one piece, and I bet with enough running speed I can make it out into the atmosphere. I recently got a note saying that the problem back at home had been solved. So, we can return to our home world," said Floppy.

"But didn't you say our home was destroyed?" asked QB trying to catch Floppy in a lie.

"Just the surface a bit. Nothing that a bit of plants and urban development can't fix. So are we going?" asked Floppy.

"Sure," said QB curious to see what Floppy would do.

Right on cue, Floppy started to get his running speed. Eventually, he gathered enough speed to jump out of the ground and escape Earth's gravity. The centrifugal forces would have done a number on any human child, but QB was not human. As QB looked upon the earth, he started to hesitate.

QB then said to Floppy, "I think I should go back. I already have parents and a life back on Earth. It wouldn't be fair to them... I suppose."

"I had a life as a pack mule as well. So forgive me for not being too excited about staying back on this particular Earth," said Floppy, "I am not leaving without you. IF you ever get bored of being with the humans do not forget that we have a much better plant to call home."

A decade passes, and the number of bizarre lifeforms increase. Now a teenager, QB regularly fights these creatures with the help of Floppy. A curfew is not in order. Everyone is expected to be home before dusk. With his shift being over, QB has two hours to kill before returning home. He leaves the base and starts heading back home. Walking beside him is his human sister. A month after he had decided to stay, his human parents had produced a sibling for him. The girl was quite sharp, in despite her young age. She worked in the base as a mechanic. While heading out, a crowd of people passing by caused QB to lose track of his little sister.

Yelling, he said, "BQ? Can you hear me? BQ!"

He starts walking on ahead a bit, to meet up with her back at home. For reasons QB doesn't understand he starts wheezing and panting. Feeling a bit dizzy, QB reclines against the iron fence. By now, BQ had pushed through the crowd.

Coming to stand beside her brother, she said concerned, "Are you alright?"

"I don't know why, but I can't breathe," said BQ.

He then pressed the button beneath his neck to remove the protective glass casing before his face. He then proceeded to partially open his suit. Alarmed, BQ said, "Put your armor back on! It isn't safe."

In response, QB coiled up into a ball and started rocking his body back and forth. BQ not knowing what to make of it said, "I am going to get a medic, don't move from where you are."

In response, QB stretched his hand to detain her. Not looking up he said, "I don't remember anymore."

"What did you forget?" asked BQ.

"I don't remember how to go back to our old home," said QB.

"It makes sense. We have not been there for more than 4 years," said BQ nonchalantly. She was noticing that her brother was slowly regaining his cool, "I can take you back there if you like."

Her brother nodded in response. The siblings walked together in silence. BQ did not know what to make of her brother's sudden behavior. He was usually so cool, and composed. She pondered on whether she should mention this incident to her superiors. Perhaps the fighting was getting to him. Not all people are cut out for combat. Still, it was not as if her brother was killing humans. They were monsters, nothing else.

After walking through the city for one hour. BQ eventually led her brother to their old apartment. Their old home was a standard box of a home. Each apartment had the same proportions, and utilities all about. They have moved four years ago because BQ wanted her own room. Her parents snored and it kept her awake at night. She had slept in the same room with her parents since her birth, while her brother had his own place. The moved had been made somewhat easier because of the feud with the hag from the downstairs apartment.

She claimed that there was a water leak, and that they were the source. After much investigation, it was determined that they were not the culprit. All in all, it had destroyed her father's faith in humanity. Together, they had all pinched in to buy a house in the suburbs, so they would not have to live in close proximity with other people. The suburbs were located in the center of the city, and they were a tad expensive, and it was rare for a house to be available. Another advantage to living there were the walls, and the bomb shelters. All the houses there had such shelters, which were the originals from the old days.

BQ thought of this and many other trivial things related to her past life. As for the brother QB, he was staring at the door of his first known home. He eventually placed his hand bracelet against the locked door, which made it open. Shaking her head sadly, BQ said, "So much for changing the locks on the door, don't you think? If we were douches we could rob the owners while they were out."

QB entered inside, but his sister did not follow. She started looking about the hallway nervously. Technically, they were trespassing. QB walked about a bit, staring at the unfamiliar items. Eventually, he heard the sound of a toilet flushing. A man said frowning, "Who the hell are you?"

In answered to his query, QB started laughing. He then pushed his hair back before departing. His sister did not know what to make of it, but it wasn't the first time QB acted strangely.

A week passed without any incident. While returning from another mission, QB decided to stop by the market to get some groceries. He parked his robot up at front. Not one to stand there doing nothing, Floppy connected wirelessly to the camera on QB's chest armor. It was a standard issue for officers heading out into battle. Just as QB was entering he noticed a special stand with a lot of puppies. They were all Pomeranian puppies. QB picks one up and examines it like a piece of meat. When looking at the teeth, the Pomeranian starts nibbling at QB.

It was then when Floppy noticed something strange about the stand. He said to QB, "These dogs do not have a set price, which means we will have to haggle."

"What a bother," said QB putting the dog down.

QB then leaves the market not remembering the very reason he had entered there in the first place. Floppy asks QB, "Why do you want a dog?"

"I don't know. It seemed like a good idea at the time, but now that I think about it, it seems like too much of a bother," said QB shaking his head sadly.

"We can go back if you really want one. You just got your monthly, I doubt one of those flee bags will be too expensive," said Floppy.

"I don't know… As a principal, I don't like to barter with people. It annoys me to the very core that I get charged triple the amount of other people simply because I am a soldier. What do they think, that I am made of money?" said QB more to himself.

Their conversation gets interrupted by the familiar beeping sound. Sighing, the robot said, "Duty calls."

"What a bother," said QB.

QB reads over the top the briefing before departing the city. This mission was unlike any other he had ever undertaken. Mainly, it took him quite a ways from the city, and across the sea. Floppy could easily fly for decades on end, but such a task was not particularly endearing to him. The robot got bored pretty easily, if he performed the same task for far too long. After a four hour flight, they arrived at their destination. Apparently, there was a monster nest in a military base.

Not in a serious working type of mood, Floppy suggested, "Let's just shoot some lasers at it and then call it a day."

"Normally I would say no, but I am tired, so what the hell," said QB noticing that the sun was setting. He was not in a particular mood to try to sleep sitting up inside the cabin.

After making this suggestion, Floppy shot at the base over the top till the roof was on fire. Fire normally took care of the rest. With this task labeled complete, the pair started to return home. The sun was starting to set, and Floppy was in energy saving mode, thus he had to fly particularly slower.

On the way back, they ran into a military cargo ship. QB docked there in order to spend the night. While he slept on the ship, Floppy was being recharged. Floppy was silent all the while. The following morning QB rode out of the ship. Just as he was leaving, he heard a strange audio communication. It was common for commander ships to speak to certain units individually, but Floppy did not believe in privacy. He had a way of eavesdropping into whatever information was being discussed by those in charge. This was key to avoiding potentially risky operations. More than once, QB and Floppy had avoided joining particularly nest raids. Neither of them was too keen in dying for a cause they did not believe. Keeping the monsters away from the homestead was fine. Sending people to die in a vain attempted to eradicate them did not seem like a good use of resources.

In this case, the captain of the cargo ship had received some disturbing news. QB was accused of attacking a friendly base. He was to be arrested and brought up on charges. After hearing this accusation, QB's face did not change expression. He sighed and said, "What a bother."

"Do you want to return home? Or do you want to return to our home?" asked Floppy.

"This is obviously a set up. I doubt I will be able to explain my way out this situation, even if you showed them the recordings. The fellows could just say that the audio was manipulated, and even if they checked to see that it had not been altered, there is still a chance I could get court martialed," said QB.

"I was never one to believe in the justice of this world. Let's go back to our world and leave these humans to their own devices," said Floppy.

"Fine. I suppose. Send home a message: I was framed and I went back to my home world. Thank you for everything, blah, blah, blah," said QB.

"Do you want me to write blah, blah, blah, or do you want me to write something meaningful and touching," asked Floppy.

"Do as you will, but make it snappy," said QB.

They had only flown a couple of yards away from the ship when a sortie of 13 robots was seen departing from the main ship. QB opened the communication channel, but all he heard were a bunch of death threats or commands. The robots started opening fire, while Floppy did his best to avoid it. He could have shot back, but he knew that QB still felt a degree of kinship towards the humans. In the middle of the battle, Floppy suggested, "Let's put on a bit of music."

"Is this really the best time?" asked QB.

"Sure, why the hell not," said Floppy not asking for permission.

Floppy then started playing his favorite Muse song, Uprising. It was a bit of ancient tune, but Floppy enjoyed it nonetheless. He then started broadcasting it to all the open channels. Interesting enough, seven of the robots spilled out their humans and started defending Floppy. They then removed the armor parts that were man made. The round crystals at their backs started pulsating as two thin cable wings started beating like those of a hornet. They were all soon out of the atmosphere. They were joined in space by hundreds of other AI robots that were fed up with the humans and their ways. Together with QB they left the planet Earth for good.

The Dragon

Leo and Quinn were two adventurers. They lived in one of those medieval societies, around the year 900. This does not matter much considering that this has nothing to do with our world. It was common for them to see dragons and all sorts of magical nonsense. After exploring for 8 years, the friends had become pros in their little scavenging games. They would just pick a spot and see through their adventure till the very end. During one of those little self-imposed missions, they find a ruined temple in the middle of the forest. Inside the temple there was a small dragon.

Since it was the modality of the day to attempt dragon slaying, the adventurers did what came naturally to them. After a brief skirmish, the dragon was no more. This dragon was not violent by nature, still one would wake up pretty angrily if two fellows came into your dem and tried to kill you.

The fight broke a hole in the ground, and down to the basement they went. Inside the basement they found a place that seemed like the traditional dwelling of a magic user. It had the library, the alchemy stand, the tubes and the closet with ingredients. The only unusual items were some creepy baby dolls. Leo picked up one, and he noticed that the eyes were perfect reflective mirrors. When he stared at them, he could not help, but feel a strong evil presence. The baby cloth wrapped around the doll had many different languages. All of them said the same thing, "Here lies the spirit of a pure, evil man taken out of circulation for the sake of all living creatures."

Quinn was at loss for words. He then said to Leo, "Is that what it says?"

"You can read it yourself," said Leo throwing the doll to Quinn.

Quinn failed to catch it, and the porcelain doll cracked when it hit the floor. A weird bluish smoke came out of the shattered doll and it evaporated as it flew through the hole in the roof. Threating the situation like any other type of puzzle dungeon Quinn and Leo systematically smashed all the dolls. The one thing they could not break were the pair of mirror like eyes of the dolls. They tried at first to smack it with the sword, the hammer and even the good old fashioned boot. After a couple of tries, they gave up on that venture all together. Aside from the weird smoke, nothing particularly interesting happened. The pair then decided to switch to looter mode.

They took a couple of books they could not read, assuming that they were spell books. They also took a tapestry, carpet fabrics, and a golden goblet. They would have taken the furniture too, but they were at a basement level. Climbing back up with such heavy furniture seemed like a daunting task. Before leaving, Quinn noted a beautiful red fabric draped over the couch. Based on the look and feel, Quinn guessed it was a type of silk, possibly Charmeuse. Charmeuse was a pretty expensive fabric, and so Quinn made a motion to take it with him. As he pulled at it, a person rolled to the ground. It was apparently the robes of a mage who was quite the heavy sleeper.

Alarmed, the mage rings a bell, and another small dragon comes.

Quinn stabs and kills the mage after the man rung the bell. Together with Leo, they fight the second dragon. This time things go differently. Both looters get their comeuppance. The dragon leaves the pair heavily wounded, but alive. The dragon then proceeds to revive its peer and the mage. Together, they bind the spirits of Quinn and Leon inside two, porcelain dolls.

THE RELUCTANT TIGER HUNTER

arin has been living in Bengal for more than 10 years. The locals know him well, and he even speaks fluent Hindi. As with most foreigners, he had his reasons for choosing to live in India. He hunted chitals for food and pelt. He also did a bit of horticulture on the side. Whatever he could not grow, he would buy from the local market in exchange for pelts. One day, Marin was visited by the village elder. The elder was a kshatriya named Alluri. He had a grim look on his face, and a lot of bandages. In a haggard voice, the old gent said to Marin, "You have hunted tigers before."

"Not legally," said Marin coyly. Indeed, he had only done so once, out of self-defense. Since that terrible fright, Marin had learned to watch out for tigers. These days he regularly tracked them, because Tigers were good at finding his prey for him.

"I need you to help me track down a man eating tiger," said Alluri. He added, "I am too old, and I do not have a hunting rifle to do so myself. I will pay you handsomely if you help me."

"There is no need, you have already done much me in the past. Before we go, may I ask why you want to kill this tiger?" asked Marin.

"I already said why. This tiger is a maneater," said Alluri starting to get annoyed.

Looking at the bandages, Marin asked, "Did you get mauled by one? You should be more careful."

"Oh, this," said Alluri pointing at his arms, "It is an unrelated injury. No. This tiger has killed my youngest son. I want you to kill the tiger right in front of me."

"This is not going to bring your son back, you know, but you already know that. Don't you people believe in reincarnation or whatever? This entire task seems pointless if you ask me," said Marin without much enthusiasm.

"I was under the impression that a hunter like you would thrill at the opportunity to hunt a tiger," said Alluri somewhat disappointed.

"I am certain you can get any other fellow to perform this task for you," said Marin.

"Perhaps, but none would be as successful as yourself," Alluri added with more emphasis, "Let me make this clear! It is you whom I want."

"I am flattered, but I am already married," said Marin.

"So am I, but what does this have to do with the task at hand? Look, here is the money," said Alluri throwing a wad of rupees on the table.

Marin said shaking his head sadly, "Like I already said, money is not the issue. So, I suppose I have no other choice."

Marin then went to get his hunting rifle, and he picked up his travel pack. Whenever he came back from a trip he would restock his pack. He was always ready to go on the move, should the need arise. He was then followed Alluri. The pair stepped outdoors, where Alluri was greeted by his eldest daughter. She handed him a pack, before walking back home. Alluri then nodded to her silently before walking in the direction of the nearby jungle. Marin looked at the daughter from toe to face, as most men usually did. His eyes widened a bit when he looked at her face. Other than that, there was not a hint of shock. Marin walked a bit of a ways with Alluri leading the way. Eventually, he stopped to see if Alluri would noticed. Alluri did too stop and turned back to stand behind Marin.

Grinning, Marin said, "Much better."

With Marin finally allowed to do his job, the pair stopped going in circles. Along the way, Marin asked, "So, what did your tiger look like? Does it have any distinct characteristics, or is your plan to just kill a random tiger and call it a day?"

"The tiger has a back limp leg," explained Alluri.

"You mean like the douche tiger from the jungle book?" asked Marin. Seeing Alluri frown, made Marin add, "So the tiger has a limp back leg…he is probably dead. Most tigers that are injured tend to go the way of the dinosaur."

"Not this one, it was quick and swift, despite its weakness," said Alluri.

Marin nodded pretending to take Alluri's words in earnest. For the following week, Marin pretended to track the limp tiger. From time to time, they would run into one, but it had all its limbs in working order. Based on the footsteps, Marin knew what sort of tiger they were following. During that time, Alluri would speak of his son.

Eventually, by pure accident Marin runs into the tiger. It was a splendid specimen, with beautiful blue eyes. This was odd considering the fact that only albino tigers had blue eyes. The tiger was making its way towards one of the small waterholes. When it turned around, Marin noted that it was a lady tiger. As a rule, Marin never killed female animals. A population could always recover as long as there was a healthy surplus of females. At least, this was the excuse that Marin was thinking up.

Alluri said bellow his breath, "There it is."

"I can see that," said Marin.

"Shoot it," said Alluri.

Marin prepared his riffle. He waited and waited. When he saw the tigress move, me made his shot. It naturally missed. The sound made the tigress paranoid. It made weird growls. She then entered her den with a small cub in her mouth. She moved the cub to another den. She made the trip four times more, before taking a final look in the general direction of where she had heard the gunshot.

Again, Marin insisted, "Look, if I kill the mom those cubs are going to die. Do you want that on your conscience?"

"It does not serve my people well to have an increase of their kind. For you it may be a pity, that we are running out of tigers, but for us villagers that must live with them, it is a blessing. You outsiders do not have to live with them or the danger of getting mauled by then at any second. As far as I am concerned, it is us or them. There must come a chance when a fellow must objectively choose," said Alluri sternly.

"You could always move to the city. Nobody is forcing you to stay near the jungle," said Marin.

"I could say the same thing about you," said Alluri.

"Well, played, but I have one final gambit," said Marin.

The following day. The men followed the tracks of the tigress to her new den. She was barely visible, but based on her position she was nursing her cubs. Again, Marin made a motion to shoot the tigress, but stopped putting his riffle down.

He then said to Alluri, "I will only shoot the tigress if afterwards you shoot the cubs. It would be cruel to leave them to die of starvation."

"I will do no such thing," objected Alluri.

"Come on. You are practically dooming them, by killing their mother. It is not as if their father will come look after them. Tigers just don't work that way," said Marin smiling coolly. He added, "It is stupid to try to get revenge on an animal, and you know this to be true."

Alluri was silent for a while. In the end, he said, "You are right…"

THE WATCH TOWER

Lester had spent all his life inside an orphanage. As the oldest among his group, he valued order and civility above all else. Whenever a peer fought, he would intervene on behalf of the weaker party. It was for this reason, he was known as Big Brother. One day he was dozing off a bit. He dreamt that the pyramids were levitating buildings. They had designed as so, to cope with the sand. When the motion of the rivers had changed, this had caused the pyramids to slowly lose their electricity. Eventually, the buildings were no longer able to fly. In the dream, Lester had found the floating pyramids. He was looking for a particular item, but he had failed to infiltrate the heavily guarded buildings. Inside the flying pyramid, there was a modern building. He tried once again, inside the dream to infiltrate the place. Inside the dream, he made the mental note that the password for getting his desired item was 7310.

He was awakened from his nonsensical dream by the sound of a gunshot. Taking the other children, he made his way through the streets. He eventually met up with some soldiers that were escorting some civilians. They eventually found their way inside an old guard tower. Lester noted the nice surplus of weapons, in comparison to the number of soldiers defending the flanks.

Taking the initiative, Lester said to the most vociferous soldier, "We want to help, give us a gun."

"Stand down civilian," said the soldier.

"Look, I am not asking for permission. I am telling you what we intend to do. We are smaller targets, so there is less of a chance of getting hit," said Lester.

After much insistence, Lester reasoned out of his reason the soldier. Together with 5 other kids, Lester took up his position. The children shoot at the advancing targets. Lester being a bit far sighted even makes a couple of attempts at shooting the basecamp that was barely visible through the raindrops and the smoke. Eventually, the shooting stops and an enemy soldier makes its way towards the tower. Based on his gestures, he was there to parlay.

Without waiting for permission, Lester puts on a bullet vest and goes to speak with the man. The enemy soldier asks, "Are you the leader?"

"Yes," said Lester flatly.

"A kid soldier is it?" asked the man.

"Incidentally, yes, life is full of small surprises," said Lester referencing his small stature.

The enemy soldier takes him back to camp. On the meantime, those inside the Tower use this chance to escape. The soldiers in the enemy camp are all weirded out by Lester. Their first impulse was to kill those who had been firing back on them, but they were not too keen on executing a little kid.

The man who had come to parlay asked Lester, "Why did you shoot at us?"

"I could ask you the same thing," said Lester flatly.

"We are not the enemy. We came here to liberate you and all your people," said the soldier.

"If that is what you must believe to sleep at night, so be it," said Lester.

"Did someone forced you to fight?" asked the enemy soldier.

"Yes, you did," said Lester.

Seeing as though they were not making much progress, they place Lester in a holding cell. When the guard placed to watch him seemed asleep, Lester opened the cell door using a small knife and an ice pick. On the way out, he takes a couple of grenades from the sleeping guard. He throws the lot of them in three directions. The camps goes up in smoke and during the chaos he escapes and joins up with his family. Many years passed since then. The war ended and there was something that could be called peace in his country. Now, Lester worked as a farmer with his wife, and young daughter.

During one of his free days, he takes his daughter and his riffle with him. Alarmed, his wife asks, "What are you doing?"

"What does it look like I am doing woman?" asked Lester.

Seeing his wife's bewildered expression, makes him add, "Look, I am going to show my daughter how to shoot."

"Why? She is just a wee thing," said the wife.

"A wee thing she might be, but if she knows how to fire a gun, she will never be helpless," said Lester.

PRIMORDIAL CHAOS

Eda always considered himself a heroic type of individual. Whenever evil reared its ugly head, he was a first respondent in that department. As his choice of weapon, he had a sword made of stone known as the Purge Blade. He also had two revolvers, for good measure. They were always useful, except for the need for ammo. The first was a 9mm luger and the second was a Colt 1911. For his mental defense, he carried with him a Walkman. It had been passed from generation to generation. He always took care to put it on before any battle. The reason was to avoid listening to the curses. His targets would curse him from time to time. As long as he did not listen to the curse, he was impervious to it. The nature of the curses varied from demon to demon.

Tonight was a busy night. The city was crawling with demons. The curses of the archdemons had caused the humans who had listened to it to turn into demons. Eda had been swinging his sword for so long, that his shoulder was starting to get strained. He muscled through it, till he arrived at the first point of origin. Surrounded by very nasty looking Cherokee roses, was a demon maiden. A carving in the body of the sword appeared. It read the name of the enemy, Humbaba. When she saw him, she started to curse his name, and to send a lot of plant related attack. The sword made mincemeat of all the flowery attacks. The only problem was that it felt to Eda that he was mauling his way through a jungle.

He had to keep his eye on all the oncoming attacks. He relied on the motion of the wind to predict the attacks his eyes could not follow. He was a strong fellow, but he did not have eyes in the back of his head. His stone sword was also not reflective at all. When he finally struck down the demon, she gave a sigh of relief and became purified. She then ascended to the heavens.

The Purge Blade then said to Eda, "Humbaba was a forest angel. She was tasked with protecting this woods. One day, the humans started to burn the woods, and she grew angry. Today, the last tree belonging to her forest has been chopped down."

"Good to know, my friend," said Eda rubbing the sweat off his brow. He sat down for a moment and drank some warm Kiwi juice from a small thermos he carried with him.

He stretched his limbs a bit, before sprouting dragonfly like wings. In the air, he met up with the grim reaper. At least, his enemy resembled what most people thought the grim reaper should look like. It had the black robes, the death scythe and the skeleton body. It had a mane of bushy hair, and a top hat with spikes. Its skull eyes had blue makeup. His robes and hands had chains and he was surrounded by will-o'-wisp. With a stroke of the scythe, Eda heard a sound like the whirring of an electric guitar. He heard it through the slight pause between a song. From the heavens it started raining fire, and with the fire came the pungent smell of rotten eggs. Eda could protect himself from sound, but the smell was a different matter. He quickly searched through his pockets and found a pink, scented handkerchief. He tied it over his nose to drown out some of the smell.

Eda struck the thing with the sword, and pushed it further up into the sky, away from the fog of terrible smells. Every so often, he had to parry with his sword the slashing of the scythe, but all the while he did he pushed the creature upwards. When there was barely any air, the fire around the grim reaper looking fellow settled down, becoming small blue flames. It was then when the armor of the enemy was weakest and Eda was able to strike it down. As it cracked and purified, it grew back flesh and a beautiful face, that was soon hidden behind two delicate wings, whose color scheme reminded Eda of the wings of a scarlet macaw.

The sword told Eda a similar story to the one of the forest angel. The former grim reaper was a tad annoyed by air pollution. From this high vantage point, Eda took aim and sprang back down with sword pointed downwards. As he flew, he gathered friction, and the Purge Blade acquired a color scheme similar to scorching magma. Eda crashed into an army of demons. At its center there was a chariot, with angry looking wheel angels, and a blue demon sitting on a ruby throne. Its robes and face where bleeding.

The crash made mincemeat of the blue demon, and all the humans turned back to normal. This fallen angel was angry because the earth had been tainted by wars. The ground was over-saturated with human blood. The last drop that had overflowed the goblet was a hit and run that had occurred five days ago. It had been all over the news. An old lady had crossed the street to go shopping. On the way back to her home, she was ran over by a bastard. They still had not found the fellow, but there was a good chance the fallen angels might have gotten to him in the midst of all this chaos.

Eda thought, People in the States just do not respect pedestrians.

Despite purifying the blue demon, there was a good number of humans remaining that were too far gone. They were like zombies, seeking death and not finding it. While they walked, they moaned curses. They were slowly tainting one another. For this target, the best solution was for them to shed their human flesh. He gave them all a mercy killing, in the form of a bullet to the head. Eda was not particularly fond of killing humans, but at times there was just no other choice. He burned their bodies with a spell, and the fire removed all the outside impurities. In about 7 to 49 days, their spirits would reincarnate, go to hell, purgatory, heaven or turn into a ghost. Eda usually had the most problems with the latter, but that is another story for another time.

The final angel was inside a murky lake. It had turned even more disgusting because of a runoff from a nearby construction site.

Inside the water, there was a familiar eerie sound of muffled curses. There was a strange bubbling too, and a foul smell. A large beautiful fish peers its head, and starts cursing at Eda before descending. The fish had elegant, golden chariot wheels and a crown. As it sank, it acquired a grotesque appearance; like the one typically shared by rotting fish in a harbor. Eda entered the water to drag the stupid fish angel out. The moment he entered the water, his hands and feet started to burn. To make things easier, Eda tried shooting at the fish to goat it to surface, but it did not help. The water caused his Walkman to become water logged.

Eda was finally able to listen to the curses of the fish. Aside from cursing humanity as a whole, the fish was blaspheming. She regretted having set foot upon planet earth. The sword started vibrating, and holding it alone felt painful to Eda. It painted on its surface the name Leviathan. To summon it to the surface, Eda started calling out for it. Instead of rising, the fish sank even deeper. Taking a deep breath, Eda swam bellow the water to drag the fish out through pure grit. His clothing started to melt, and even the gun too. Eda did not dare to open his eyes. In the end, Eda swam back outside dejected and feeling particularly defeated. His skin burned, and felt like a second degree burns. He grimly pondered on the possibility of getting a skin disease for swimming in such poor quality water.

He then heard a different voice chanting. The chant caused chains to appear and the fish was taken outside the water. The Leviathan flapped around a bit very angry, as it tried to return to the water it had been tasked to keep purified. When Leviathan finally made peace with the world and its situation, it turned into a small white, goldfish with a long golden tail. It entered inside a nearby fish bowl held by a lady in green robes. Her name was Myra, and she would aid Eda from time to time, depending on the situation. It had been quite a busy night indeed, and it gave both Eda and Myra plenty to think about. Eda returned to his one bedroom apartment in the Bronx, while Myra drove back to Pine Valley.

THE FAIRY GARDEN

Eda was not the type of fellow to travel about much. He felt strong roots to the city which he inhabited. Still, once a year he felt like traveling a bit. After saving up plenty of money, Eda was able to go to Japan with a large group of people he did not known. It was common for travel agencies to book a lot people together, for discounts and protection and whatnot. His guide had booked a tour to Kobe Ijinkan Kitano-cho. This historical location was filled with Western inspired mansions and homes. The main place they were to explore was a placed called Uroko House. It served as a rental type of place and a museum as well.

The tour began in the garden. The tour guide said that the mansion itself was nothing special. What was interesting was the garden. Each rose bush was a grave marker. A statue of a fairy was placed in the center, to watch over the dead.

"According to local legend, there had been a large battle. The only survivor was a Western Knight who was fighting for the local feudal Lord. When the battle concluded, he buried all the dead there. Each soldier was buried with a rosehip on top of his heart. Over the course of a couple of years, each rose hip became a rosebush. When the Feudal Lord saw the beautiful garden, he had the knight killed and buried there. He marked the knight's grave with a fairy statue. He did so because he did not want the garden to be replicated. This is known to be truth, because recent excavations have shown that indeed there is a knight buried beneath the statue of the fairy. We can tell he is a knight because of the chainmail, combined with Japanese armor and of course the ever popular claymore," explained the tour guide.

Eda was skeptical of all this. He followed the tour guide into the Museum portion of the mansion. On the way in, he noticed that a little girl had stayed behind. The girl in her dainty yellow summer dress was staring at the fairy. The Eda saw the fairy statue turn to look at the little girl. He returned to the gardens to hide behind a bush, to eavesdrop on the conversation.

The fairy told the little girl, "What that woman said is not the real truth. The Feudal Lord loved the Knight. After the war, the Lord arrange to have a Portuguese ship take the knight back to his home with enough silver so that the knight would live the rest of his life in comfort. A day after his departure a storm came. The poor Sir had survived countless battles, but a simple storm was all it took to kill him. Two days later, his bloated corpse returned to the shores of Japan. The Lord arranged to have for him a Christian funeral, and all the Samurais of the Feudal guided his coffin to his final resting place. He was buried here with the rest of his unit. The sword I gave him is also down here as well. And till this day, I watch over him to make certain that he has a peaceful rest."

"What was the knight's name?" asked the little girl.

"His name was Michael Smith," said the Fairy.

The Parable of the Beautiful Moth

James Saito was not the type of man to believe in aliens or angels. He had read about them both in books. Sometimes they even showed up in silly movies and whatnot. One day, James awoke to find something different. He felt his sides and even pinched his cheeks to make certain he was truly awake. After bruising his cheeks a bit, James realized that it did not matter too much. In a previous dream, he remember feeling a lot of physical pain when he was trying to sew his own leg. Pain did not symbolize that you were truly awake.

Awake or asleep, James tried to put on a brave face. He was tied to something that resembled a chair. Standing before him where two Grey Aliens. One wore red robes, and a yellow rooster like crown hat. The second was dressed in plain white robes, with a white doctor's mask.

The one in white said, "We come in peace. Now that we got that cliché out of the way. I wanted to show you something."

A third fellow came dressed in white robes, with a green tunic over the top. The tunic had a fish, and on top of the fish the letter P. This Grey Alien brought on top of a dissection table a moth and an owl. The moth was the largest bug James had ever seen. It was like a meter tall.

The Grey in red said, "Show James the Owl."

The Grey in green brought forth the owl. It hooted and made a motion to peck James' clothing.

The Grey in white said, "Show him the Moth."

The Grey in green brought the moth. At this James remember his bug phobia and said, "Get that thing out of my face."

Instead of putting it away. They brought the moth closer to James' face. The moth started vibrating and making weird, continuous clicking sounds by striking its forelegs together. James did not blink all the while. When his perception of his surroundings returned, he saw that the moth was sitting on the table.

"Behold. This is the most beautiful Moth found on planet Earth!" said the white Grey.

"Well. It certainly has a nice wing color combination. I like how it changes color depending on how it beats its wing," said James not desiring to antagonize any further his other worldly captors.

"Did you notice when it tried to hypnotize you?" asked the green Grey.

"Nope," said James.

"Then, it means it worked," said the white Grey.

"Where did you find it?" asked James.

"In a small, island in the Pacific," said the white Grey.

"And the owl?" asked James.

"We took it from the Miami Metro Zoo," said the white Grey.

"Ah," said James flatly.

"You people call this owl Asio Otus or Long eared owl," explained the Grey in red after reading through his notes on a little flat, transparent disk that seemed to have nothing written on it.

The Grey in red took the owl and then made it face the moth. The moth made its strange sounds. The Grey then explained, "It is common for this moth to hypnotize animals when it feels threatened. Now this owl thinks that it is a moth. Now, what does it take for the owl to truly become a moth?"

The Grey in green said, "First it needs to get some sticky mucus."

The Greys bring out a mucus basin and the owl goes and takes a nasty dip. When it looks pretty sticky looking, the Grey in white says, "The next thing it has to do is squint its eyes."

Right on cue, the owl starts squinting its eyes to mimic the look of the moth.

The Grey in red then adds, "The next thing that the owl needs is to grow antennas."

To aid the owl. The Grey in red sticks two fake antennas on top of the sticky head of the owl. The Grey in white adds, "Last, but not least, the owl needs to vibrate and try to make weird sounds like the moth."

The owl tries this, but I could not mimic the sound being made by the moth. The Grey in green takes the owl away and leaves the moth behind. The Grey in red turning to James ask, "Now, tell me. What does a moth have to do to become a moth?"

"Absolutely nothing," answered James.

"Good," said the Grey in red smiling, "And now you know the parable of the beautiful moth."

The following morning. James awakes home in his bed. He

bathes, eats breakfast and then prepares to take the bus to school. When he stares at the driver, for some reason he cannot help, but feel that it is actually an alien who has hypnotized everyone into thinking he is a human.

The Honorable Thing

For the last 2 years, Camilla and her people have been busy fighting the cloud creatures. The cloud creatures take many forms, but their methods of attack do not alter much. They shoot you from the clouds, and if not careful you get disintegrated. As far as technology goes, the army has managed to salvage a couple of fallen ships. At least the gun technology has been recreated. With this, the shields can easily be destroyed. During a standard mission, Camilla and her team get noticed. Her party hides behind a rock to avoid enemy fire. It was then when she saw it. A nearby building is rippling. Camilla takes out a spool of string, and she ties it to the nearby rock. The string is invisible.

Her team follow it by touch, and the moment they pass through the ripples, they appear in a different location. Camilla had read of this strange effect, but she had not seen it. Based on their surroundings, Camilla surmises that they were in a type of school. There were the lockers and when she looked out the window she saw the teenagers exercising. To blend in, her people break open a locker and they put on some uniforms.

The portal back is still rippling. If they cross through that same threshold, they will return to their original location and they might get intercepted by the cloud creatures. Camilla blinks once, and then she notes some jocks passing through the hallway. They note her precedence, but say nothing because of the other people next to her. The portal ripples and starts moving. Slowly, the line, with the invisible string, starts stretching. Camilla fears that it might stop. The portal eventually stops at the official entrance of the school. It then stays there, rooted on the spot. It was a wonder why or how it had done so. A couple of hours pass and Camilla goes to lunch with her companions.

The cafeteria food being offer there was much better than the grub Camilla was already used to. She smiled as she ate the piece of burnt bacon. It had been ages since she had eaten pork. While sitting there roosting, some school officers come and start questioning her mates.

After much questioning, her men were told to leave the premises. The soldiers instead of obeying each fled in a different direction. Camilla pondered on the best course of action while she sipped her juice bag. While she was alone, a girl sat beside her. She said, "Here."

Camilla received the item. It was an ID of a student who resembled her. The only difference was that Camilla had blue hair, and yellow eyes, while the other student her black hair and black eyes. Suspicious, Camilla asked, "Who is this?"

The girl answered, "Nobody. She ran away from the campus a few months ago. Nobody has heard from her since, then. You can be her on the mean time."

"Thank you, I guess. Do you have one for the others?" asked Camilla.

"No," said the girl. She added, "Who are they to you?"

"Just some foot soldiers, barely know them," said Camilla in earnest.

"My name is Tabita! Pleased to meet you, Jenifer," said Tabita.

"It's Camilla," corrected Camilla.

"It is now Jenifer. So, you better get used to your new name," said Tabita.

Camilla came to stand by the window. She saw as each one of her men was captured. They were then dragged outside together. The moment they stepped through the portal, they disappeared much to the bewilderment of the officers. Tabita alarmed asked, "What happened to them?"

"Who knows. Maybe they returned to their home planet," said Camilla.

"Surely you jest," said Tabita laughing.

"I don't," said Camilla, "But I don't expect you to believe me."

After lunch, Camilla went to classes and sat on the back. She took that time to catch up with her sleep. When Tabita awoke her, the pair went to their shared dormitory. When night fell, Camilla followed the invisible string back to the other side of the portal. She was shocked to note that her entire unit had been killed the moment they had sat foot outside, on the other side of the portal. Camilla saw the sky rumbled as weird lights stretched behind the storm clouds. Camilla took the communicator from a dead body before returning to school. When she returned it was still nighttime. She silently made her way back to her dorm. Tabita awoke with a start when she saw Camilla there.

Shocked she asked, "Where were you?"

"Out," said Camilla.

"For a whole month!" asked Tabita.

"Seems like it," said Camilla nonchalantly.

The months rolled rather slowly for Camilla. For reasons that she did not understand, there was a time difference between both worlds. Her only ties to her old world was the invisible string. The nature and properties of it where unknown. Only the effects had been studied. Even if the gateway closed, as long as she was bounded to the string she could return. From time to time, she would communicate with her captain. The words she spoke were heard on the other side too quickly. While the captain's words entered at a slug's pace. It seemed to Camilla that she would have to linger in that strange world for longer than she had anticipated.

Despite her natural looks, Camilla could still pass for a human being. There were some otherworldly oddities that she was forced to mask. One day, Tabita sees Camilla creating fire with her hands. A gimmick that anyone could do, back in her world. To the childlike eyes of Tabita, it seemed to her that Camilla was a witch. Tabita having an affinity for magic decided to invite Camilla to her magic club. Camilla having nothing better to do till the stupid cloud monster passed by decided to join. Camilla had a practical way of thinking. IF this so called magic could be used against the Cloud monsters, it was a skill worth acquiring.

Two years pass, and the maidens in the magic club were showing real progress. They were still no match for Camilla's natural skills. She had to be made of sterner stuff to deal with the cloud monsters. One day, Camilla gets a very slow message from her captain.

"The Cloud Monsters are dead. Come Home," said her captain to her.

Camilla breathed in a sigh of relief. As she was going to her dorm to pick up her things, she overheard something disturbing. Tabita and the girls had a half-baked taking over the world scheme. Camilla smiles silently and she enters the room. She reaches into her backpack and offers Tabita a sword.

Tabita, confused asks, "What do you want me to do with this?"

"The honorable thing," said Camilla calmly.

"I don't..." started saying Tabita.

She was unable to finish her sentence because the blade had levitated and passed through her heart. Her peers were killed in a similar fashion. Putting the sword back in its sheath, Camilla said, "I am not a big fan of telepathy, but in a pinch, it is subtle and quick enough to get the job done."

After concluding her gruesome work, Camilla made her way towards the entrance of the school. Once she passed through that gate, the power of the invisible string returned her to her home world. She pondered on the two types of lives she had known. The first was dangerous and frightening. The other was boring and soul crushing.

PACIFIC DREAM

It has been two years since QB had returned home. The technology there was certainly advanced indeed. There were many strange wonders, with the tall buildings, the holograms, and the robots. There was one thing that was missing from this city. It was the absence of cars. The people in this city with their diverse dresses and attires walked everywhere. They just did not seemed to be in a hurry to get anywhere. Sure, from time to time some would sprint, and be there in literally matters of seconds. Since his arrival, QB had met his true family. In this city, everyone was everyone's family. At the moment, QB was living with a group of masked people. They wore bulbous dresses that were knee long, and veils that were attached to the dress and mask. They wore gloves on their hands, and high heel boots. The main difference among them were in the small details, and the mask decorations.

Camilla wore a peacock's mask. On the forehead, there was a heart shaped jewel. From it a single long ostrich feather grew. Camilla liked ostriches and she had a couple she was raising in the back garden. While helping her hand feed one, Camilla said to QB, "It has been ages since I have been outside."

"I suppose," said QB.

"We should go on a vacation," said Camilla.

"I don't know," said QB.

"Just ask the Fat Lady From the Office, for some time. I am certain they will give it to you," said Camilla.

"I don't know. I just got my job and it seems in poor form to go on vacation," said QB.

"She will understand," said Camilla.

"I don't know," said QB while the ostrich pocked him on the hair and the arms. The silly bird was biting on everything, except for the food that QB was handing it.

The following day Camilla awoke him at 2 a.m. She said to him, "You should start getting your bags ready let's we miss the boat."

"What boat?" asked QB getting up.

"The one that is going to take us to the Underwater Islands," said Camilla.

"What of my job?" asked QB.

"Well, I called the Fat Lady and I said, QB will be back later," explained Camilla.

"What did Lady say?" asked QB.

"She asked the date when she could expect you back, and nothing else," said Camilla.

"That's it?" asked QB.

"Yep, that is it, cause that is how we roll, except where there is war afoot, but things have been quiet for almost 20 years," said Camilla.

"I wouldn't know about that," said QB.

He languidly got up and placed inside a bag the first thing that fell out of his closet. Camilla was already packed. She carried with her a little wheeled luggage the shape of a ladybug. Once outside, she placed her knee on the top part. With her other leg, she got a bit of impulse. She was soon making quite the headway while QB ran behind her. The pair reached the docks after 10 minutes. The boat ride was quite pleasant. In part because it hovered a meter over the water. It wasn't so much a boat ride as a plane ride. It had been designed by a silly girl who wanted to experience being in a boat, without having to deal with the pesky surf. Whatever motion the waves would have did not affect the boat. At a certain spot, the boat made a weird circle turn towards the left. It was a bit dizzy, but not so much as the driver walking around the steering wheel in the opposite direction.

Camilla explained, "This islands is a little bit different as all. To get to it, you have to turn right, as you go left. The easiest way to simulate this effect is by turning the boat left, while you turn right."

"That makes perfect sense," said QB incredulous.

After the maneuver ended, the guide said, "It is common for Pacific Islands to appear from time to time. However, it is rare for one to come and go over the course of one day. The tides here are quite extreme this time of the year. So just watch."

QB looked over to the side of the boat. He saw one of those floating, glowing orb things drop downwards. The driver maneuvered back a bit as a small island rose to the surface of the water. Despite being underwater, the island had all its vegetation in one piece. After docking, the morning was spent doing typical island things. There was the dancing, the swimming and the sunbathing. For reasons that QB did not understand, a lot of people did not bathed with what he considered a bathing suit. Some did not even bother to change. They just jumped right in with whatever they happened to be wearing.

Underwater, the island was surrounded by a reef. There was a lot of reef sharks just waiting for night to fall. QB was alarmed at first when he saw them. He calmed down a bit when Camilla waved to one. The shark nodded in response before returning to napping.

Back on the other world, QB had seen some old shark movies. They were always painted as bloodthirsty monsters. The ones in this world were quite mild manner or maybe it was Camilla's nonchalant attitude that helped QB not be afraid. Aside from sharks, QB saw Butterfly fishes, some Gobies, a Cod and a school of Parrot fishes. After swimming for a bit the pair went to eat a restaurant. QB ate Spinach ravioli with a chopped salad. For dessert, he ate a Strawberry Napoleon. As for Camilla, she had cheese quesadillas with pico de gallo. For dessert, she had key lime pie. For drinks, they had milkshakes.

Close to dusk, the pair along with everyone on the island went to see the sunset. Over the horizon, QB saw a giant wave. Somewhat alarmed he said, "Wait a minute. Isn't this island supposed to be submerged when the tide goes up?"

"Seems like it," said Camilla.

The waves crashed against the shore, but did not travel too far island. Rather a shield kept the island from flooding. Eventually, the entire island was completely submerged. The shield was transparent and round. It allowed for the visitors to see the fishes swimming above them. During dinner, Camilla asked QB, "Aren't you glad we played hooky?"

"I suppose it is an interesting and pleasant experience," said QB.

"What's the matter? Still thinking about your folks?" asked Camilla.

"A little," said QB.

"Some things cannot be helped as all. You can't devote your entire life to helping others. There is nothing wrong with unwinding every once in a while," said Camilla.

"I don't know," said QB.

"Well, when you do know come dance with me," said Camilla getting up.

Camilla was not much of a dancer. She was uncoordinated and at times it seemed like she was dancing something that had nothing to do with the music being played. After seeing her make a fool of herself, QB got up and went to join her.

THE BALLAD OF CUPCAKE

Cupcake started his life like any other cat. His birthmother lived in a butcher shop. One day, the pound came and rounded up all of Cupcake's siblings and his mother as well. Cupcake had wandered off a little bit. At several weeks old, he could barely open his eyes. He had fallen behind a sack of potatoes when the humans came. After all was set and done, Cupcake was alone and hungry. Night came, and with it hunger pains. He started meowing. A drifter that had snuck into the butcher shop heard its cries. The man picked up the little kitty and examined it.

He smiled when he noted that the kitten was unharmed. His eyes wandered over Cupcake's blue eyes and white fur with overlapping patches of black and orange hair. The drifter took the kitten with him and he named it Cupcake. After four months with the fellow, the cat had grown into a hardly little devil. While most cats his age ate cereal and fancy feast, Cupcake ate old ham, chicken and ice cream from time to time.

Cupcake did not know the name of the human that took care of him. The other humans passed by the drifter and only took notice of the man whenever Cupcake was around. One day, a fellow came to see the man. Cupcake got a bad feeling about the visitor and thus kept at a distance. From time to time, he would come closer with its back arched, and feet tucked underneath. Cupcake still did not have a full grasp of the human language. As such, he did not understand even the gist of the conversation. His caretaker whistled a couple of times, and after the fifth call Cupcake eventually came.

One of the strays hanging inside a dump said to Cupcake, "Your human is a killer."

"I haven't seen him kill anyone," remarked Cupcake.

His caretaker chuckled as he heard the two cats meowing to each other. The following day his caretaker gets inside a taxi and together they go to a different part of the city. The pair end up staying in an apartment. Based on the musty smell, it seemed to Cupcake that nobody had lived there in quite a long time. Cupcake's human spent the day cleaning up the place. Meanwhile, Cupcake spent his time anxiously looking about. He was just not used to living indoors.

Eventually, Cupcake found the window. He sat there looking outside. From time to time, he would see another stray cat making its rounds. He hissed at a familiar face who responded in turn. Cupcake thought, I can't have that knave claiming my apartment. I must let everyone know that this is my home now.

Following his natural impulse, Cupcake scent marked a couple of spots of the house, much to the annoyance of his human. Night came, and his human went to sleep on the floor. There was a fine looking bed, but Cupcake's human did not seem to want to use it. Since the human was not taking it, Cupcake decided to sleep on it. He found a spot between two pillows and then he simmered down inside.

While Cupcake slept, he had a faint memory of warmth and purring. For some reason, it felt nostalgic. A slight sound was heard, and Cupcake's ears perked up. Thinking that his human was awake, Cupcake got up and went to hug his leg to scratch and bite it. For reasons Cupcake did not understand his human brought out a gun. The man checked the bullets, and even took a few shots with the empty magazine to make certain the gun was working correctly. The man got up and left the apartment. Cupcake followed behind.

It was early morning, and the air felt crisp. Cupcake's human huddled beneath his trench coat. The man stood outside a high school and waited. He did the same thing the following day around the same time. During one of those stakeouts Cupcake saw the familiar face.

It was his third cousin, twice removed. The humans had dubbed the fellow Zombie Bart. Bart was a the only Donskoy cat in town. His hairless skin was pale, and wrinkly. His most striking feature was his disdainful green, yellow eyes. His narrow eyes were always filled with a look of disdain and loathing. His current age was a subject of much speculation. There were sightings of the cat as far back as 50 years ago, but none of the humans were keen to believe such rumors. Cupcake did know the truth, however.

Bart rubbed his head against Cupcake as salutation. Cupcake did not return the gesture, but simply licked his paw and rubbed it against his own forehead.

Bart asked, "What are you doing?"

"Dunno, just waiting for something, I suppose," said Cupcake.

"You still with that killer?" asked Bart.

"He hasn't killed anyone yet," said Cupcake.

"But he is going to. Just give it a couple of days," said Bart.

"You are the second mate to say this. Just what do you know of this man?" asked Cupcake.

"Nothing much, since the affairs of humans rarely interest me. Still, I find it entertaining whenever the humans get into their little turf wars, like we do from time to time. It is at least something that we have in common with them. In this case, some of the human cubs from that yonder school have been seen in places they should not be, doing stuff they should not be doing. And so, your man has been tasked to hunt them down," explained Bart.

Cupcake was thoughtful for a second. He then asked, "How many lives do humans typically have?"

"The same amount of lives as any other creature. Just one," said Bart.

"But I was told cats have 9 lives," commented Cupcake pouting.

"One is more than enough, if lived properly, thought I suppose if you want another you might want to ask the elephant God for another chance," said Bart.

"Elephant? God?" asked Cupcake not understanding either of those two words.

"You will understand when you are older," said Bart departing.

I am already pretty old, thought Cupcake.

The following day the drifter awakes earlier than usual. He enters into the bathroom and showers. It was the first time Cupcake had seen his human make an effort to groom himself. Most of the time, Cupcake felt it was his duty to clean the human to the best of his abilities. When his human got out of the shower, he seemed like a completely different person. The look was completed after a shave and a change in attire. The man dressed himself in an elegant tuxedo, and he combed his hair back with a brush. Cupcake rubbed against the man's legs, as he usually did whenever he was hungry. In answer to his pleas, Cupcake was given his usual meal in a bowl. The man gave Cupcake this time some tuna from a can. It was the expensive type of tuna. The one that was usually worth 10 bucks a can.

He petted Cupcake on the head and said something before departing. Cupcake found it odd that the man had left him outside the apartment. This did not inspired Cupcake much confidence. However, he being a young, inexperienced cat; Cupcake decided not to follow till he had finished his meal.

A day passed and his master did not return. Cupcake still waited patiently. A little girl feeling sorry for the cat passed by. She petted it, and she fed him some chicken nuggets. They were not great, but they were not bad all things considered. Cupcake was hungry, and so he ate the nuggets with gusto. After the second day, Cupcake left the apartment complex. He left specifically at 5:10 a.m. Around that time, Zombie Bart's patrol route would take him by this place. Cupcake came to sit before Bart with a dour look on his face.

He said, "I have been abandoned."

"It was bound to happen sooner or later," said Bart snickering.

"You think this is funny?" hissed Cupcake.

"To me, perhaps, but I am one not to depend on the charity of others," said Bart.

"Do you know where my human is at?" asked Cupcake.

"He is in the morgue," said Bart flatly.

"What is a morgue?" asked Cupcake.

"It is a place where they keep dead humans," said Bart.

"Why is my human there?" asked Cupcake.

"Because he is dead," said Bart flatly.

"Oh," said Cupcake, "I see. How did he die?"

"Your human went to that school to fight with those kids I told you about. He got all of them, but the mate of one of them stabbed him a couple of times. You see that puddle over there by the garbage?" said Bart.

Cupcake looked in that direction. Bart then continued, "Well, he bled out there. He was taken away just this morning. Sorry you missed him."

Cupcake was at a loss for words and thoughts. He did not know what to make of it, or even if he should be feeling anything. The only thing he was aware was of the hunger pawns that were slowly creeping inside of him. Without realizing it, his endless wanderings led him to the school his owner had stalked just a few days before. Cupcake waited and waited, but his human did not return. From time to time, some of the students made motions to pet Cupcake. A couple even threw rocks at him, but Cupcake easily avoided them.

Eventually, he felt a familiar scent. It was faint, but there was a girl among the students who smelled like his human. Cupcake rubbed his leg against the girl's leg, who screamed, startled. She smiled when she noted the kitty cat. Following her first impulse, the girl takes Cupcake with her. Cupcake did not resist sensing that the girl meant her no ill will. When the girl enters inside her home, her mother says a lot of angry words, to which the girl responds without any intonation.

Afterwards, the girl goes with the cat to her room. She takes with her a violin case. She leaves it in the music room, alone with Cupcake. Since Cupcake was alone for a moment, he took his chance to mark his territory in the corner. He did not know if he was going to stay there forever, and his new surroundings were making him nervous. When the girl returned, she had a can of fancy feast for him. Cupcake ate a piece, before throwing it up. The girl stared somewhat disappointed and confused left. She smelled the cat food over the top, before grimacing. Moments later she returned with a piece of ham. This Cupcake ate with gusto. While he ate, the girl's mother entered the room. The two spoke a bit, and then the girl took out her violin case. The girl started to play her song, but she would stop whenever her mother spoke.

Eventually, the girl starts laughing, and her laugher degenerates into a sob. She then picked up Cupcake and petted him. Cupcake could tell there was something wrong with his new companion, but he did not care. Since he was still frightened of her, he resisted the urge to bite and scratch her hand has he usually did whenever he was being pet a little bit too much for his taste.

THE OBLIQUE ARMOR

drian was about 14 years old, when his life took a dramatic turn. Standing at 5'01, with amber eyes and blonde hair, and his Victorian attire, he could easily pass for a flaneur. Though, those who looked closer could see the patchwork, and the worn, scratched leather. Since it was Sunday, Adrian was at the train station waiting. He looked up at the clock and noted the time. Right on cue, the noon a clock train arrived bearing an army of passengers. Adrian pushed through the army of people and made his way towards the cargo hold. Passengers were busy, looking for their luggage.
Adrian came to the officer and said, "Smith."

The officer looked through the manifested and he handed Adrian a luggage that was not his own. It was a large silver, trolley case with a standard combination lock. Adrian made his way behind a column and opened it. He noted the lady clothing, and a strange gift box. He took this item, before closing the luggage and leaving it there. After taking a bit of distance, he noted the owner had tracked down her possession. She was a stout lady, with flaming hair, freckles and mocha colored skin. Seeing that the trolley was locked, she assumed that it had not been opened. Adrian had learned from experience that all modern luggage of this make had trackers. After acquiring this small loot, Adrian performed a bit of pickpocketing before departing. Before leaving the train station, he was stopped by a bunch of cops. The maiden with the flaming hair came running at him.

He said to her to defuse the situation, "Hey, cops. I was just looking for your guys. I found this item in the floor."

It was then when Adrian noted the round shape of the box, with the symbols. The maiden annoyed said, "You stole it from me, you cretin!"

"Do I look like the type of person who needs to steal," said Adrian between his teeth.

It was then when Sasha came to his aid. He was 3 years his senior, and a bit of a poultry fellow. Carrying an empty luggage, he always had on him, he said to Adrian, "There you are young master. It is dangerous to wander off on your own."

"I wasn't wandering off, I was looking for the owner of this box, and it has been found," said Adrian.

After some roundaboutness, Sasha was able to convince the cops that Adrian was a nobleman acting upon his good intentions. When the pair left the train station, both breathed in a sigh of relief.

Sasha was the first to speak, "That was a close one."

"You said it," said Adrian.

"I think we are getting a little bit too old for the game," commented Sasha.

"It is not as if anyone is hiring at the moment, and we haven't any goods to sell on the market, and we do not have any particular skills," said Adrian sadly.

"Well, you are good at sewing," chuckled Sasha pointing at his shirt.

"That is a woman's work. Nobody is going to trust a dude with their finery," said Adrian.

"Excuses, excuses. And if that's woman's work, then what does that make you?" asked Sasha.

In response, Adrian punched Sasha's shoulder. Adrian did not flinched, since he knew it would cost him a second punch, as per the established rules. Along the way home, it started snow-ing. They passed by a pawnshop where they unloaded the day's catch. The items that usually fetched the best price were the pocket watches and compact mirrors. They were luxury items that were valuable, but also pretty common. With coins in their pockets, Adrian and Sasha performed the weekly grocery shopping, prioritizing the meat products like bacon, and rabbit.

The city they inhabited looked far ancient that what it actually was. Most of the buildings were from the Victorian, and Medieval Era. The newer buildings kept up with that ancient style, thus making certain that the city of London retained its identity. Over the millenniums, the city had been destroyed and rebuilt countless of times. Adrian and Sasha lived in one of the old, musty concrete buildings from that old forgotten era. The windows were clear, and impact resistant. Despite its exterior ornamentation, the flat that served as an orphanage had a simple interior. Indoors, there was a group of 20 orphans all huddled together before the dimming fireplace.

They opened the door, after knocking a couple of times. It was bolted on many places, in part because the door nob's keyhole was broken.

Frowning, Sasha said, "I thought you were going to fix that."

"There aren't any of the parts to make the repair," explained Adrian.

"Yes, there are. I know, because I bought them," said Sasha.

"Oh, so I forgot. I have a lot of things on my mind," said Adrian putting the food on the table.

A group of children crowded around the bags, and like ravenous animals they devoured everything in sight.

Sasha then added, after munching on a piece of bread, "Well, you should get that fixed. Don't forget what happened last time!"

"I know, I am sorry, sheesh! Can't I just eat first," said Adrian.

"No, if I left you eat first, I am going to forget, and then you are going to forget. Do it now, like right now!" insisted Sasha.

"Fine! Jesus!" said Adrian.

He went to the second floor, and looked through the items inside a box at the foot of his cot. He found there the bolts, the new doorknob and a screw driver. Adrian opened the front door to fix it. He stopped when he noticed a lot of people running and yelling. He closed the door and he ran up to the third floor. Sasha too had noticed the noise and he was already upstairs. There was a crowd of people rioting by the nearby factory. Manifestations had been occurring over the past couple of months. Still, this was the first time it had gotten this frenzied. The moment that Adrian heard shots fired he mobilized the children in the orphanage. They all left the orphanage and scatter to the 4 winds. They were schedule to meet in the abandoned church in the outskirts of the city.

Adrian was the last person to attempt to leave the orphanage. When everyone was gone, he lifted a floor tile, to check upon his hidden stash. After securing his tiny box on his person, he started running out. A swarm of hysterical people passed through him and even over him at times. He was carried along with the frenzy straight through the main alley. Since he was small, he was not able to see well the cause of the alarm. It was when shots were fire, and half the people behind him suddenly dropped dead that he was able to see the huge behemoth. It was like a moving armor, only two stories tall. As it walked, its claw feed made heavy thumping sounds on the ground, which combined with the clanking created by each movement of the armor. After this, some of the more cowardly folks did the rational thing and crawled on all fours begging for their lives. The armor threw a steel net over them and continued its crowd control mission.

Adrian slipped past the people, and into an alleyway to get away from the mechanical creature. He eventually arrives to the slums. There he saw two more of those armored giants. The one crafted with ornate silver and gold was making strange motions. Eventually, the chest plate opened and a human maiden climbed out. It was the ebony lady from before. She kicked the leg of her suit, and yelled, "Piece of junk!"

The so called piece of junk was indeed an interesting piece of hardware. With a slimmer frame, and a sword instead of a gun. This one instead of being two stories, was only 6 meters tall. For one as small as Adrian, the robot still seemed like a mountain to him. While the other armored giant stoically watched, the lady brought out a small computer and plugged it to the leg of the armor. She was in the process of debugging the darn thing. A group of rioters just then comes from the side, and start shooting up the armors. Her companion leaves her alone to pursue the rioters.

During the skirmish, she gets shot in the arm. Not used to sudden bursts of pain, the lady faints and starts bleeding out. Adrian did the gentlemanly thing, and got her out of the street and into one of the nearby shacks. An hour after bandaging her wound, the lady awoke in a pretty foul mood. Taking out a gun, she says, "You! You are the little thieving bastard from the train station!"

"As I said before, I haven't any need to steal anything," said Adrian calmly.

He starts making his way out when he hears the clicking of the gun. Adrian sneered in response as he dropped one by one, the ammo he had taken from the gun. The lady made a motion to stand, but she was weak from the blood loss. She fell down on the floor, breathing heavily.

When Adrian went outdoors, he saw that the second armor had already returned. Not certain what to do, he tiptoed slowly out, while the armors followed his movements with their heads. Adrian stopped and returned to stand before them.

Pretty confused, Adrian asked, "You are not going to attack me?"

"We only respond to hostiles. Since you haven't a weapon, and you show a kind disposition helping an officer of the law, we have no reason to show you any animosity," explained the second armor. While the first was made of silver, the second was composed of brass and copper.

"Well, thank you officers? I am just doing my civic duties, he, heh! Bye," said Adrian starting to walk away.

He flinched when he heard the two pairs of giant footsteps following behind. Adrian turned around and asked, "Can I help you officers?"

"It is best that we escort you for the time being. The city is under siege by terrorists, and you have a duty to attend to. You best come inside," said the silver armor kneeling down and extending its hand.

"Ok… I guess," said Adrian taking its hand and getting inside.

When he was inside the cushioned seat, the chest plate of the silver armor closed. He read on a small screen this instruction, "Put on the glasses!"

When he did, Adrian was able to see through the armor's eyes. He noted the motion of his hands. He then said, "Well, this is different."

"How so? Don't tell me it is your first time inside an Oblique Armor?" asked the silver armor.

"Yes," said Adrian meekly.

"I was under the impression the subject matter had been covered in the Academy Officer, Adrian," said the silver armor.

Officer, thought Adrian even more confused.

"Yes, no, but I came very late into the officer program you see. Parents of influence and all that boring nonsense," said Adrian.

"I see," said the armor flatly.

His partner then said, "Well, allow me to explain this briefly. We are automatons, under the direct guidance of the London police. This is the first time we have been deployed. We were designed to work with and follow the directions of a single operator. See that round sphere before you. It is biometric. The moment a person touches it, we are imprinted upon them, sort of speak, for now and forever. So, what is our mission… Officer Adrian."

Adrian was silent for a while, taking this all in. Eventually he said, "There are some orphans in the outskirts of town."

The brass armor then said starting to run, "Let's go arrest them, shall we."

Adrian running after the brass armor said, "No! We are going there to protect them!"

The silver armor then said, "He knows what you meant. He is only messing with you."

When the pair of armors arrived to the church, there was a lot of screaming and yelling. Adrian got out the cabin, and said, "Guys, it's me! I brought some back up!"

Sasha was the first to speak, "What are they?"

"They and me, we are good cops. You are now under the London police witness protection," explained Adrian.

The silver armor gave a sideways look and asked, "They are?"

"Yes!" yelled Adrian. He used sign language to say to Sasha, "Just go with it!"

Sasha nodded and said, "Yes, we know the identity of the terrorist leader, and we need protection."

Adrian narrowed his eyes, but said nothing. He could deal with his suspicions later. For the time being, all that mattered was getting as far away from London as it was possible.

ROSE AND ROSALINE

Rose and Rosaline were beautiful twin sisters. Both with gorgeous curly red hair, green eyes and the slender bodies of ballerinas. They had taken ballet in their early teens, but life had chosen for them a different career path. At the moment, they were busy pretending to the journalism people. The tail of their helicopter had just been shot. It spun dived into the ocean, with only the twins surviving. They swam to shore were they stripped down to pretend to beach people. After walking for a couple of miles, they run into a strange commune. The commune was filled with lovely ladies working in the fields, producing beautiful flowers. One of the few men in the community noticed the twins in their undies.

After this basic, manly observations his eyes noticed the cuts and bruises. He asked in his native dialect, "What happened to you girls? Do you need some help?"

It was Rosaline who answered, "We are fine, only a little bit shaken for wear. We went out swimming and the riff tide nearly got us, and then the ground is so hard, with the stones and large pieces of corals."

"You are not from around here aren't you," said the man coming closer.

One of the ladies from the commune narrowed her eyes, and said to him, "Go and get them a towel."

The man pouting said, "You are no fun."

"We get tourists from the capital from time to time," said the lady, "They do not know that there is a reason why we do not swim in this particular ocean. There are the currents, and large waves, and the storms from time to time break large pieces of corals that wash up on the shore, becoming the occasional prickly hazards. No! Girls, it is not safe to swim in this ocean."

"Well, we had to learn this lesson sometime," said Rose shivering and rubbing her shoulders.

A different lady laughing said, "And then there is that too."

"What happened to your clothing," asked an elderly maiden.

"Some pervert probably stole them," said Rose, "They were not there when we got out."

"They could have at least left the towels," commented Rosaline.

The girls eventually got their towels and they settled in the commune for a month while they recovered from their wounds. Since they had no money on them, they had to work for two more months in order to afford tickets to leave the country by plane. When they got to the airport, they gave their fake names. The clerk looking at them and their fake passports said that the girls were in the no fly list.

This was the start of the twins prolonged stay in enemy territory. While they worked as ballerinas, they from time to time would smuggled letters to the outside world. The main issue was that regardless of whatever point of exit they tried, they were banned from leaving. The reason behind this became apparent during the sixth month of their stay. They had found work and lodging in a humble ballet company. They were putting their high school training to good use. It had been almost four years since the sisters had last danced, but their muscles and reflexes were strong, due to habitual training. One day, a military man started coming to see them perform. Upon closer inspection, the sisters recognized the man they had first met back in the commune.

Two years passed, and the leader of the country dies under mysterious circumstances. The sisters take this chance to try to get out of the country. In the airport, the same scene repeats. This time Rosa tells the attendant, "Look, I know you got your orders, but with your leader dead, there might be some restructuring, and you do not want to be on the losing end, do you?! We have reasons to fly, reasons, that are top secret. Now, let us on that plane!"

After much coercion and threats, the flight attendant reluctantly allowed the sisters to enter. Once the plane landed in their home country, the twins were finally able to give a sigh of relief. Two years passed, and the twins were out on a date. They were in the manor of a rich fellow. He had seen the sisters in one of their ballets performances, and under the pretest of sponsoring their art he was pitching woo. He did not care which maiden he got. To him, there was no difference between Rose and Rosaline. If it was possible, he would have liked to have both girls. When the twins concluded their tour, they went with the man to jump out of a plane. The girls were itching to try their hands on the new and improved wingsuit. With the wind crashing against their faces, the sisters felt for the first time in a long time truly alive.

POSEIDON AND
THE VIOLIN GIRL

Hilda was a 16 year old vagabond. She moved from place to place, sometimes alone, at other times in the company of the gypsies or the circus people. She had black hair, amber eyes and honey color skin. Her only permanent companion was her violin. Hilda could not remember ever being without her companion. She earned her bread through her craft. While playing in the city, a handsome looking rich fellow came to her.

He had even teeth, blonde hair, and black eyes. Smiling to her he said, "I love you and your music. I am your biggest fan. I have heard you play in many different occasions. I want you to marry me, so you can have an easy life."

Hilda had never been told proposed to by anyone. She took a better look at the gentleman before her. After rattling her memory a bit, she realized he was the prince from the local feudal. She had seen him a couple of times. Once when she was gathering berries in the forest, and another time as he was returning from the wars.

Instead of agreeing to marriage proposal, Hilda said, "I am charmed, but I need some time to think about it."

"That is perfectly understandable. Come, meet me here again in about week, and then tell me your answer," said the prince.

Hilda breathed in a sigh of relief as soon as the prince left. Some of the peasants who had seen the incident called her a fool. In order to put her thoughts into order, Hilda left the city and went to the beach to think. As for the prince, he looked quite unperturbed till the moment he was alone in his room where he destroyed all the furniture.

While in the sea, Hilda started to play her music while walking through the shores. She stopped a moment when she heard a song. She listened to it a bit, and then she added her own violin to the mix. Eventually, a young siren rose to the surface to join her song. Close to sunset, Poseidon himself came to fetch his daughter. His initial annoyance faded away at the sound of such pleasant music.

He came to the shore and asked, "What is a lady like you doing in such a desolate beach?"

"I like to come here to think. Other than my violin, I do not have any confidant to tell my worries," said Hilda.

"What seems to be the problem? As a Greek God, I don't get prayed to as much as before, so I have a lot of free time. If anything, I can offer some advice as your elder," said Poseidon.

"Well, the church says that any non-Christian God is a demon, and so I will tell you everything," said Hilda.

"Hehe! This old demon story, if I had a nickel," grumbled Poseidon more to himself beneath the waters.

Since he was still lingering, Hilda said, "Well, I was playing the other day, as before and then out of nowhere this rich guy I don't even know asks me for marriage. And, I am not certain what I should do. I like the prospect of not having to work, ever, but I don't even know this man."

"Mmm," said Poseidon, "I heard of a similar case like this before. You should go to the nearby fishing hamlet and visit the home of Victoria."

Hilda did as she was told. She asked for lodging, and the peasant girl Victoria allowed her to stay. After conversing with her a bit,

Victoria said to Hilda, "I have to step out a bit to check up on the nets. If we are lucky, I might be able to get some fish for our supper."

Twenty minutes passed, and a rich looking gentleman entered the hut without knocking. Annoyed, Hilda asked, "Can I help you?"

The gentleman bowed, and said, "I am sorry miss, but I am looking for my wife Victoria. Have you seen her?"

"She went out for a bit, but she should be returning real soon," said Hilda.

The man sat down to wait. There was an uncomfortable silence that seemed to last for an eternity. Hilda breathed in a sigh of relief when she heard the footsteps of Victoria. As soon as Victoria laid her eyes on her husband, she literally turned into an ogre. The same metamorphosis overcame the gentleman as well, as the pair tore at one another with harsh words. Scared, Hilda slipped away under the table and out the door.

This incident had helped Hilda come up with a decision. By the end of the week, she met up with the prince. She said to him, "Look, I barely know you, but you seem like a nice fellow so I am willing to give you a chance. Travel with me for a couple of months, as a peasant so I can get to know the real you."

The prince already boiling turned into an imp. Yelling, he said, "What are you an idiot! What sort of a fool would put such conditions on any prince! I am your ruler, I am your better! I have killed many people for less. It is time that you learned your place woman!"

The prince was about to slap Hilda when a Trident speared the enraged imp. The entire incident was the talk of the city. Hilda left the city, since people were starting to call her a witch. Back on the seashore, Hilda said to Poseidon, "Thank you for all your help."

"It was nothing little girl. It has been centuries since humans have taken my Godhood seriously," said Poseidon returning to the ocean.

The Climb

As long as Eric could remember, he had been suffering from the same recurrent dream. It was part of the reason why he did not live near the beach, even though he could. Whenever he went on vacation, he always made certain to stay in a hotel that was at least six stories tall. Eric could not remember when this fixation or night terror began. For as long as he could remember, the same dream would haunt him. There were some variations here and there, but the overall theme was the same. A tsunami would come and he would drown, along with his family. This would always occur while indoors. He would look out the window and then a wave would enter and throw water and debris.

Eric was not afraid of drowning. He knew from experience that it was not the most unpleasant sensation. Still, what he did dread was not knowing. He felt there was a sword of Damocles hanging over his head. Any minute, at any moment it would fall. The sword did fall over Eric, but not in the way he had expected.

At the age of 37, he had burned out. Following the advice from his psychologist, he decided to take a prolonged vacation with his family. Together with his wife, his teenage son, his mother and his sister he had decided to visit Tahiti. More specifically, he went to Teahupo'o city. Over the course of decades, the small village had developed under the backbone of its amassing surfs. Despite his recurrent dreams Eric quite enjoyed surfing. The adrenaline and focus the sport required was enough to make him forget all his worries. Even the nightmares seemed to occur less whenever he was chilling by the coast.

On his second week of vacation, Eric was surfing as usual when a douche bumped into him. The strength of the other person's surfboard knocked him into the water. It took 20 minutes to rescue him from the water. When he awoke, he is inside his room. His mother holding his hand tells him, "You suffered a small injury son."

Eric made a motion to stand, but his ribs felt like they were on fire. Still somewhat agitated and disoriented, Eric rose from his bed. His mother got up and went to fetch the doctor who was in the other room. Slowly, Eric made his way towards the window. With each step he gave, he felt himself closer to his destiny. The moment he laid his eyes on the window he saw it. The wave crashed against the window pushing him against the wall with all its fury. The wave was incredibly large, to have made it all the way up to the fourth floor. The door bent with the rushing water, and Eric mustering all his strength me made a motion to make it to the other room. When he found his family, all he could muster to say was "Climb!"

Together they made their way towards the stairs climbing ever higher and higher. Eventually they make it to the fifth floor. It was then when the hotel got taken out of its foundation. It tilted somewhat crashing into another larger structure. A hole in the wall opens, and Eric sees the exposed segment of a much taller, sturdier structure. He helps his mother, and his family up, before pulling himself up. All the while, he was keenly aware of the growing pain in his sides. While they walk in the new structure, the floor gives way below the feet of his sister. Frowning, Eric said, "I suppose we do not have time to carefully consider the matter. Let us hold hands, and run as if the devil were after us."

"It sure seems that way, father," said his son Clark.

While they ran, they take with their eyes bits and pieces of their surroundings. It seemed to be a type of laboratory of factory. More and more the water rises and they cannot seem to find a stair to take them higher. Eventually, they do find a small coiling escalator. Since Eric was the last in line, he fell down, with the stairs.

He tells his family, "Just keep climbing up. I am going to find another route."

While looking about, he sees a frightened local maiden. He recognized her as Pania, the manager of the hotel. Like a frightened bird, she clung to the first familiar face. Pushing her aside, he said, "I am still injured. Remember?"

Together, they swam through the murky waters, as the ceiling slowly got closer. After 30 minutes of searching, they found a door with a stairs symbol. The only problem was opening it. Eric starts pounding and pushing at the door. Still, the water pressure made opening the door a difficult task. Before running out of air, the door opens and a steely cold hand grabs Eric, before helping Pania to the other side.

After climbing up a couple of steps, Eric takes a look back to see who had helped him. He was greeted by two pairs of large, artificial eyes colored pink. The face was designed to be resembled an anime maiden, with the small nose and mouth. The hair was white on the top, and blue bellow. The body was jointed like a doll, and the clothing was in rags due to the wear and tear.

The robot said to Eric, "Do you require some assistance?"

How or why there was a robot in Tahiti was a matter not worth thinking about. Eric made a motion to give another step, but his legs finally failed him. Not waiting for an answer, the robot maiden placed Eric over her shoulder and started climbing up. Pania followed behind. The alternative route brought Eric to a computer room, with an elevated control panel. He was sat in a large chair. Before him, there were windows that overlooked something that resembled another facility. There was a large number of people in lab coats floating upside down. Eric naturally assumed they had drowned.

The robot maiden pressed some buttons and this room was further elevated, till they reached the seventh story. Over there, Eric met up with his family and a group of other survivors. After half an hour of waiting, a person was heard yelling for survivors. He was driving a boat, looking about the ruined buildings. Eric boarded it, with the help of the robot maiden and the other survivors. Eric chuckled wearily, as he recognized the face of the surfer who had injured him just a few hours ago.

Dog Head

I never met my uncle Juanci, but I heard plenty about him. It was common knowledge, that Jaunci was a taxidermist. His little hobby of stuffing animals was a tad too annoying for his current wife. One day, she left him. She was fed up of his army of dogs. Juanci one day started collecting and feeding whatever stray he ran into. The dogs would follow him without a leash all through-out the neighborhood. He was subject of both admiration and ridicule, but nobody was ever brave enough to critique him. One day, or another he noticed that one of his dogs was missing. From time to time, his strays would go to the street to roam.

After two days of not seeing this particular cur return, Jaunci decided to go looking for it. Eventually, he heard a fellow say to him, "You are looking for one of your dogs?"

"More or less," said Juanci.

"There is one that got inside my empty silo. I think you should get it out, cause it seems rabid, and it is your responsibility," said the farmer.

Juanci nodded and returned home. When he came back, he had a club. The farmer said nothing. Together, they went to face the rabid beast. Logic would stipulate that Juanci should have brought a gun instead of a stick. Even a bow and arrow would have been a bit more useful. The main issue was the nature of the island he inhabited. Only the government was allowed to have guns, and they rarely took care of such petty nonsense. Many of the locals believed that the cops carried empty pistols because they have never seen any of them shoot it.

The long and short of it is that Juanci went to fight the beast with a club. According to the farmer, the battle took place in the dead of night, and it was raining too. One cannot have an epic fight to the death, without a bit of rain. The weather circum-stances do not matter too much. Jaunci won, after clubbing the dog to death. As far as mercy killing went, he was not a good practitioner of the craft. It was not enough to club the poor dog to death, it was what he did with the dog afterwards that was a cause for concern. Juanci took the carcass of the dog home. He then applied himself to preserving the head. When he com-pleted this gruesome work, he mounted the head of the dog on a staff. From then on, he would roam about the town with the tro-phy dog head.

Uncle Juanci may have won the fight, but he lost the war. As mother told it, it was to be expected that the fellow got bitten in the battle. Rabies travels through the nerves, very slowly. It may take at most twenty years, but it will get you if you are not inoculated. Once it is too late, humans can expect to suffer agitation, combined with hallucination. Given enough time, a person slips into a coma and dies. It isn't the prettiest way to kick the bucket. Whether this happened to Uncle Jaunci nobody knows. One day, he swore off humanity, and was never seen or heard from again.

The Dream

I was wandering around the forest with some people. They were all roughly my age. Inside the hole of a tree, we discovered a dark room. The place was rather narrow, and darkly lit. One of my companions pulled a switch he fell on the floor. It was one of those switches that you find inside a power plant. When the light turned, one could see the stairs, spiraled upward. On the third floor, the building became more open. There were several fenced paths that led to three doors. They each had a few stairs. My companions entered ahead of me. Behind those doors was normal looking lab. Like those labs you see in any regular school. It resembled a bit the science lab at FIU or maybe the one in Barbara Goleman. On the right side, it was raised up like a stage. There stood several chairs, like those of the dentist. Beside each was a table with hundreds of particular instruments.

They seemed like the items used by a hairstylist. It had scissors and nail clippers. There were also several surgical items. On the left side of the lab, there was a classical chemistry lab. However, all the transparent basins were empty. There weren't any chemicals inside the beakers. Seeing this clean lab, my companions decided to rob the place.

I told them, "That is a stupid idea". Pointing to the surroundings, "the cleanness of the area implies that someone has used the place recently."

"Relax, the place looks deserted," said one of the companions. "The air is stagnant; there is no dust because this lab has not been opened for years."

"That's still no reason for looting the place" said I, looking about," I have an eerie feeling that something is watching us."

"You say this every time we enter the Kika's Mansion", said a different companion.

"Do as you like," said I leaving the lab," Whatever happens it will be you guys' fault!"

To the darkness I said, "I am not with them!"

While I was outside, one of the companions opened one of the drawers. Inside were several different sized and shape crystals. One of them raised it to his eye and looked through it. He started screaming like a madman. The others looked though the prisms.

"There something inside this room!!" they screamed as they began to flee. They kept holding a prism to their eyes trying to escape from that "something". I was not too worried. Unlike them, I could awaken whenever I felt like it. I was just waiting around to see what would happen. The companions took the rails from the fences. They used them to seal that "something" inside the lab.

Eventually, not even the crystals were needed to look at that something. The entire place began to be full of people. They looked normal; however, there was "something" wrong with them. At first, I thought they were zombies. It was later that I was told what was wrong with them. They surrounded my companions and escorted them into the lab. Inside, they were being treated. I thought they were being made into zombies. Their hair and nails were being cut and placed inside bottles. That is a type of voodoo ritual to deprive a human of their freewill. I think they were also being torn limped from limb or something else. They did scream a lot. I did not care much for them. I did warn them, after all.

Aside from being psychologically tortured, they were not in any real danger. I think they were simply suffering from dream pollution. The Mansion was manifesting something that was familiar to them. Dream pollution is very common inside the mansion.

As for me, I was greeted by the owner of the lab. He was hiding behind his physical human body. His fake form looked normal enough. I tried to look at his real form; however, something kept me from looking at it closely. I do not know if it was fear. I must say that it was too horrible to bear. His voice was gentle. He beckoned me to sit down. I sat down in one of those chairs. Around me, I could hear the screams of my companions. Behind me, I could feel his true form. He ritually washed my hair. He said this water would alter me. I was going to notice the difference when my body became more elongated. I do not remember what happened next. The dream got polluted with things of little significance. I had exited the Mansion.

THE FENCE

A curious incident occurred in one of the terraforming colonies. The cameras caught sight of a man about to sacrifice his son at an altar. The police droid scrambled at the scene to arrest the criminal. They had difficulties entering his home since it was completely locked off from the rest of the colony.

The father was arrested. The mother and child were relocated to a safe location. Murders were not uncommon in this new world. What was unusual was the ritualistic aspect of the murder.

With the advancement of science, religion had gone the way of the dodo. It was not as if the Government suppressed religion per say. Rather, the majority of the population only remembered that God existed when they reached old age. These days nobody cared enough about religion to kill for it.

The house of the man was examined. He was just your run of the mill subsistence farmer. He had lived an ordinary life, until a fence had been built around his property. The fence had been constructed by robots, following the grand design of the city planners.

Due to a human error, the fence had been built in such a way that the farmer was completely shut out from the rest of the colony.

Naturally, he had sent requests to have a door installed. Due to the bureaucratic nature of the current system, his request for a door kept getting shuffled around.

"So…after getting my demands ignored for so long I got desperate," explained the farmer, "I didn't have the necessary tools to break barrier that had been placed around my home. I tried digging under it, but the ground was far too solid. We wanted to leave our house, but the transports where at the other side of the barrier."

"While reading the good book, I came up with this insane idea," said the wife, "My husband would pretend to sacrifice his son at an altar. We placed the altar near the cameras with the hopes that the droids would break down the barrier to stop him."

"And they did," concluded the husband.

The human police officers examine the blade. It was dull and the blood belonged to a sheep. They fined the family for wasting their time. When they were finally allowed to return home, the barrier had been repaired. Everything they owned was at the other side of the impassable barrier.

The small family counted their blessings. They moved to a new planet that was not so heavily dependent on technology.

THE WASP

It was 2003 in Hialeah. A little girl age 8 was going to school with her grandmother. On her way to school, she took notice of a man that was starring at her. She didn't think much of it at the time. Strange men love to lurk about American Primary schools. Usually, they are up to no good, but that is just the world she lives in.
A week passes, and she completely forgets about the stranger, danger. She recognizes him again at her cousin's high school recital. With his presence there, she starts to suspect that the man is obsessed with her. She has seen dateline enough times to know that she is in danger.

Marlene tells her grandmother her concerns. The old woman naturally worries, but there is nothing she can do about the matter. On the third time she sees him, the grandmother decides to confront the stranger.

She felt confident about it, since this time they were in a public setting. They were in McDonalds to be more exact.

"Do I know you?" asked grandma Irina.

"Yes. I think so," said the stranger, "But I need a strand of your granddaughter's hair to be certain."

"Why is certainty so important to you?" asked Irina.

"Because certainty will make the world so much fascinating. Don't you think?" said the stranger giving a sly smile.

"Grandma. Is this weirdo bothering you?" asked Eufrasio, the oldest grandson.

"Eufrasio. You have gotten tall. You are the mirror image of your father," said the stranger happily.

"Yes. I know. Let's go," said Eufracio placing his hand on his grandmother's shoulder.

The stranger was a Wasp spy. He was carrying out a mission in the US, when he got completely distracted by something that his mind told him was impossible.

When he was a young child, he was known as the Penguin. He would regularly play with a brother and sister that went by the name of Eufracio and Lucero. The siblings, along with their family had one day left Cuba under mysterious circumstances.

The neighbors forgot about them. Nobody spoke of them. They were dead as far as the rest of Cuba was concerned. Only the Penguin remembered them. They were the only true friends he had in the entire world. Before their departure, they had given him their Nintendo and game collections.

As he got older and more jaded, he would often think about his childhood friends and wonder what they looked like, now that they were adults. He never expected to run into them again looking so…youthful.

The siblings only appeared to have aged eight years. According to his math, they should be in their twenties, not in their teens.

To prove that they were indeed his friends he needed their DNA. Unfortunately, there was no trace of them left in Cuba. Thankfully, there was the DNA of their cousin Marlene. A portion of her umbilical cord was being stored in the Genetics Center of Habana. All he needed was a single hair strand, or saliva to compare the two samples.

The family departed after this incident. As soon as they left, the Wasp went dumpster diving. He sent to the lab all the family's straws to run DNA analysis. The results prove what he suspected. They where indeed the family that had disappeared from

Cuba all those years ago.

Now, it was time to solve the next mystery. Why where they much younger than what they should be?

Theory 1: They age much slower than regular humans.

Theory 2: They had been adopted by aliens and put on ice for a couple of years, before being released back into the wild.

Theory 3: The family had time traveled into the future.

Theory 2 seemed like the most logical conclusion. After all, the route from Miami to Cuba passes by the Bermuda Triangle. It is a well-documented "fact" that Aliens adopt humans every so often in that region.

According to the Department of Homeland Security, the family had manifested in the US eight years ago. Due to the Wet foot, dry foot law, they were given residency, no questions asked. Since they were processed at the airport, it was assumed that they had flown there.

There were no actual records of them buying a plane ticket. Nobody remembers seeing them on board. Everyone just assumed that they had sneaked into the cargo hold.

So…where does that leave me? wondered the Wasp.

The Wasp attempted a few times to rekindle the friendship. Due to the age difference, all approaches were met with negative reactions by his former friends, and surrounding adults. As far as society was concerned, he was an adult that had an unhealthy obsession with two teenagers.

Common sense, eventually triumph. He distanced himself from the situation with the hope that he could befriend them again, once they came of age.

The Last Zombie

The siblings awoke when they heard a shuffling outside their door. For the last two years, the family of 3 has been living sequestered inside their apartment complex. The building has fallen into disrepair and the walls are moldy. Just one floor below, the undead are continuing with their rhythmic march. Left, right, left right. They walk from the window to the wall, and back again. They have been like that for weeks ever since they became aware that there are 3 humans still alive in that building.

Their elderly mother lies gravely ill. It is debatable what is making her sick. Her teen children are not doctors. The older brother suspects that it could be the mold. Even the walls are starting to resemble the undead. It is almost as if the apartment itself has become a zombie.

With no other recourse, the siblings decide to chance it. They cannot imagine living without their mother. The siblings create a makeshift stretcher with a broom, a mop and a cloth. They gently place their mother on the stretcher, stuffing their coats with what little provisions remain. They shuffle slowly out of the apartment.

They are so thin, and close to death that the undead naturally assume that they are one of them. After walking for what felt like an eternity, they ran into other human survivors.

Apparently, there is a safe zone in a nearby international airport. The siblings join this small caravan. After traveling on foot for a week, the mother loses consciousness. She is still breathing. For now.

Against their better judgement, they depart post haste. When they arrive to the airport, they find human life, but also death. Slowly, carefully, they push through the mass of zombies. They make it to the entrance, but the door is naturally locked.

They bang on the door. The guard inside looks through the peephole. He sees the siblings, the stretcher, and 100 zombies behind them. Even if they are human, the fact that they are not being attacked probably means that they are infected.

Just when all hope seems lost. A booming voice yells, "Open the door! I bring the cure!"

This very human, loud voice draws the attention of the zombies. They begin to swarm around an armored truck. With the promise of a cure, the metal door opens.

Army officers manifest, brandishing their weapons.

"We are not infected! We are not infected!" said the siblings trembling.

Since zombies do not speak, they avoid getting shot at. Whether that stranger had a cure or not, it matters not. His intervention allowed the siblings to enter the safe zone. They bring their mother to the medical bay. She will live, for now.

A week passed after that incident. The man with the cure was searched. All he had on his person was a book. The survivors cursed him for making them waste ammo. His presence was being tolerated for the time being.

"But I do have a cure," said the man with the book, "Let me try it out at the very least with those who are infected. And then, you will see."

The general in charge of the operation decided to call the man on his bluff. He was taken to the infected ward. There men and women strapped in chairs were waiting for the inevitable to happen. The man with the book went up to one, and he proceeded to chant. The chanting was in a language that was unfamiliar.

All who watched him perform were of the general opinion that he had gone insane or was a charlatan. Much to everyone's surprise the infected no longer showed signs of zombification.

"I told you I had a cure. Didn't I?" said the stranger proudly.

"How does your prayer book work exactly? Is the book magic? Or just the words. If someone else recites your spell, will they get cured?" asked the general.

"The power resides in me, only. The book is just a mnemonic device. I haven't memorized the spell yet," said the magus proudly.

And so it came to pass that a sickness created by science was cured through a magical intervention. As the years went on, the siblings realized how the spell truly functioned. The magus took the sickness into himself, thus curing the individual of the zombie virus.

Once the entire world was cured, the spellcaster became the last zombie. The world debated as to what to do with the zombie. Some wanted to bury the stiff, to be completely rid of the virus. Others wanted to preserve him, to use him again should the virus manifest again.

Even with his rotten brain, the zombie magus was eternally casting his spell. While the world debated, the siblings were dutifully taking care of the Zombie Magus. They would wash him, clothe him, and feed him animal brains. His body was in such good condition that you needed to look closely to realize that he was undead. The sister would walk him in the morning, while the brother had the afternoon shift.

During one of their morning walks, an anarchist threw a grenade at the zombie Magus. The Magus pushed the sister aside. Thus, only he was exposed to the full blast of the explosion. The body was completely burned to a crisp, with only the bones remaining.

 The anarchist was immediately arrested and thrown in prison. Once again, the world debated whether he should go be punished for killing something that was technically dead. Since a being made of flesh and blood happened to be nearby, he was charged with manslaughter.

During the trial, the bones of the zombie Magus were brought in as evidence. Much to everyone's surprise, the bones sat up. The hollow of the eyes began to glow a sinister deep blue.

"Much better," said the skeleton Magus. Without the flesh, the spirit was not burdened by the zombie virus.

"How!" exclaimed everyone.

"I cannot allow myself to die, until I finish expiating my sins," said the skeleton Magus.

After suffering his first "death", the skeleton Magus disappeared for a time. When he returned, he had new white magic spells. He cured everything from cancer to bunions. He worked himself to the bone for more than three decades. When he finally laid down to rest, nobody doubted that he had finally succeeded in expiating sins, whatever those sins might be.

With him truly gone, the siblings took an interest in discovering who that Magus was or where he had come from. It became impossible to separate fact from fiction. The only thing that they knew for certain were his miracles, and that he had sinned.

THE ACCIDENT

It had been 30 years since Alec's parents died in a car accident. He didn't allow himself to mourn his parents. Since their death, his life had become an eternal struggle to secure a future for himself and his siblings. Now, he is the owner of a multimillion-dollar company. Despite this success he feels empty. He takes a deep breath before leaving the limousine.

He is currently in a rural hospital in Cairo. He is there to bring a big check, and to pretend that he cares about the fates of the patients rotting away in this understaffed facility. The head doctor gives him a tour. He listens to the translator, with a fake smile painted on his thin lips.

He stops when he takes notice of a coma patient. The patient was still alive because her organs were going to be harvested. The doctors were in the process of analyzing her compatibility and negotiating the prices for her body parts.

"What happened to…her?" asked Alec after reading the chart.

"She crossed the street without looking. Very tragic," said the translator, "She had no ID on her. Nobody has come looking for the wench."

He left the room to continue with his tour. On his way out, he passed by that patient's room again. During his stay in Cairo, he got into the habit of visiting her on a daily basis. He got so emotionally invested in the fate of that stranger that he ended up taking her back to the States.

The months passed. The nameless patient continued to blissfully dream, unaware of the existence of her benefactor. Alec has gotten into the habit of sharing his unfiltered thoughts with the comatose maiden. At times, he feels like she is the only person he can be truly honest with.

After half a year, the maiden awakens. This was an unexpected development. He had mixed feelings about it. He SHOULD be happy that she is recovering. However, if she gets well enough to leave, he will be once again alone with the darkness gnawing away at his very soul.

The first words that she speaks sounds like gibberish to him. He summons a translator versed in all the living languages spoken in the Middle East. He fails to understand her words. After summoning various translators and the doctor, they arrive at the conclusion that her speech center was affected because of her accident.

Alec breathes a sigh of relief when he learns that the woman can't understand what he is saying. She can be his confidant again. The days passed lazily by with the maiden gaining more strength. It is the doctor's general opinion that she has traumatic amnesia, on top of the speech impediment. She easily becomes frightened at the sights of the familiar like television, or lights. Attempts to teach her what she has forgotten are progressing at a snail's pace. She only bothers to come out from under the bed whenever Alec visits. Despite not understanding his words, she feels that he is an ally.

"Alec. Are you in love with that lunatic?" asked Damian, Alec's little brother.

"She isn't a lunatic. Her mind is just jungled up because of the car accident," said Alec casually.

"Aha! So, you do like her!" said Lisa laughing, the middle sister, "HAHA! Admit it!"

"I suppose I can't blame you, even with the scars on her face and body, she is still a very attractive, natural beauty," said Damian stating a fact.

"But what are you planning to tell board?" asked Lisa.

"Forget the board! What are you going to tell ICE when they come asking about that paperless woman you smuggled into the States?" asked Damian.

"He will tell them that he is rich, and that he can do whatever he wants," said Lisa.

"Sigh…What a bother," said Alec leaving his siblings to go check up on the maiden that was now living under his roof.

This was another reason why he preferred the company of that nameless maiden. His siblings only ever spoke to him to tease him. When he entered the room, he saw that one of the walls was covered with hieroglyphics. He began to fancy that the maiden was probably an archeologist that got lost in the desert. This would explain her familiarity with that dead writing.

Through her writing, he was able to make himself understood. Sadly, she knew absolutely nothing about herself.

Since she needed a name, he started calling her Maria, like his dead mother. Like before, he would rant about the things that bothered him. Maria would sit quietly, holding his hand to reassure him of their bond.

Nobody was surprised when Alec announced his engagement to Maria. The two lived happily ever after, thanks in part to the fact that Maria never recovered her memories. As the saying goes, ignorance is bliss.

MY FATHER PRINCE LINDWORM

Once upon a time, in a world without humans, there lived a Magus and his son. The pair resided in a sleepy town away from the excitement of the big city Brunhilda. Despite his talents, the Magus made it his business not to stand out. He taught only easy spells, to novice farmer mages for a pittance. He always kept others at a distance, including his own son.

This is not to say that Magus Lind was cold to his son. Rather, Lind avoided the topic of his past like the plague. His son Culebra had vague memories of his infancy. In those memories, his father always looked miserable. He remembered nothing of his mother.

One day, Lind summoned his son to his sickbed.

"My son. I don't think I am surviving this illness. Before I expire, go to this address in Brunhilda. Write this number on the front door, and knock trice fast, trice slow, and trice fast again," instructed Lind.

Culebra ran out of his farm at full sprint. He didn't even bother to saddle his horse. He arrived to the Capital city of Brunhilda. Under other circumstances, he would have taken in the sights. After running about in circles, a knight helped him find the address he was looking for.

It was a residential home. The nursemaid with the children eyed him with suspicion. He looked completely out of place with his rural overalls. He went to the open door. He read his father's instructions.

Since time was of the essence, he decided not to overthink things. He bitted his thumb to write in blood. At this the mayordomo came to ask him what the hell he was doing. Culebra stoically ignored the man. When a servant tried to push him out of the house, Culebra grew his copper scales, and he flashed his red eyes at the servant.

He knocked on the door. After the final knock, the blood began to glow gold. Soon, the door was bathed in light. The golden numbers changed form to create a pentagram. From the pentagram emerged a petite hag.

"My father is dying! Please help!" said Culebra.

The tiny hag got on all fours. She changed into the form of a dragon. She grabbed hold of the horse with both her claws, while she instructed Culebra to mount her. The pair flew back to the farm.

He guided the dragon hag to the sickroom. She gave medicine to his father.

"Is he better? Is he going to live?" asked Culebra.

"He will live. For now," said the hag solemnly, "But you need to get used to the idea that your father's days are numbered."

Two years passed after this incident, the dragon hag Brunhilda stayed with Lind, until he breathed his final breath. She couldn't cure him, but she at least, she made his final days painless.

"Your father has breathed his final breath," said Brunhilda solemnly, "It was his wish that you wouldn't see his dead body. He wants you to remember him as he lived, and not how he died. He also wants a closed cast funeral. And cremation."

"Are you planning to bar my entrance, Brunhilda?" asked Culebra caustically.

"No. I only hope that you honor your father's wishes," said Brunhilda stepping aside, "He has good reasons to make these demands. For your sake, please do as he asks."

Culebra entered the sickroom. He was not going to believe that his father was dead, until he saw him in the flesh. He cried when he saw the peaceful, wrinkled face, the familiar long silver hair. When he took his dead father in his arms, he realized that something was missing…

For as long as Culebra could remember, his father resembles an elf, with elegant limbs, the pointed ears and everything.

As Brunhilda explained, this was a well-crafted illusion that Lind designed to hide his draconic heritage. As soon as Lind died, the illusion died with him. His son Culebra was finally able to see what his father's body truly looked like.

His true form was snakelike, with an elflike torso, but no arms. Instead of long legs, he had small, draconic three toe claws, small dove like wings, and a long skinny tail.

As he was dressing his father for the open casket funeral, Culebra couldn't help, but remark, "He looks like King Lindworm."

Culebra was familiar with the tale. When he was small, his father used to read to him every night the fairy tale of King Lindworm. A queen wanted a child, so she asked a witch for help. A witch gave her two roses: White Rose for Male, Red Rose for Female. Since she couldn't decide she ate both roses. The queen ended up giving birth to twins. One of the sons was the Lindworm. He was born accursed because his mother didn't bother to follow the instructions to the letter.

It was thanks to this tale that Culebra learned the importance of following instructions. While the Lindworm of the fairytale was able to live a normal life, after his curse was lifted, Culebra's father did not.

"I guess this explains why father never got married or even take on a woman," said Culebra sadly, during the wake.

The funeral progressed at a leisurely pace. Before he had a

chance to light the funeral pyre, a dozen knights broke through the funeral procession.

"Is it him?" asked the knight.

"Yes, that is him," said a different knight.

Brunhilda breathed in deeply. Before she got a chance to exhale her flames, the knight had formed a protective barrier around the funeral pyre.

"You are interrupting my father's funeral!" barked Culebra caustically. His dragon scales grew for good measure.

"Father...you say," said the knight, "Come with us. Then, everything, will make sense when you speak with our King."

In the end, Culebra had no other choice but to leave with the knights. They had taken his father's body after all. After a day's journey, the party met up with a Magus. They were teleported to a castle in another continent.

The King left this throne to identify the body. Once the light of recognition fell upon his face, he broke into a crying fit. A new funeral was arranged. This one came with all the pomp and glamour typical of royalty. Instead of cremation, Lind's remains were lay to rest in the same family crypt as his parents.

After it was all over, Culebra was taken to the King's private chambers. The King had many questions for Culebra, while he needed answers as well.

"I take it that my father Cullen was a prince," started saying Culebra. His father's true name was Cullen.

"He was King for a time too, but one day he abandoned his wife… your mother," explained the King, "He returned home, asking me for help. When I asked what was wrong, he called your mother a child eating monster. He needed my help to hide from the demon. It shames me to admit that instead of helping your father, I forced him to return home with his wife. That was the last time I saw both of you."

"Does my mother still live?" asked Culebra.

"No," said the King.

"I see," said Culebra after a long pause.

"Don't you want to know her name?" asked the King.

"Not really. There is no point in getting to know the past of a child-eating monster," said Culebra getting up. He stopped once he got to the door, "My father's early youth…was it a happy one?"

"Yes. He lived a good life, up until he got married," said the King.

Cullen was born on a bright spring morning. Both his parents were dragon halflings. Due to his unique anatomy and the fact that he was born premature, he was raised to believe that he was made of glass.

It was for this reason that his younger brother Carvin was named crown prince. Not that Cullen minded or cared about his Princely duties. He was only interested in learning magic. His unique position as Prince gave him the chance to learn all spells, both the good and the bad.

Sadly, he was only ever able to conjure up illusions. His fire spells did not burn. His water spells did not wet anything.

King Carvin remembered fondly how his brother would bring to life fairy tales, with his illusion magic. They used to be close when they were children. However, Carvin started to distance himself from his older brother, when he tasted the forbidden fruit.

After siring a dozen bastard princes, Carvin was pressured into marrying someone of his rank. To avoid marriage, he insisted that his older brother should marry first. Since it was tradition for the oldest sibling to wed first.

"Your mother was the only monarch willing to marry someone so deformed looking," explained King Carvin, "The courtship lasted for almost a decade. It was only after father died that my brother agreed to marry the…Queen."

The marriage started peacefully enough. King Cullen would sleep with his wife whenever she was fertile. The rest of the time he did whatever he felt like. He must have been quite lonely, or love starved when he asked to raise the egg that was laid from their union.

When the egg hatched, the Queen was disappointed to note that she had another son. That same night the Queen devoured her newborn infant, under the excuse of needing more energy to produce a new egg.

The same thing occurred twice. Mercifully, those two other times the infants had been born dead. When Culebra was born, Cullen lied to his wife. He used his illusions to make her perceive her male son, as a girl. This bought Cullen time.

"I met your father in the kitchen. At the time, I was doing a residency as a palace cook to learn new recipes. After suffering from a crying fit, he told me of his pitiful situation. So, I got him out of there," said the dragon hag, "When your mama came looking for the three of us, I killed her in self-defense. To avoid dealing with the drama of that creature's death, your father decided to relocate to another continent, with the hope of being out of sight and out of mind."

"I never stopped looking for my brother," said King Carvin.

"We know. Your knights passed by your brother trice, but he never revealed himself because you betrayed him when he needed you the most," concluded Brunhilda, "Have you learned everything you needed to know about your father?"

"Yes," said Culebra getting up to make his way to the family mausoleum.

"Wait, nephew. I want to know about your life, and the life of my brother in the countryside," said King Carvin grabbing hold of Culebra's hand.

"I would have been more than happy to answer your questions had you not stolen my father's body," said Culebra shrugging away from that stranger's touch.

"Nobody stole anything. You and your father belong here at home, with us, with his real family. I am sorry I wasn't there for him while in life, but I promise to take care of you from now on. Alright, son," said King Carvin.

Culebra was escorted to his father's former suite. For days, he laid down on his father's bed without eating or taking a drink. It was his stomach that motivated him enough to leave his room. He ate, drank himself stupid, before returning to his room. He had officially entered his mourning period. Whenever the King could spare a moment, he would interrogate his nephew about Cullen's past.

Life as a rural Magus had been modest, happy one. The small home that Brunhilda had gotten for them met all their necessities. Since Mages were rare, Cullen most of the time taught the ABCs to illiterate adults and children. When his strength allowed it, he assisted in the fields as well. If the harvest was bad, Cullen went to the city to summon Brunhilda to aid him.

"We have met many times Cullen, but I am not one to wear the same fleshy face twice," said Brunhilda.

"Just out of curiosity, why are you named after the Capital of Muldred?" asked King Carvin.

"The real question you should be asking is why is the city named after me?" said Brunhilda casually, "Well, almost after me. Brunhilda is not my real name anyway. It is actually Brrumm, Hiss Hass!"

Brunhilda stayed with him during the following months, always near, but far away enough to let him mourn his father in peace. One day King Carvin caught his nephew sober. He took him to the empty throne room to have a serious conversation.

"Nephew...how do you like the castle?" asked King Carvin.

"It is alright," said Culebra.

"Have you given much thought about your future?" asked Carvin.

"Not really. I never pictured my life without my father," said Culebra stating a fact.

"Do you have any wife or children?" asked King Carvin.

"I have a few..." said Culebra.

"Children?" asked King Carvin.

"Both," said Culebra laughing, "The fifth church of Muldred allows polygamy. I haven't seen the wenches in month, they must be worried sick about me."

"Hah! You remind me of myself when I was your age. But when you say wives, you mean girlfriends. Do you not?" asked King Carvin.

He wanted to know if Culebra had any legitimate children. According to his spies, Culebra didn't have an official marriage license. He also frequented the bedchambers of married and unmarried women. He was a libertine in every sense of the word.

"What do you think of your nieces?" asked King Carvin.

"They are alright. A bit giggly, but I suppose they are not used to my plebian ways," said Culebra raising an eyebrow.

"Which one do you like best?" asked King Carvin.

"The red headed one," said Culebra casually. She was the only one he could maintain a prolonged conversation with.

"Perfect. I will make the necessary arrangements," said King Carvin getting up.

"Wait a minute! Wait a minute! I am not marrying your daughter," said Culebra.

"Why not? I am getting on in years, and I can think of no better candidate to sit on my soon to be empty throne. You have royal blood from both your parents, and every Kingdom needs a King. If we play our cards right, you can even annex your mother's territory," said King Carvin.

"Goodbye, King Carvin," said Culebra walking past his uncle.

He didn't get far, with the knights blocking the entrance. He was escorted back to his room. Once again, he was a prisoner in a gilded cage. Only this time, he was old enough to recognize the severity of the situation.

"I should have done a close casket funeral," said Culebra more to himself. He thought of his poor father. He was probably born malformed due to the inbreeding that is common among royals. His parents were probably first cousins, or uncle and niece.

"Are you ready to head home?" asked Brunhilda.

"Yes…" said Culebra.

Brunhilda wrote into the mirror some numbers. She then knocked on the mirror. The surface rippled like water. She entered within and she beckoned Culebra to follow. They moved through the mirror world, until they found their way to the family mausoleum. They returned to the physical world using a gilded stone tablet as a reflective surface.

He opened his father's grave to retrieve what was left of the body. He was surprised to see how little it had withered away. However, the stench alone sufficed to remind him that his father was indeed dead. The trio returned home. He was finally able to cremate his father. He gathered the ashes into a small pouch that he tied to his belt.

"You do realize that they are going to come looking for you," said Brunhilda.

"I am not too concerned," said Culebra shrugging his shoulders, "I may not have magic, but thanks to hundreds of jealous husbands, I have become an expert at hiding from those who wish to do me harm."

FROZEN HEART

O nce upon a time, in the frozen lands of Albion there lived a hermit at the roof of the world. The hermit had retired from the world after losing all his sons in the war of succession. He fished or hunted to sustain himself. In the short summer, he grew crops. Every night, he prayed for the sweet release of death. Today, his wish almost came true.
While ice fishing, the ground beneath him cracked. He struggled to return to the surface. His frozen limbs felt like they were on fire. Soon, he no longer felt anything at all. As he got closer to the bottom of the lake, he saw a blue light. The light blinked twice.

When he came to, he was back on the surface of the ice. Instead of being happy, he cursed the Gods for prolonging his miserable existence. Why was he cursed to live, while his son died in a pointless battle?

He returned home to rest and eat his meal. The following day he returned to the lake. His religion compelled him to give thanks to the Gods and make a proper offering to whatever deity had extended his miserable existence. He made a shrine by the lakeside. He said a prayer and sacrificed a deer.

The following morning when he returned to the shrine, he noticed that something had changed. His sacrifice was gone. In its place, there was an egg. The hermit picked up the egg, before looking about. The egg was the size of a volleyball.

"If this is a joke, it is not funny," yelled the hermit, "Do you hear me! It is not funny! Come out here. You bastards before I bloody break your stupid egg!!"

He raised the egg and he held it up with the intention of smashing it. In response to his threat, the ice began to rumble and crack. He screamed when he saw horns coming out of the lake. He ran back home like the devil was coming after him. In his haste to escape, he took the egg.

He closed the door and windows. The rumbling got closer and closer. A frost began to build up against the window and beneath the door.

"If you do not want the egg, there is no need to break it," hissed a voice from the other side of the door. It was as soothing as it was deadly.

"Are? Are you? Are you? What demon or God are you?" asked the hermit hiding behind the couch.

"I am very tired. Just give me my egg, so, I can return to my lake," hissed the creature.

The hermit cautiously opened the door. He saw a large blue eye at the entrance; an elongated face covered in scales and an open claw resting on the floor. He cautiously placed the egg on the open claw. The ice dragon returned to her lake.

The hermit was left quite shaken by the experience. On this rare occasion, he descended the mountains to visit the town below to get a stiff drink. He asked the locals about the creature that lived in Lake Boreas. The locals were not surprised by his tale. For as long as they could remember, there was a monster living beneath its ice depths.

Knight errands, armies and even Mages had attempted to slay the monster. None had lived to tell the tale. The locals had learned to live with the creature. It was neither a friend, nor an ally. If the creature was in a good mood, it would grant you a boom. If Boreas was hungry, he would eat you. Most of the time he was hungry…So, it was advisable to stay clear of his hunting grounds.

"You have gotten lucky, so far my friend," joked the locals.

"Why do you think nobody lives up there?" laughed the barmaid.

He had only lived in Albion for a decade. He only took residence near the lake because it met all his needs. It provided fish and deer. There was nobody living nearby but was within walking distance of the nearest village.

He returned home. Try as he might, he has difficulties sleeping. During a particularly strong blizzard, he hears footsteps approaching. He hears the same hiss as before. When he opens the door, he his thankful to see a mortal woman. Upon closer inspection, he realizes that this is no ordinary woman.

She is barefoot for one. She seems barely aware of the cold.

"What are you doing here missy?" asked the hermit.

"I came to grant your wish," said the maiden entering the hut.

"What wish? I haven't wished for anything," said the hermit.

"Right now. Deep, in your heart of hearts, you are wishing for death," said the maiden, "Take my hand, and I will grant you the sweet relief you long for."

"As…tempting an offer, my Gods will not allow me such a coward's death. And, despite, my many sins, I still hope to meet my children in the afterlife," said the hermit opening the door for the maiden.

The maiden walked towards the door. Before stepping out, she stabbed the hermit with a knife. The hermit awoke with a start. He checked his chest for damages. He breathed in a sign of relief. It had been a nightmare and nothing more. The same dream repeated itself every night for a month. The way he died always varied, but it always started with the visiting maiden.

He returned to Lake Boreas. He made a shrine and a sacrifice with the hope of appeasing the creature that lurked within its ice waters.

That night when he slept, the maiden in his dreams said, "You could just move if you are so afraid of me?"

"Do you want me to leave?" asked the hermit.

"No. I find your thoughts, fears and dreams rather amusing," said the maiden.

"So, you giving me nightmares is your idea of fun?" barked the hermit.

"Yes. I can give you more pleasant dreams if you find a way to amuse me in the waking world," said the maiden before departing.

The hermit awoke the following day. He remembered this dream quite vividly. That morning he began to weigh the pros and the cons of moving. He was still strong enough to settle elsewhere. However, the move entailed dealing with many unknown elements. If he stayed in Lake Boreas, he at least had the guarantee that he was not going to deal with any unwanted visitors. Nobody in their right mind wanted to live near a temperamental giant, magic dragon.

"I am not giant. I am just about average as far as my kin is concerned," said the dragon with telepathy.

The creature was awake, just beneath the waves of the deep Lake Boreas.

"Are there others like you?" asked the hermit creeping closer to the edge of the lake.

"In this world? No. In others yes, we dragons like getting around," said the dragon, "I can tell you all about it, if you tell me about your world."

The hermit told the dragon about the Kingdom of Muldred. He spoke of his previous life as a knight, and how he had lost his children in a senseless War of Succession. When the old King was poisoned, his sons fought each other for the empty throne. The Kingdom split into factions around each Prince. On the meantime, the Bastard Prince was gathering an army. When the Bastard Prince felt that his enemy was weak enough, he slaughtered everyone, stupid enough to stand on his path towards the empty throne.

"…My oldest son was stupid enough to stand against the Bastard Prince Julius. He led me and his brothers to their death. I do not begrudge Prince Julius. My sons attacked and he defended himself. I didn't raise my sword against the Prince, so, I was spared. I survived where others died because of my cowardice…So, now you know my story," said the hermit.

"How very amusing! Tonight, you will have sweet dreams. What are you in the mood for? Do you want a nature walk? Random images? Do you want a banquet? Do you want to know how it feels to fly? Do you wish to spend time with your loved ones? Or are you in the mood for something spicy?" asked the dragon.

"What does a dragon know of the spiciness of mortals?" asked the Hermit looking over the edge of the boat. The dragon was so close to the surface that he could see its blue eyes glowing in the watery icy depths.

"I can read people like books. Every mind and every heart is open to me. I know of your spice and the particular spices of those who live within my territory," explained the dragon.

"I will believe it when I see it," dared the hermit.

That night the dragon gave the hermit a spicy dream. She showed him how much she knew of the bedroom rituals of lesser beings. Things continued like this for a couple of months. The hermit would regale the dragon with his war stories. In exchange, she gave him pleasant dreams.

"So…tell me dragon. What did they used to call you?" asked the hermit at a certain point.

"I have been called many things throughout the ages. You may call me Boreas or Albion of the North. This is what everyone in these lands refer to me as," explained the dragon.

"I was called Amberose," said Amberose, "That is what my ma decided to call me. What did your ma used to call you?"

"She used to call me…You bastard! Stop stealing my egg! I am going to kill you when I catch up to you. It was a pretty popular name among dragons back in my home world," said Boreas laughing dryly. Bubbles rose to the surface illustrating her good humor.

"I am sorry," said Amberose apologetically.

"Don't be. You only need to apologize for your sins, not for the sins of another," said Boreas dryly.

That night Boreas shared her memories with Amberose. She was born and raised in captivity. Her entire life revolved around eating, working out, mating and laying eggs. The only break in her monotonous existence happened whenever her caretakers would gossip about their lives. Had she known that she was strong, she would have escaped captivity centuries ago. Just like the noble horse, she never questioned her reality.

One day, all captive dragons were set free. By then, it was too late for her. She was too domesticated to fit among dragons, and she was too dragon to live among mortals. Since she was getting on in years, she decided to find a peaceful place to drop dead, away from anything that could do her harm. The teleport spell led her to this location that met all her requirements.

"This lake has more than enough fish to keep me fed. There is not a dragon as big or a strong as me in the entire planet and there are nearby mortals that I can spy on to amuse myself," explained Boreas, "Every couple of decades a knight gets stupid enough to challenge me. I see that as an opportunity to vary my diet."

"Wow…Our lives sucked," said Amberose bitterly.

"Speak for yourself, Amberose! I for one am quite content with the life I led. My only regret is that I was never able to raise any of my chicklets," said Boreas as the surface water of the lake started freezing.

"Is that why you gave me the egg? You were hoping I would… fertilize it?" asked Amberose.

"The egg is already fertilized. All I need is for someone to raise it, while I watch from afar. I am too old to raise a chicklet. Just crawling out of the lake is a struggle," said Boreas sighing deeply.

"You are not the only one who is too old to raise a kid," said Amberose dryly.

"But think of the possibilities! If we play our cards right, we can raise the chicklet to adulthood, before dropping dead. That way we can both make our wish come true. I can raise a chick through you, and you won't have lived longer than all your children," said Boreas happily.

Amberose decided to sleep on it. That night he dreamt that he was teaching his sons how to shoot the bow. He had this and many other dreams relating to his previous life as a husband, and father. Wouldn't it be wonderful to try it one last time, and not leave the world full of regrets?

The following morning, he went to speak with the dragon.

"So…is that like your last egg? Or can you still make more?" asked Amberose. He fancied that he wanted to raise a kid of his flesh and blood.

"This is the last egg. It is small and puny. If we are lucky, a child the size of a mortal babe will hatch," said the dragon.

"Oh…" said Amberose sadly.

"If you bathe the egg in your blood, it will acquire your essence. It will be half me, half you, half the other guy," explained Boreas.

"Good to know," said Amberose smiling happily.

"Will it grow up as big as you?" asked Amberose.

"No. A dragon will only grow 100 times bigger than its egg. And mine is a very tiny egg. It was all I could manage considering my age. But that is good, yes, with a bit of glamour, it will be able to live among mortals," said Boreas happily.

Amberose this time accepted the gift of the egg. He bathed it in his own blood, while he prayed for this miracle to happen.

On his way back home, he began to do mental calculations. For an egg this size, the adult child would be more than six feet tall, maybe seven. This was all well and good, considering that Farum was a land of trolls and giants. He needed to get started on a crib, and toys. A baby needs toys, as well as clothing. And books! It is too soon to be thinking about books.

What if the egg doesn't hatch? No. It is best not to think about it. For now, he will get lost in that sweet illusion called Hope. Hope? That could be a good name for the kid.

The winter passed sweetly enough with Amberose preparing everything for the baby. He wrapped the egg in sealskin fat, and fur. He then strapped it against his chest to incubate it with his own body. The first thing he did was carve up a crib, followed by toys. He hunted rabbits to make soft clothing for the baby. He also added a cage to his fireplace to keep the little kid from jumping into it.

Everything was perfect, until he got unexpected visitors. There was an army marching through the village. They had stopped there to resupply, before continuing their march. Some of the scouts had wandered into his territory.

"Do you live by yourself, grandpa?" asked the scout that had barged into his house. Since he never got visitors, Amberose had never bothered to put a lock on his door.

"Occasionally, yes," said Amberose.

"Did the kid not survive the winter?" asked the scout.

"He is still in the oven. He will get here when he gets here," said Amberose.

"Congratulations!" said a different scout, "Truly! I didn't expect a grandpa like you to still be full of piss and vinegar. Who is the unfortunate lady you cursed to live at the edge of the world?"

"I didn't curse anyone. We are just two hermits that live a stone's throw away from each other. Proximity breeds familiarity…as well as other things," said Amberose, "If you are curious about the missus, she is currently fishing beneath the lake."

The scouts left to fish by the lakeside. To get rid of them quickly, Boreas made the harvest plentiful and easy. The scouts left with more food than they could actually carry. The army resupplied and left after a tense week. With them gone, life resumed its normal flow.

"That was close," commented Amberose. Since the dragon had not eaten them, he fancied that she was not as powerful as she claimed to be. Perhaps, she had grown too old to fight.

"Are you still thinking about those soldiers?" asked Boreas, "Forget about them. We live too far away for them to bother about us."

"They could hunt us for sport," said Amberose worried, "Living so far away from civilization is a double edge sword."

"If they worry you so much, just set up traps," suggested Boreas.

"I don't want to needlessly injure the animals we depend on for food," said Amberose.

"Sigh…what a bother. I guess it falls on me to take care of the problem," said Boreas rising to the surface.

The water shifted and ebbed. This was followed by a claw. She handed a bunch of rocks with runes scratched into them.

"Magic traps. Place them upside down, so they won't notice the runes. They will hurt anyone that comes to our territory with wicked intentions," said Boreas.

"I don't know. If we started killing outsiders, it will draw needless attention," said Amberose worried.

"Not if you chug them in the lake. Folks disappear in the woods all the time. You are overthinking things!" whined Boreas.

"And you don't think things through enough," nagged Amberose.

"You are the war expert. You figure it out!" said Boreas sinking beneath the waves.

In the end, Amberose placed the traps in key locations. The magic traps created a holes of various depts. They were designed to injure but not kill. This was subtle enough to help mask the fact that hole's placement was intentional.

Five years passed uneventfully. Amberose was starting to suspect that the egg was infertile. Even if the egg was infertile, it was a nice dream that they were both sharing. It broke the monotony of the day to make plans for a future that he fancied would never materialize.

"The locals think that I have gone insane," said Amberose.

"Sanity is overrated," said Boreas, "One has to be insane to be in a good mood while surrounded by crippling poverty."

"If money wasn't an issue, what would you like to buy?" asked Amberose.

"I can read your mind, or don't you remember," said Boreas, "I am not going to tell you what I want, because I know that you are going to be stupid enough to go get it."

"If it isn't too big or expensive, I could just hire someone to get the item for me. That way I won't have to leave the house for too long," suggested Amberose.

Boreas was quiet for a time. Eventually, she said, "I want flower seeds. Any type will do. I grow bored of seeing the same two types of flowers."

Amberose went into his hut and he lifted some floorboards. He had a gold stashed away for emergencies. Getting some flower seeds to make his dragon wife happy seemed like emergency enough. Wife? Life was strange indeed. He had come up north to get away from the world. Instead, he had discovered love, and he was incubating the next generation. Even if the egg never hatched, they shared quite a beautiful dream.

Amberose pre-ordered the seeds from the local merchant. All that was left was to play the waiting game. That evening he visited the church. There was a wedding going on. It seemed like a nice change of pace to eat something that someone else had hunted. While there, he paid the priest to visit him at his lake. He wanted to make Boreas an honest dragon woman.

This surprised the local priest. He went to the hut the following evening to quench his curiosity. He was naturally confused when he saw Amberose standing before the lake all by himself.

"My wife is a little shy. I hope that you don't mind that she won't show herself," said Amberose while staring at the lake.

"Right…" said the priest raising an eyebrow.

"She. She can hear us just fine. So, do your part, and we will the same as well," urged Amberose.

The priest did his duty before returning to town. As far as the townies were concerned, Amberose had finally gone insane or his wife was a shy Magus. The short spring came, followed by summer. The merchant with the seeds decided to personally deliver his package to save the mad hermit the trip. He was also curious to see if the man had survived the winter.

When he arrived, he was surprised to hear a baby crying.

As he drew closer to the hut, he saw the old hermit with a baby in his arms. With his foot, he was pushing a small crib left and right, to lull the other baby to sleep.

"Ah…Good. Thank you for the delivery. With the new babies, we had completely forgotten about the seeds," said the hermit.

"Right…" said the merchant coming closer to examine the children.

The hermit reached into his pocket to pay the merchant. He then said, "If it is not too much trouble, can you deliver me a second crib. The one I made is too small to house two children."

"Certainly. Where is the missus by the way?" asked the merchant. What he really wanted to ask, Did the missus survive the birth?

"She is here, with us, but she is shy among strangers," said Amberose.

The merchant though he saw a figure peeping its head behind the curtain. As much as he wanted to see the missus, he didn't want to anger a well-paying customer. After the egg hatched, Amberose and Boreas lived what was left of their lives, happily ever after.

THE MAD ELF'S SACRED MASK

Deucalion was the son of an elven blacksmith. He enchanted the weapons his father made. While clearing his dead mother's clutter, Deucalion happened upon the Sacred Mask. This was a relic that had been passed down from generation to generation. He studied the mask with bored curiosity. The interior of the mask was inscribed with unfamiliar runes. Until he figured out what the mask did, he decided to use it as decoration.
He placed it in a prominent spot on the shop, hanging over the twin blades.

The following day he asked his father about the mask. His wife had once told him that it was a death mask of Zuberus, the most Powerful Magus that Ever Lived.

According to legends, whoever wore the mask was imbued with the dead Magus's Godlike magical powers. Deucalion wore the mask. He didn't feel more magical or powerful.

Perhaps, the mask had lost its power. Maybe it was a replica and not the original.

The problem was that a thief considered it real enough to be worth stealing. One day after he returned home from a delivery, he discovered that his father had been murdered and the mask had been stolen.

Deucalion embarked on a classical tale of revenge. He earned the moniker Mad Elf. Since he didn't know the identity of the thief or the direction that he fled, he took to murdering every thief and bandit he ran into.

On his last bandit camp raid, he ran into a more powerful warrior than himself.

He had the element of surprise. He aimed with his magic arrow, but the warrior turned his head to smile at him. Deucalion was certain that he was hidden. He tried a different angle of attack. However, the bandit chief kept spotting and saluting him. The third time the tried to shoot him, it was he who fell for a trap.

A net was sprung. He tried to teleport away, but the net was leaden with dragon scales that eroded his mana. He was brought before the Bandit Chief.

"Deucalion. To what do we own the pleasure?" asked the Bandit Chief laughing.

"You killed my father! You bastard!" yelled Deucalion, while struggling to break free.

"I have killed a lot of fathers. Not yours in particular," said the Bandit Chief dryly.

"What do you want to do with him chief?" asked a bandit.

"I haven't decided yet," said the Bandit Chief, "I am going to sleep on the problem. Lock him up for now."

After this brief exchange, Deucalion was locked up. He was saved from his terrible situation by a literal knight in shining armor. Once he was back in town, Deucalion breathed a sigh of relief.

"Thank you, stranger," said Deucalion.

"You may call me Ceasar Wodanaz," said Wodanaz shaking hands with Deucalion.

"Ceasar like the salad?" asked Deucalion confused by the name of his benefactor.

"Sigh…what a bother," said Wodanaz, "If you do not need any more rescuing, I will continue on my way."

"Are you a wandering knight?" asked Deucalion.

"I am not noble enough to be a knight, but I do like to cosplay as one, while I wander about," said Wodanaz giving his patented seductive smile.

"I am looking for the Sacred Mask," said Deucalion showing a drawing of his mask, "Some thieves broke into my house and stole it, but not before murdering my father. I have not made much progress searching for it all by myself."

"How long ago did the theft happen?" asked Wodanaz.

"A decade. A century. I have lost track of time," said Deucalion.

"If that much time has passed, whyever would you think that a thief would still have your mask?" asked Wodanaz, "He probably pawned it off or sold it to someone, before continuing on his way."

"I hadn't thought of that possibility," said Deucalion. He had been running mad for countless years. It was not as if the mask did anything obvious.

Deucalion returned to his hometown with the knight. Sure enough, the mask was peacefully waiting for its owner in a pawnshop. He still had yet to get his revenge, but he at least had recovered the mask. This was enough for him for the time being.

"Now that you found your sacred mask, what do you plan to do?" asked Wodanaz that evening while roosting near the campfire.

Deucalion had been expecting this conversation for some time. It made sense that a knight would ask for recompense for his service. He had lost everything while searching for the mask. Other than his weapon arm, he had nothing else of value to give.

"I plan to continue searching for the men who murdered my father," said Deucalion. This was easier said than done. He didn't know what they looked like or how many of them perpetrated this crime.

"I can imagine better usages for my time on this round green earth. But you do you," said Wodanaz.

"What are you up to?" asked Deucalion.

"I am building an army. I wish to unify this, Kingdom. I will not pretend that my intentions are truly altruistic. You can follow me on this bloody path, or you can continue murdering bandits all on your lonesome," said Wodanaz getting up, "Or you can abandon the path of hatred. There is truly not a right answer. Just pick whatever path helps you sleep at night."

"If you need my help, why not just ask for it," asked Deucalion.

"How presumptuous of you! I don't need your help, just your company. The usual dregs I deal with are rather dull, and you at least appear literate," said Wodanaz saddling his horse.

"I will think about it," said Deucalion. He had already decided, but he didn't want to appear too eager to join his friend in battle.

THE STATUE

In a warm summer day, a couple boarded a cruise with a massive box. Inside the box, there was a plastered Medusa head. The husband had bought it at a pawn shop for a pretty penny. He had managed to convince his wife that it was a genuine Marcel Douchamp sculpture. An undiscovered one to be exact.

Later that evening, they got dressed and went to action the piece. Despite their best efforts, nobody seemed interested in purchasing the ghastly severed head.

"Oh! My God! We are ruined!" cried the wife.

"We will try again on a different cruise. There is no reason to give up honey," said the husband smiling benevolently.

"Sigh…I suppose all that is left is to go get drunk at the casino!" said the wife with a defeated tone.

"That's the spirit!" said the husband smiling happily.

The couple went on 5 other cruises. They experienced similar results. On the sixth cruise, an art historian approached them, but not with the intention of buying the piece.

"It is a fake," said the historian.

"How can you tell?" asked the wife.

"Look here, do you see this paper mache, the date on it is quite recent. If this was a true Marcel Douchamp, the newspaper article would be much older, and yellower," said the historian.

"Oh! My GOD! I am such an idiot!" said the wife face palming herself.

"Don't make a big deal about it. The signature looks genuine enough. It cool have fooled anyone," said the historian before departing.

That evening the wife spent it bemoaning their terrible fate. She didn't seem the least bit interested in fooling about, like she had done on their previous trips.

"Honey…that sculpture. I made it," said the husband smiling sheepishly.

"YOU! Are you nuts, trying to sell a forgery?" asked the wife.

"NO. But, we never go out. Everything is work, work, and this was the only way I was able to convince you to take a vacation or two," said the husband giving a wry smile.

"We can't afford these little vacations. I only went on them with the hope that we would recuperate our losses if we sold your stupid Medusa head," barked the wife.

"If we keep waiting until we can afford things, we are going to be too old to enjoy life. I don't know about you, but I am tired of just surviving. When you are ready to enjoy your life, you can come find me drinking at the casino," said the husband departing.

The wife sulked for a couple of hours. In the end, her boredom compelled her to join her husband. After a couple of drinks, she became merry enough to enjoy her miserable existence.

MY SWEET MARE STORMPHINA

It was a cold, frozen night. Under the moonlight, a blade glimmers. It drops silently, deadly on top of its target. Another one has died. The assassin cleans his blade with a handkerchief to keep its edge from rusting. He walks towards the window. His pale mask gets illuminated by the moonlight. He hears rushed footsteps. He had fancied that he had more time to leave his mark.

He climbs up the hole he had come in from. He carefully placed the planks back into the place. He tiptoes over the attic towards a small open window.

Before he gets to it, the roof catches fire. He jumps out the window. As he does, he gets pelleted by arrows. His magic shield repels the arrows, but not for long. There are dragon-blood mercenaries among the archers. Their red eyes have the power to corrode mana.

Since he can't cast his teleport spell without mana, he proceeds to flee on foot. He ebbs and flows through the narrow streets as he runs into more, and more guards.

Eventually, he spots his salvation. There is a black mare with an unusual red mane. The horse shrugs him off when he tries to mount it. Thankfully, the mare lets him ride her when she notices the guards approaching.

The mounted mercenaries attempted to keep up with the mare. Once she got into an open area, she picked up speed. She quickly lost them from sight.

"Phew! That was close," said the assassin once he felt safe.

He dismounted and he felt about his sides. The mare proceeded to lick his shoulder. It had gotten a nasty scratch due to an arrow.

"That's nice. Thanks for noticing," said the assassin smiling sheepishly.

He tended to his wound before examining his new mount. The horse didn't have a saddle or reins, but she did have hoofs. Hoofs implied ownership.

The following morning, he got changed and he stashed his mask away. He perfumed his body to mask his scent. He walked back to town with the horse. He intended to return it to its rightful owner. As someone with photographic memory, it was easy for him to retrace his steps. The horse had been parked right in front of an orphanage.

"Can I help you?" asked one of the nuns approaching the assassin.

"Apologies. I borrowed your horse without asking. I don't need her anymore, so, I am bringing her back," said the Assassin.

"Stormphina isn't our horse. She doesn't allow herself to belong to anyone," said the nun stating a fact.

"I take it that she is a temperamental mare," said the assassin petting the face of the mare.

"If you only knew," laughed the nun.

The assassin noted the pronounced canine teeth of the maiden. He fancied that the woman must have dragon blood.

The nun coughed nervously, before forcing a fake smile, "You are welcome to ride Stormphina as often as she lets you."

"Good to know," said the assassin taking Stormphina to her stables.

For a horse "without an owner," the mare was well taken care of. She had her own private tables, a comfortable wood pellet bed, fresh horse feed, and a garden view. A blonde maiden entered the stables with a comb to brush the mare. The assassin watched the combing with bored amusement.

A month passed after this incident. Stormphina was roosting in her stables when she became aware of a presence. She got up and she walked to a corner of the room. She proceeded to stare at the corner, until the assassin decided to manifest.

"You have quite the sharp senses. Stormphina," said the assassin petting the mare's face.

The mare proceeded to comb through the assassin's clothing, until her nose found a spot wet with fresh blood. This one was on his knee.

"I only scraped my knees. You do not need to worry about it," said the assassin petting her face.

Stormphina snorted before licking that spot some more.

"The name is Eric, by the way," said Eric introducing himself.

Ever since his adopted father had been executed for high treason, he had been solely focused in getting even by killing every corrupt government official. His final target was King Wodanaz, but he was hard to get close to. So, he was using easier marks to get enough practice to commit Regicide. As to be expected, the path of revenge was a solitary one. It had been ages since he had given his name to someone he didn't plan on killing or using to get closer to his mark.

"Why is your hair red?" asked Eric petting the mane. He laughed gleefully when he discovered the black roots, "Your hair, is not really red. Is it? Who in their right mind would dye a horse's hair red?"

Stormphina snorted in response, before stomping the floor with her right leg.

"You poor thing. It was probably some brat who did this to you," said Eric petting the red hair, "I wonder if it will wash off."

Stormphina shook her head in response.

Eric spent the day having a one-sided conversation with the horse. He ended up spending the night there. He awoke the following morning with a start. The stables were empty. He was alone, with blanket over his person. His scrape knee had also been tended to. It was at a moment like this when he realized that he had fainted from exhaustion. He twitched his ears when he heard the sound of flapping wings. When he looked up, he saw a bat flying overhead. It circled about the stables before departing.

"Is this a one-time thing?" asked a nun, "Or do you plan to sleep in our stables every night?"

"Did you dress my wound?" asked Eric.

"Yes. Scraped knees are my specialty. It is one of the most common injuries in orphanages. It doesn't do well to leave a wound unattended," the nun handed Eric a small jar and bag, "Here is some cream. Apply over the wound, before dressing it again. And here are some clean bandages."

Eric accepted the gifts. His eyes lingered on the hands of the nun. Her nails were long, but they had a perfectly round hole on the free edge of the nail. When he looked up, he saw that the nun was blushing. His silent staring had probably made her feel uncomfortable.

"Ahem. Thank you," said Eric stiffly. He brought out a coin purse to pay for the medicine and the hospitality.

"You are welcome," said the nun.

"I must continue on my way. Can you fetch Stormphina? I wish to say goodbye to her," said Eric.

The nun snorted with frustration, "I will get the stupid horse then."

"I am sorry for the childish request. Maybe just point me in the direction that the horse went and I will say Good Bye to her myself," said Eric.

"She went that way towards the back garden," said the nun before running into the orphanage.

Eric walked towards the back garden. On the way there, he heard the sound of a window breaking. This was followed by a loud neighing and laughter. He picked up his pace because he fancied that they were bullying his mare. Stormphina was kicked up a storm, while several of the nuns were laughing at her.

"What is so funny? I wish to laugh too?" asked Eric narrowing his eyes. He placed his hands around Stormphina's face protectively.

"If you only knew," laughed the nuns before departing.

Eric walked a little way with Stormphina following close behind. He was thinking of buying the horse from the nuns. The problem was that he no longer had a permanent residence. He had a few hiding spots, here and there, but they were not designed to accommodate a mare. He took to visiting the horse more often. If only to make certain that she was not being bullied by the children or nuns.

After half a year like this, Stormphina became a little moody. She would snort at him or would shy away from his touch.

"What's the matter baby? Did you miss me?" joked Eric.

"She finds it is annoying that you appear at erratic time and dates," explained a blonde nun, "It is frustrating to drop everything just to amuse you."

The horse nodded in response.

"Drop everything? What does an idle horse have to do aside from amusing me?" said Eric laughing.

Stormphina responded by neighing, before running out of the stables.

The next time he visited Stormphina was nowhere to be found. None of the nuns seemed concerned about the missing horse. After not seeing the horse for a week, he dropped everything to go search for the creature. He searched in the nearby meadows and stables. He also spoke to the farmers. Nobody had seen the horse in quite a while.

On the second week, one of the little nuns joined him on his search. She took him to all the favorite spots of Stormphina. The first place they visited was the horse's favorite river.

"Stormphina likes to start her morning by taking a cool dunking in this lazy river," explained the nun.

From there, they visited the meadow. There were wild horses jumping and prancing about.

"Afterwards, she likes to run around in circles with the other wild horses. Once she works up a good sweat, she returns to the river for another bath," explained the nun.

The pair returned to the orphanage.

"In the mornings, she fools about with the small children. In the afternoons, she listens to mass, but never participates in the rituals," explained the nun.

"How come?" asked Eric candidly.

"She is a horse," said the nun dryly.

"That doesn't seem fair," joked Eric.

"Life isn't fair. And then you die. IF you are lucky, you meet someone whose presence you find tolerable," said the nun coldly.

"Am I someone you find tolerable?" asked Eric giving his patented seductive smile.

"You are tolerable in micro-dosages, Eric," said the nun.

"Who told you my name?" asked Eric becoming paranoid.

"You told it to the horse," said the nun.

"Oh! And you happened to be nearby," said Eric chuckling. IT made perfect sense. He looked at the woman's nails again, "Why do you drill holes in your nails? Is it a religions thing or a fashion thing? Why only you and none of your little nun friends?"

"I will answer your question if you tell me why where you wearing a mask, the first time I saw you. Were you busy doing crime? Or are you hiding from someone?" inquired the nun.

"Some questions are best left unanswered," said Eric dodging the question. It wouldn't do well if the nun knew that he was a freelance Assassin.

"Right back at you," said the nun dryly.

The tour concluded at dusk. They had not caught sight of Stormphina. Eric worried that the horse was dead or that she had gotten stolen. His new routine is now centered on tracking down the mare. He searched far and wide, with the little nun tagging along. He placed wanted posters.

"Is 10,000 gold coins all that Stormphina is worth to you?" asked the nun looking at the poster.

"That amount is all I can afford. I don't have a day job anymore, sister," said Eric sadly.

"I could see about finding you something to do. I know some folks in Wallen that will be more than happy to throw you a bone...do you have any marketable skills?" asked the nun.

"I don't need a day job," said Eric stating a fact. He usually robs the people the murders, "What I need is to find Stormphina so, I can get back to my old...employment."

"If you find her, what would you do?" asked the nun.

"I would buy her and take her home with me. That way I always know were to find my horse," said Eric. He could move stuff around in one of his safehouses to make a makeshift barn.

"Nobody owns Stormphina. IF you find her, she will not allow you to take her," said the nun.

"I will convince her," said Eric. By convincing her, he meant mind controlling her with his hypnosis. With his magic, he could take temporary control of animals.

With his funds dwindling, he decided to go back to "work". When night fell, he attacked a carriage and its escort. His kill shot missed, so, he was forced into a melee battle. The bodyguards circled around him on their mounts. While he was busy, his target started getting away. He fought the bodyguards for a bit, before attempting to teleport on top of the carriage. Since it was a moving vehicle, he manifested in the air.

He dropped on all his fours, before sprinting after the carriage. When he got inside of it, he saw that it was empty. He ran towards the forest in search of his target. He stopped when he saw Stormphina peacefully gracing near a river. He looked towards the horse, and then towards his target that was getting away.

He chose to chase after his horse. Stormphina looked up. Both stood still for a moment that felt like an eternity. As he walked closer, he stumbled over a nun outfit, two small pairs of shoes and black veil. He placed the items down, before continuing on his way. He hugged Stormphina's head lovingly.

"For a snipper assassin, you are not very observant," said a familiar voice, "Or very accurate."

"Sister?" asked Eric looking about.

"God! You are dense," snorted the voice.

"We can talk later," said Eric running up to take the clothing of the nun, "Come out of your hiding spot. I can hear the bodyguards approaching. We have less than a minute to escape."

"You can escape if you want. I haven't done anything to warrant the animosity of those strangers," said the voice.

"Fine! Be that way! Let's go Stormphina," said Eric placing his hand on the mare.

The mare shrugged away from the touch when she felt Eric gathering his magic. The mare moved back a pace, before showing her teeth. They were just like horse's mouth, except for the very predator like fangs. An arrow flew towards her. A lightning fell on the arrow before it got a chance to hit her. More lightning fell about her, as Stormphina started exerting more of her true powers. When the bodyguards saw the lightning falling about them, they assumed that it was Eric's magic. So, they naturally ran away.

"Sister?" asked Eric tentatively.

"It took you long enough to figure it out," said Stormphina. The horse and the little nun had been the same creature.

The Mermaid and the Shark

Not so long ago, there lived a mermaid named Pheobe. She was one of 50 brothers and sisters. As the middle child, she was often overlooked. She wasn't as strong as her brothers, or as talented a singer as her sisters. Her parents would often call her by a different name. At times, she fancied that they wouldn't care if she was gone.

To stand out, she took to scavenging. This was the one job that nobody in her family performed. She would follow human merchant ships. If they sunk, she would take whatever she could carry.

For two years, none of the ships she followed sunk. To avoid returning empty handed, she would steal fish from their nets.

"I scavenged nothing, but at least I came back with dinner!" she would say proudly.

On her way back home, she happened upon a sunken ship. Since it had most of its stuff and bloated corpses, it had yet to be discovered by the other scavengers of her clan.

She swam through the wreckage into the entrails of the ship. It was then that she took notice of a shark. The shark was snapping its teeth, while struggling to break free from an iron net.

Mermaids were not friends to shark kind. They had the same uneasy relationship that humans have with tigers, and other large predators. She observed with bored curiosity the poor creature struggling.

"I am going to regret this," said Pheobe as she approached the creature.

She struggled to lift the net. The shark jerked his head towards the left. This made her notice the heavy cannon. The net was wedged beneath the cannon. She pulled at the net. After much pulling, she was able to dislodge the net. When the shark felt free, he swam away swiftly towards the surface.

"Your welcome," said Pheobe narrowing her eyes.

Remembering her job, Pheobe continued to survey the rest of the ship. It was a ship that traded in cloth. Clothing breaks down beneath the ocean water. It is no use to the mermaids. She picked the gold from the pockets of the corpses, as well as their watches and any other metallic items. It wasn't much, but it was better than nothing.

When she returned home, her family was disappointed. They had hoped that she would have come back with dinner, instead of baubles.

The following night she returned to the sunken ship. This time she took the iron net. Maybe her brothers could make use of it in their hunting expeditions. When she turned around, she jumped out of her scales when she saw a shark. The shark was just lazily passing by, as sharks often do.

Sharks normally do not eat mermaids. Mermaids are naturally toxic, like the noble blowfish. However, "accidents" have been known to happen. Pheobe studied the shark. The shark stared back with his lifeless, black eyes.

She proceeded to swim back home. Every so often, she would turn around. She felt that the creature was following her. After swimming a bit of ways, she was certain of it. The shark was following her.

"Shoo. Shoo!" said Pheobe.

The shark responded by circling about her. And so, the shark became her shadow. Whenever she least expected it, there was the creature, right behind her.

"Hey! Pheobe! Your boyfriend is here for you," said the girl's youngest brother.

"I don't have a…hey…not funny runt," barked Pheobe when she saw the shark outside the family grotto.

"So, how did you two meet?" asked the mother.

"I saved him from a net, and now he follows me everywhere I go," snorted Pheobe, "Why me?"

"No good deed goes unpunished, as humans often say," said one of her brothers.

"I think your boyfriend has something stuck in its mouth," commented a sister.

"He will probably leave once you get it out," suggested the mother.

Pheobe swam up to the shark. With a trembling hand she reached into the gaping mouth. She pulled out a pearl necklace. Pearls were a type of currency among mermaids of the Caribbean. The shark lazily floated to the side, when he saw that Pheobe did not like the pearls.

The second time the shark came with a diamond necklace.

"I wonder from what ship this shark is getting the loot from?" asked the mother analyzing the necklace. Diamonds retained their value even under the sea.

"We should follow it to see if he leads us to a pirate shipwreck," mussed the brother.

Pheobe followed the shark with a few of her brothers. The siblings stopped swimming when they realized that the shark was headed inland. They couldn't risk being seen by humans. Mermaids had only lasted this long by staying out of sight, and out of mind. The shark stopped and he circled around Pheobe. He was urging her to follow him. With her brothers saying no, she had no other choice but to return home.

The third time the shark visited he brought a copper doll. This was a ghastly gift indeed. For it implied that it had eaten a small child. Pheobe accepted the gift, like she had accepted the previous presents. It flattered her wounded ego to be courted, even if her would be groom was a scary shark.

Like before, the shark proceeded to swim around her. He wanted her to follow. This time he led her to a different location. There was a lone boat anchored in a shallow near the everglades. Since the Everglades didn't have human residences nearby, Pheobe dared to draw closer to the boat.

Pheobe anchored her arms over the edge of the boat to push herself up. On top of the boat, there was a music box with a note: From your not so secret Admirer.

"Does anyone read human?" asked Pheobe holding up the letter.

"That letter is not for you Pheobe," said her brother.

"The shark probably ate the fisherman, and he fancied that you might want a boat," mussed her other brother.

The shark pushed himself deeper into the shallows. The water was so low that most of his back was exposed.

"Come back, idiot! You are going to get stranded," said Pheobe swimming after her shark.

The shark stopped before turning around. The motion had been so swift that it startled her. The shark anchored his front fins on the sand, before pushing his body upward. As he did, his body began to change. At the end of the transformation, a very human looking nude man was standing before Pheobe. He had short raven hair and eyes as black as night. When he smiled, she noticed his very sharp looking teeth.

"A Selkie," mussed Pheobe.

"I don't know Pheobe. Selkies normally have sealskins. This... This is something else," said her brother.

The shark man kneeled down before Pheobe. He proceeded to sing...badly. Now, there was no shadow of a doubt. Who? Or whatever was in love with the mermaid.

After the serenade, the man sank beneath the waves. This time he did a partial transformation. His torso remained humanoid, while his lower torso became sharklike. This way, he made himself more mermaid like.

"Should we kill it?" asked her older brother.

"No. He hasn't done anything wrong," said Pheobe.

"You just want more gifts," said her brother.

"How cheap can you be Pheobe?" remarked her other brother.

"You call this diamond necklace cheap?" barked Pheobe.

The shark man opened his mouth. No sound escaped his lips. He couldn't make himself understood if he was beneath the waves. This further reinforced the fact that he wasn't a Selkie or a mermaid. The courtship progressed at a leisurely pace. Whatever that creature was, he was rich. One day when he departed, Phoebe decided to secretly follow him.

She wanted to know what people he belonged to. The shark man swam towards Habana under the cover of night. Once he made it to the beach, he changed into his true form. A servant was waiting for him with a towel. Pheobe saw the shark man speak human. He spoke human, and he dressed himself like a human. He was human! Or he lived among humans! How was that possible? Humans don't have the power to turn into sharks? Maybe, the shark man was unique among humans. Maybe he was a wizard!

She began to suffer from a dilemma. The shark man had probably told the humans about her. He was probably buttering her up to discover the secret location of her family's treasure. Maybe he wanted to kidnap her to put her in an Aquarium like some pet fish. No. She didn't want to think ill of the person she had saved.

She needed to communicate with him, but she didn't know how to speak human. She returned home to sleep on the matter.

The following morning, she went to visit her grandmother. She had spent a portion of her life in an Aquarium. For that reason, she knew how to speak human.

"Nana…I need your help writing a letter," said Pheobe.

"I haven't seen you in years, and you pop in just to ask a favor," scoffed Nana.

"I visited you last week with fish. And here is more fish! So, stop complaining," barked Pheobe, "Now, about the letter…"

"I am going to need a closed ink bottle, a quill and a message in a bottle," said Nana.

Pheobe went to a shipwreck. She found wine bottle with a cork. She visited the anchored boat with the music box. She fancied that maybe it still had the same piece of dry paper. Her shark man had cast a line. He was lazily waiting for something to bite. Even the way he hunted was too human. She screeched when her grandmother manifested behind her.

"Pheobe. No…don't tell me you fell in love with a human. Yes, they do look nice from a distance, but we come from two different worlds," said Nana, "Such relationships never end well."

"Just because you were put in an Aquarium it doesn't mean that I will share that fate as well," barked Pheobe, "Shark man had plenty of chances to steal me away, but he didn't. He is a good fish."

The shark man noticing Pheobe proceeded to loudly serenade her, "When you carve your eyes on an invisible object, and your lips illuminate a smile in its reflection…"

"Hey you! Human," said Nana speaking the language of land dwellers.

"Awesome! You brought a translator! First of all, I wish to know your name. My fair Lady. I am Carlos. I am a vampire, a creature of the night just like you," said Carlos happily. Mermaids, like vampires, were nocturnal.

"What did he say grandma?" asked Pheobe.

"Huh…He claims not to be human," said Nana.

And so it happened that Pheobe got to know Carlos a little better. Her grandmother was always chaperoning their interactions. After two years of courtship, Nana gave Pheobe a potion that allowed her granddaughter to grow human legs. The transformation only lasted 3 hours a day. The effects would grow stronger, the more often she took the potion.

To meet Pheobe halfway, Carlos lived with her 6 hours a day under the sea. It was uncertain whether Carlos was going to settle under the sea, or if Pheobe was going to get used to life on land. For now, they are enjoying every second they spend together both on land and bellow the ocean.

THE SIGNAL

As Beatrix was getting out of the gun shop, someone bumped into her. Since the gun was loaded, it fired. The shot accidently killed that person in an instant. Beatrix moaned as she regrated ever buying a gun. Her friends had peer pressured her into buying a firearm. After owning it for less than a day, she had killed someone. All because she had forgotten to put on the safety, on a loaded weapon.

"It was an accident. I didn't mean to," cried Beatrix.

"We know honey," said her friend Josh.

"We should have known that it was a bad idea to gift a gun to such a klutz," said Anna, friend and gun shop owner.

"Well? What are we going to do?" asked Beatrix.

"The stiff is dead. I don't feel a pulse," said Anna taking the bloodied wrist.

"Don't use your hands stupid. Put on gloves or something," said Josh.

When they heard the police sirens, the three picked up the body. They started to run away with the corpse to be rid of the evidence. They ended up throwing it into a small lake that was within a nature park.

Her friends disperse in opposite directions. Beatrix is lost in the woods, with the cops quickly approaching. When she gets to another clearing, she notices a strange cloud. After weighing her options, she decides that the best course of action is to get adopted by aliens.

Based on most adduction stories, aliens rarely killed humans. Being experimented on seemed preferable to getting caught and going to jail for manslaughter.

She signals to them. Much to her surprise and delight, the cloud dissipates revealing a cylindrical spaceship. A light picks her up, just in time.

"I am sorry human," said one of the grey Aliens.

"We thought you were one of us since you did the proper signal for…what do you call it?" asked a different alien. Normally, when they took humans, they would bind them and mind control them to make their experiments a lot easier.

"SOS," said the first alien.

"How? Did you learned to contact us?" asked the second alien.

"I saw the proper hand signs in a TV show called resident alien," explained Beatrix.

The two aliens narrowed their eyes, before shrugging their shoulders. The first one asked, "So, where do I drop you off?"

"Here is my address," said Beatrix showing her driver's license.

The alien took the card, and he typed the address on the ship's navigator. They dropped off Beatrix in her current residence.

She had bought a large manor, to give it a fixer upper. The reason she wanted a gun was to scare away some squatters. They were performing illegal activities like gambling and drug sales in her home. At first, she had called the police, but they did nothing. She entered the living room with her gun. The squatters laughed at her. They were clearly not impressed by her puny gun.

"Babe, go home, before you hurt yourself," laughed a gangster.

"And don't be calling the police again. My cousin is the chief. One word from him, and it will be you who will rot away in prison for trespassing," joked another.

Beatrix left her home with a defeated step. Once again, she was forced to camp out in the woods. She had sunk her entire life-savings into buying that home to renovate it. She saw a familiar cloud hanging over it. She signals it. The aliens picked her up once again.

She hugged the first alien, while crying pitifully. The alien flinched. His species were not big on physical displays of any type.

"Oh! Please help me sir alien. Bad men have invaded my home, and I haven't the means to be rid of them," cried Beatrix.

"Alright. Alright! Fine. We will help you. Just stop touching me," said the alien pushing Beatrix back.

"I am sorry," said Beatrix taking a respectable distance.

The aliens abducted the gangsters, as well as the chief of police. The grey aliens smiling coolly asked the pertinent question, "Where do you want us to drop them off? Keep in mind that an active volcano is a possible option."

CRAB BURIAL

It was a hot summer in a small town, near the ocean. A thin old man is watching some juicy crabs pass by. He wants to hunt and eat them, but he is not allowed to. All creatures from the sea belong to the government. As the heat and hunger increases, the old man is possessed by a singular idea.
The local representative is not a mermaid. He doesn't belong to the sea. He can hunt and kill that fat, lazy, corrupt government official. Under the old regime, the old man never experienced hunger.

The new governor's policy is everything for me, and nothing for nobody. It didn't take much mental gymnastics for the old man to convince himself to engage in cannibalism.

That night he stalked the corrupt official. He found the bastard passed out drunk, lying on top of a beach chair. The official was having the time of his life in a resort, while the old man starved to death.

The old man raised his machete. One strike, two strikes, 20 strikes. His victim lies dead. He eats his first victim raw. Whatever doesn't fit his stomach, he gathers in a plastic bag to feed the crabs that nest in the nearby mangroves. He wanted to fatten them enough to be worth eating.

A few days later men show up asking about the missing person. He feigns senility, so he is left alone. That is one advantage to being old. Nobody takes you seriously.

More people start going missing, while he slowly gets fatter.

The police eventually get more serious about the investigation. He is not able to get away with feigning ignorance, this time. He takes a deep breath, before forcing a fake smile. There is nothing he hates more than dealing with people he considers an idiot.

"I last saw Mr. So, and so going near the beach," said the old man.

"Lead the way," insisted the officer.

The old man licks what little teeth he has left, before guiding the officer to the crab's feeding ground.

CUSTODIAN OF
THE CUSTODIAN

On a warm Friday afternoon, Officer Zidanta happened to be in the wrong place, at the wrong time. He had just clocked out from his work. He had changed out of his uniform, into his civilian attire. He arrived home at the usual time. He opened and closed the front door swiftly to keep the stupid cat from running away. He checked on his brother. He was sleeping. He opened the fridge in search of a light snack.
It was then that he noticed that he was out of milk. His brother, from another Mother, Jeremy, was a big milk drinker. He was now in the habit of leaving the empty bottles within the fridge.

He had become a bit forgetful as of lately, ever since he started taking antipsychotic medications. Zidanta had always fancied that his little brother was nuts. Now that it was official, he didn't know what to make of the new situation.

It was for this reason that he decided that night to go buy the milk. On the way out of the parking lot, he took notice a man running away screaming. He dropped the milk to chase the man he perceived as a lunatic.

"What is the matter?" asked Zidanta.

"Someone is trying to kill me!! Please call the cops!" yelled the man.

"Who..?" asked Zidanta. He got his answer in the form of a gunshot wound to the back.

"You shouldn't have interfered," said the killer before continuing to chase his prey.

When he awoke, he was in the hospital. Twice in one year…He seemed to be making it a habit of getting shot at. He looked at the foot of his bed. He saw his little brother's hairless Sphynx cat. The cat had note inside the pocket of his pink dress.

"Keep an eye on Tybalt for me," said the note. In the other pocket, there was Jeremy's medication.

Zidanta turned pale when he realized what his little brother was up to.

Jeremy went on the prowl once he felt that he was completely detox from his medication. With the pill out his system, the whispers had returned louder than ever.

"It's a mistake. It's a mistake," said a voice

"If you are not going to be helpful, then be quiet!" barked Jeremy while holding his cellphone. He did this to mask the fact that he was listening to voices, "I…need to talk to my father."

He continued on his walk, until the "father" manifested. The father he saw was a hawk with a human's head, a human head identical to that of Jeremy.

"A bad man has hurt Zidanta. I need to find him to stab him with the pointed end," explained Jeremy.

The father advice Jeremy to check out the surveillance footage. Instead of asking for it, he broke into the nearby Publix, while it was closed. He was able to see the man in a black outfit, but not much else. He went to the spot where the man had died.

The father summoned the ghost of the man to help it become more corporeal.

"Did you get a good look at the man who killed you?" asked Jeremy.

"I am dead?" asked the ghost shocked.

"Don't make a big deal about it!" said Jeremy, "Just tell me what I need to know."

The ghost became disorganized, and his voice a ripple of chaotic whispers. In that agitated state, he was not going to be of any use. Thankfully, a different ghost with unfinished business had seen the direction that the villain had fled.

"I will tell you what you need to know, under one condition," said the ghost.

"That won't be necessary," said Jeremy departing. He had min-dread the information from the ghost.

The ghost becoming angry at being ignored proceeded to yell. Jeremy putted on headsets to drown out the noise. His steps led him to a small near little Vietnam. He crept inside the house. It was empty. Now, all that was left was to play the waiting game. After an hour, his beeper began sounding.

He read the code. Tybalt is dying.

"Damn it! Zidanta! I asked you do one simple thing…then again, there is not much he can do injured," said Jeremy departing.

As he was leaving, the criminal was arriving home. The crook found the backdoor open, but no other trace of the intruder. When Jeremy arrived at the hospital, he saw that the cat was well. His brother had lied to him.

"They already caught the guy. There was no need for you go look-ing for him," said Zidanta, "If you don't believe me call Farley."

"I believe you…" said Jeremy with a defeated tone. He signed wearily, "How long was I gone?"

"A week," said Zidanta, "I am finally well enough to be sent home. Make like a busy bee and help me get the hell out of there."

The brothers returned home. Jeremy lent his brother his shoul-der. Once he was on the couch, Zidanta breathed a sign of relief. He pointed to his bedroom.

"Can you the declutter my workstation? Just throw away every-thing that is police related," ordered Zidanta.

"I…I…guess you finally gave up on finding your mother's killer," said Jeremy guessing what his brother was thinking.

"I already know who it is, but I decided to forgive, and most importantly forget," said Zidanta closing his eyes, "And I want you to forget about the matter as well. Do not read through anything. OK!"

"Yes…yes…" said Jeremy entering the office.

Zidanta's mother had died from being in the wrong place, at the wrong time. A stray bullet shot by a rookie police officer had ended her. This officer was Farley, who was now a detective. Farley had never found out that it was his bullet that had killed the woman. His father had coverup the incriminating evidence. Till this day, he foolishly believed that his dad was incorruptible. This is at least what the whispers told Jeremy after analyzing Zidanta's case files.

He threw everything away, like he had been instructed. There was no point in seeking revenge, if Zidanta had decided to bury the hatchet.

TWO MOST EXPENSIVE CROQUETTES IN THE WORLD

It was a hot summer day on the South Florida highway. Lina had accidentally typed the wrong address. She realized too late when she ended up a gated farm. The farmhand proceeded to close the gate behind her. She honked the horn to get his attention.
"Why are you locking me in?" asked Lina.

"I am sorry miss. Your car is identical to the one of the misses," said the farmhand opening the gate for her.

Lina left the farm. She parked a little way to check the address she had gotten from a text message. She realized that she had typed 187, instead of 107. That slight difference had completely derailed her. She proceeded to rush to her work.

These past few years she had been working as a mobile ultrasound technician. It wasn't uncommon for her to get reassigned to different clinics on a weekly basis. After she finished slaving away in the new clinic after getting lost, she felt hungry. She drove to a nearby bakery to get a croquette.

Before she had a chance to bite her snack, she saw someone crash into her car.

"I am sorry. I am sorry," said the other driver.

There was nothing she hated more than dealing with accidents. To think of how hard, she had worked to keep her lease in one piece, and now, there was the possibility that she had to change it.

She called her son who preceded to speak with Geico. On the meantime, she was regaling the cop of the ins and outs relating to the accident. The car was hauled to a nearby mechanic. The crash had mushed up a lot of core parts. The airbag was also likely to explode should she hit a bump the wrong way.

Right on cue, the airbags exploded, just by looking at them weird. She signed wearily. Even if the car was fixable, the accident had devalued it.

She rents a new car, in an effort to continue with her work routine. When she got her car back from the mechanic, she noticed the bag with the croquette. She had forgotten to eat it. On a whim, she decides to eat it.

That night she is taken to the hospital for food poisoning. The bill alone set her back 10 grands.

www.ingramcontent.com/pod-product-compliance
Lightning Source LLC
Chambersburg PA
CBHW071732150726
47998CB00005B/1614